THE
SHOOTING

Book **Nine** in the
Munro Family Series

CHRIS TAYLOR

Copyright © 2015 by Chris Taylor

All Rights Reserved

LCT Productions Pty Ltd
18364 Kamilaroi Highway, Narrabri NSW 2390

ISBN. 978-1-925119-20-6 (Paperback)
ISBN. 978-1-925119-19-0 (Ebook)

The Shooting is a work of fiction. Names, characters, places, brands, media and incidents either are the product of the author's imagination or are used fictitiously. Any resemblance to actual persons, living or dead, events, or locales, is entirely coincidental.

Published in the United States of America

All that glitters is not gold…

Tom and Lily Munro have been married for sixteen years. They love each other and are happy in their respective, successful careers. With a cute teenage daughter and a son who has never caused them any grief, their life is just about perfect.

Then Lily becomes a victim of a school shooting and is left fighting for her life. Tom's beside himself with fear. What will he do if she dies? How will he live without her? And what about the suspicious lump he's found in his breast? Does he have the courage to find out if it's serious?

In the midst of his fear and panic and indecision, his daughter begins acting out. With Lily still gravely ill in hospital, Tom's at a loss what to do. He has so much more going on right now. Finding time to delve into the reasons for Cassie's behavior are almost beyond him. He wants to believe it's nothing more than normal teenage rebellion, but his heart is telling him it's so much more…

His once-perfect life is falling apart—shattering before his very eyes.

Can he stop the carnage before it's too late? Will this Munro family ever be able to pick up the pieces?

THE MUNRO FAMILY SERIES

THE PROFILER
(Book One—Clayton and Ellie)

THE INVESTIGATOR
(Book Two—Riley and Kate)

THE PREDATOR
(Book Three—Brandon and Alex)

THE BETRAYAL
(Book Four—Declan and Chloe)

THE DECEPTION
(Book Five—Will and Savannah)

THE NEGOTIATOR
(Book Six—Andy and Cally)

THE CHRISTMAS VIGIL
(A Munro Family Series Novella)

THE RANSOM
(Book Seven—Lane and Zara)

THE DEFENDANT
(Book Eight—Chase and Josie)

THE SHOOTING
(Book Nine—Tom and Lily)

THE MAKER
(Book Ten—Bryce and Chanel)

DEDICATION

*This book is dedicated to my sister, Marina Wiggins
and to my friend, Grace Anselmo and to all of the
hardworking and committed teachers in our schools and as
always, to my high school sweetheart, my husband, Linden.*

ACKNOWLEDGMENTS

As usual, no book comes into being without a lot of help and support by my friends and family. A world of thanks must go to my friend and fellow author Angela Bissell, critique partner extraordinaire, and a girl who loves the Munro family as much as I do.

To Pat Thomas, the best editor in the world. I love working with you. You turn my humble offerings into something truly amazing. I couldn't do it without you.

To Alisha of damonza.com, thank you for yet another fantastic cover. To my sisters, Nicole Guihot and Catherine Coster, thank you for your excellent editorial comments and suggestions. I hope you like the final result.

To Grace Anselmo, a quirk of fate has brought us together and I now can't imagine writing a Munro Family story without your input. Thank you once again for all of your suggestions. They are highly valued.

To Detective Superintendent Michael Kilfoyle, thank you once again for all of your technical expertise. Any mistakes are wholly my own.

To Amy Atwell and her dedicated staff of miracle workers at Author EMS who are so much more than book formatters. Amy, once again, heartfelt thanks for working your magic.

To the fantastic writer organizations such as Romance Writers of Australia, Romance Writers of America and Romance Writers of New Zealand for all the help, support and encouragement they offer new and aspiring writers, including me.

To my readers, thank you for your support and love for the Munro family. Your encouragement and enjoyment make this journey all worthwhile.

And lastly, to my friends and family, especially my husband and children. Thank you for putting up with late dinners and even later conversations as I've emerged day after day from the sometimes scary but always enthralling world I've created on my computer.

PROLOGUE

Roseville, Sydney—present day

Brady Sutton steadied both hands and pointed his virtual AK-47 machine gun at the television screen. A second later, his finger squeezed the trigger on the game console. It vibrated and throbbed in his hands. A sharp *rat a tat tat* echoed through his bedroom. *Man, the surround sound speakers his dad bought for him last Christmas were so cool.* It sounded so real, as if he were there, right in the thick of it.

The asshole he'd been pursuing in his virtual stolen car through the back alleys of Los Santos fell over in a lifeless heap on the road in front of him. Bullet holes peppered his chest, all of them leaking blood. Even more blood pooled on the ground beneath him.

Brady pumped the air with his fist. "Yeah! Take that, you son of a bitch." A fierce surge of satisfaction rushed through him and left him tingling. He pulled the console toggle toward him and floored the accelerator pedal of his virtual car. He reversed out of the alley with a squeal of rubber, spinning his wheels. The body in the alley now forgotten, he went in search of another target, wishing that he could eradicate his real-life enemies as easily as he did playing on his PlayStation.

His dad had bought him a new game a few months ago.

Brady couldn't believe it when his father pulled the package out from behind his back and showed him. *Grand Theft Auto V* was all everyone talked about around the corridors of school. It was R rated for one and had been banned for sale in Australia by two department stores. Of course, that instantly made it the most desirable PlayStation game in the modern world. There wasn't a kid at school who didn't want it. Only a handful had played it.

Thanks to his dad, Brady was now among the elite. His mom would have been appalled if she knew about it. His dad wasn't stupid. It was the reason he'd snuck it upstairs without her knowledge. He'd given it to Brady and had then sworn him to secrecy. They both knew what would happen if his mom found out.

Sometimes, Brady wished his dad still lived with them. He could be really cool. Like when he'd brought him the game. And sometimes Brady missed having him there at night, like when he woke up and thought he heard strange noises in the dark.

But there were plenty of things he didn't miss: like the fighting and arguments between his parents and the days of cold silence when they wouldn't speak to each other and it was like he was living sealed off from the world in a suffocating cocoon with no one to talk to.

Brady's mom disapproved of him spending so much time on his PlayStation 4. She'd go ballistic if she knew about *GTA V*. He hadn't been allowed to have any of the *GTA* games. His mom didn't think they were appropriate for an eleven-year-old—or any kid, for that matter.

Lucky for him, his dad felt differently. Besides, she wasn't here now and she'd never know. He didn't have to worry about Vanessa, either. She was supposed to be babysitting him until his mom got home. From what he could tell, she spent all of her time texting on her phone or talking to her boyfriend. She barely paid Brady any mind other than to offer him a plate of cookies when he arrived home from school. She never ever ventured upstairs.

That suited him just fine. It meant he got to play *GTA V* all afternoon without fear of interruption. He didn't care that the game was violent; in fact, he relished the fact he could hunt down anyone he chose and slaughter them without a backward glance. He even had the means to torture them. It was kind of fun to capture a crook and rough him up with a pipe wrench and then pull out most of the fucker's teeth. It was great. It was empowering. Almost as good as strapping sticky bombs to a heap of cop cars outside the police station and then waiting for all the cops to come out before detonating them. He'd watch the bodies get ripped to shreds. Some of them were burned alive. It was sick. He couldn't get enough.

For once, *he* was the one in control. Brady Sutton was the one calling the shots and the fuckers he captured and killed were the ones who were begging for his mercy. Too bad he couldn't do it to the cocksuckers who walked the corridors of his school. Now, that would be something.

He smiled at the use of the obscene language. The words felt good on his tongue: sophisticated, mean and nasty. It was "don't fuck with me" language. He wished he was brave enough to say it at school—like Michael and Franklin and Trevor were on *GTA V*. They didn't put up with any shit. How sick would it be to swagger up to Ian Little and give him a mouthful of cheek before whipping out an assault rifle and blasting the fucker's head off?

It would feel fucking fantastic, that's how it would feel. If it weren't for the fact he didn't have an automatic weapon and he'd be called up to face his mother, he could almost bring himself to do it.

Most kids would think having a mother who was the deputy principal would be kind of cool, but Brady knew the truth: It sucked, big time. Kids picked on him because of it; others accused him of getting special treatment. There was always someone who'd been hauled before Ms Sutton for bad behavior who took it out on him at every opportunity. Sometimes he didn't even know the kids who cornered him down near the bike sheds and pummeled him into the wall.

His mom never said much about it. Most times, she didn't

even know. The bullies took care to hit him in his chest or his belly or his back, where the bruises were concealed beneath his school shirt. He'd given up trying to talk to his mom about it. She worked long hours and by the time she set aside the never-ending pile of paperwork she lugged home with her every night, he'd often gone to bed.

Sometimes he wished he had a brother or even a sister to share the time, but his parents had struggled to have him. Even then, he'd been born ten weeks early and most everybody thought he would die.

His mom used to love telling visitors the story about how she'd watch him in the neonatal intensive care unit, or NICU as it was called by those in the know at the Royal North Shore Hospital. He weighed less than four hundred grams and battled for every breath. Against all odds, he rose to the challenge and survived the critical first weeks. His mom would shake her head and laugh when she got to that bit and say that right from the beginning he was a fighter and that nothing would ever get in his way.

He wished it were true. He wished he was a fighter like Michael or Franklin or even Trevor, the heroes of *GTA V*. They knew how to stand up for themselves. They never let anyone get in their way. So what if they went on crime sprees for the fun of it?

They went after what they wanted. No one pushed them around. No one dug a sly elbow in Michael's ribs or stuck out a foot and tripped Trevor over, laughing hysterically when he fell flat on his face.

No, the heroes of *GTA* didn't take shit from anyone. They knew how to get on in the world: with a revolver in one hand and a machine gun in the other. That was the way to do it. Nobody fucked with you then.

Brady chuckled at the thought and imagined the look on Ian Little's face if he fronted up to school like that. He could almost picture himself calling out to the bully from across the playground and waiting for the cocksucker to get close. He'd probably be flanked by his suck-up buddies. Russell Smith and Cory James rarely left his side. In fact, it would be even better if they were with him. Brady could take out all three.

He'd have his weapons hidden behind his back and would wait until the very last second. Escape would be impossible. Then he'd whip out his guns and blow them to pieces, just like he had in the game. Blood would pour out of the bullet holes and pool all over the grass. He'd stare down at what was left of their bodies, pleased and exhilarated, and wishing he'd done it years earlier.

His mother would be mad, but she was the one who kept telling people how stubborn and determined he was. Forget about trying to get her to intervene, he'd fight his own battles, thank you very much and boy, word would soon get around. The bullies would learn to steer well clear of him. School would become a whole lot more fun.

The more he thought about it, the more excited he felt. *He could do this. He could take control.* He didn't have an AK-47, but he did have the .22 caliber rifle his dad had given him. He even had a box of ammunition. His dad had told him to hide the gun and the bullets underneath his bed and not tell his mom. She took things way too seriously and she'd be furious if she found out.

Ever since his dad had been convicted of assaulting Brady's mom, his dad wasn't allowed to keep firearms or ammunition in his house. At least, that's what his dad said. Brady was more than happy to look after them for him. It just went to show how much his dad trusted him. It made him feel grown up and important. It made him feel good.

In a few more months, he'd be allowed to get his own gun license. He'd looked it up on the Internet. He could get a minor's gun license at twelve. It wasn't too far away. In the meantime, he'd learned how to load the .22 by watching videos on YouTube and thanks to *GTA V*, he'd had plenty of practice firing one. By the time he was old enough to get his license, he'd be an expert.

Setting aside the PS4 game console, he lifted his bedspread and wriggled under his bed and reached for the gun case on the floor. It wasn't heavy and he easily managed to drag it out and put it on his bed. The sight of the camo-patterned case made him smile, like it usually did. His father really was way cool.

Taking his time, Brady unzipped the bag and lifted the gun out of its case. He ran his hand over the smooth wooden stock. His dad had told him the gun had been his grandfather's and was a treasured family heirloom. It was one of the reasons why Brady's dad had given it to him. He said if the cops found it, they'd take it and he wouldn't get it back.

Brady wasn't going to let that happen. He told his dad he'd guard it with his life. His dad had grinned and chucked him under the chin and said he hoped it didn't come to that. Brady hoped it wouldn't either, but he wasn't afraid to die. People died all the time. He only needed to spend a few minutes on *GTA V* to work that out.

Killing someone was easy. *Bang! Bang! Bang!* And they were dead. Just like that. Easy. Just ask Michael or Franklin or Trevor. *Just ask Brady Sutton.*

CHAPTER 1

Chatswood Elementary School, Sydney—present day

Hannah Sutton tucked a loose strand of hair behind her ear and sighed. The spring break was over and the final term of the school year had begun. She was hoping it would be better than the previous three, but from the length of the printout of disciplinary reports entered into the computer system over the last few days, this term promised to be just as trying as the others.

As Deputy Principal of Chatswood Elementary School, one of her jobs was to oversee discipline. In a school with enrolments well over five hundred kids, it was no mean task. Today was no different. With the weather warming up and many more outdoor activities on offer during their breaks, Hannah expected a decline in the number of fights and petty misunderstandings. Weren't the kids too busy fielding a ball or scoring a goal to bother with arguing?

She glanced at the printout and sighed again. Apparently not. Including her son, if the reports about his behavior were to be believed. She shook her head and fought against the wave of helplessness that threatened to overwhelm her. Ever since she'd kicked Colin out, it had been an uphill battle every step of the way. Not that Brady resented her for asking his dad to leave. In fact, she thought her son was probably happier now that all the fighting had stopped. She was certain their life had taken a turn for the better, even if it meant it was just her and Brady braving it alone.

But being a single parent wasn't for the fainthearted and as much as she was glad she didn't have to deal with Colin's petty jealousies and insecurities any longer, having another adult around to help with the parenting responsibilities had certainly made life a little easier. She and Colin had been separated for nearly a year. Neither of them had taken steps to make it official, but it was more from a lack of time on Hannah's part rather than any inclination to once again try and find a way to make things work.

The night Colin hit her, she'd vowed never to let him near her again. As far as she was concerned it was the one and only time it would ever happen. She'd ordered him out of the house there and then and had collected Brady from his bed upstairs and had filed a report at the police station the very same night. The humiliation of having to recite the details of the assault to a perfect stranger would never be forgotten, but her actions had the desired effect and for that, she was grateful.

Colin was charged and a restraining order put in place and they'd managed to live their lives in relative peace. She'd allowed her husband access to his son, but only when he was stone-cold sober and she made sure she never found herself alone with him. It seemed to work and over the months, they'd formed a fragile truce. Sometimes, she even missed him.

With an impatient sound in the back of her throat, she pushed the foolish thought aside and collected the file on the top of the pile on her desk. *Roland Hall.* He was a well known visitor to her office and for all the wrong reasons. The twelve-year-old had been on suspension for fighting with another student and threatening him with obscene language. Right now, he and his parents were waiting outside to meet with her and go through his re-entry interview. No doubt, it would prove tiresome, as usual.

She stood and took a moment to adjust her tailored

jacket and skirt. She touched the sensible bun at the back of her neck and then opened the door to her office.

"Mr and Mrs Hall, Roland. Please, come in."

Brady Sutton snuck into the corridor, careful to keep the gun hidden behind his back. He'd timed his entry perfectly. The bell signifying the end of roll call had sounded twenty minutes earlier and most everyone was in class. The corridor was quiet and empty. All was going according to plan.

He'd woken that morning knowing today was the day he was going to make those cocksuckers pay. Just like the heroes of *GTA*, today he'd take control. He'd stride through the corridors and destroy his enemies. Ian Little was number one on his list.

For as long as Brady could remember, Ian had made every one of his elementary school years an agony to be endured. In the early days, it was minor stuff, like stealing his lunch box or hiding his school bag. Once, in the second grade, Ian had upended a whole tin of paint all over Brady's shirt and then claimed it was an accident.

Over the years, the bullying escalated until it was downright hurtful. By then, Ian had recruited Russell and Cory. They all took delight in tormenting him. The beatings were a daily event. He couldn't even go to the bathroom without being set upon in some utterly disgusting way.

Ian had been in Brady's class since they'd both started school six years ago, despite his pleas to his mother that she use her influence to rearrange them. But she'd done nothing, telling him it was out of her control. She wasn't in charge of curriculum or the structure of the classes, she'd said. That was Mrs Brian's department.

In the end, he gave up asking.

But that was yesterday and all the other yesterdays. Today, he was going to make a few changes and set his own course to freedom. Maybe he'd blow Mrs Brian away, too.

Just like he did when he was playing *GTA*, Brady stealthily stalked his prey. According to his timetable, his Grade Five class was having music with Mrs Munro in the classroom at the end of the hall.

A momentary surge of regret flooded through him. He liked Mrs Munro. She was one of his favorite teachers. She and his mom were friends. Sometimes, they lunched together. He hoped she wouldn't be too scared at the sight of Ian's blood.

He'd emptied his school bag of everything. He wouldn't need any workbooks today. His satchel now hung from his shoulder, with nothing in it save the box of ammunition. It was a shame the old .22 rifle wasn't automatic, but he'd done what he could to compensate. He'd filled the clip to its hilt.

Ten bullets were in the magazine. He hoped it was enough. He'd brought along the box of spare ammunition, but there was no guarantee he'd have time to reload. He'd just have to make sure he made every shot count. Like he did during *GTA*.

If you lost concentration, you were dead. Game over. It was as simple as that.

———————

Detective Senior Sergeant Tom Munro walked out of the tea room brandishing two fresh cups of coffee. The morning was early yet and all he could hope was that the day would be uneventful. His squad had attended more than their fair share of emergencies over the course of the past week. It was nice to sit around the squad room of the North Sydney Police Station and do nothing more than answer emails and the occasional phone call. Besides, it gave him time to think about his upcoming wedding anniversary and what gift he could possibly buy for his wife.

He'd been married to Lily for sixteen years. Together, they had two teenagers, a daughter and a son. They were good kids and Tom was proud of them. They both attended a high school in Chatswood, not far from their comfortable home and the elementary school where Lily worked. It was a good situation all round and most of the time Tom was content with how things had worked out.

If only Cassie wasn't acting out...

He shook his head and pushed the thought aside. It was probably just part of the normal course into adulthood. At seventeen, she still had a lot to figure out, like Lily kept telling him. Determined not to dwell on it, he forced a smile and deposited one of the coffee cups on the desk of his partner and fellow police negotiator, Andy Warwick.

"Thanks, mate. Appreciate it. After the night I've had, I need that coffee like I need my next breath. It's a matter of survival."

This time, Tom's grin was genuine. "Sounds pretty rough. Which one of the kids was sick?"

"No, it was Cally. She's been laid low by a terrible flu. Was up and down all night. Painkillers, throat gargles, tissues. It seemed like every time I closed my eyes, she was asking me to get something else. It wouldn't be so bad if she wasn't pregnant. She can't take anything stronger than paracetamol. I'm just relieved Jack and Grace don't have it."

Tom nodded in understanding. "I can still remember the years when Cassie and Joe were that young. It seemed like one or the other of them was always coming down with something." He grimaced. "A by-product of attending a daycare center. It's a hell of a way to build up your immune system."

Andy grinned. "Yeah, you have that right. Throw in the fact that Cally's teaching kindergarten and you have a fine old mix of germs coming into our household on a regular basis."

"She's over at Hornsby, isn't she?"

"Yeah. It's a bit longer commute than the last job, but she loves it over there. Is Lily still at Chatswood?"

"Yep. She's been there since she finished college and

even before. She did her teaching practicums there. The only way they'll get her to leave is to carry her out of there in a pine box," he joked.

The phone on Tom's desk rang, interrupting their conversation. Tom set his coffee cup down and leaned over to answer it.

"Tom Munro."

"This is dispatch. We've received an emergency call from Chatswood Elementary School regarding a possible shooting. Crews from Chatswood have already responded and an ambulance has also been called. Details are a little sketchy. At this stage, it's not known if there are any injuries. They're calling for a team of negotiators to deal with the shooter."

Tom took down the details. By the time he hung up the phone, adrenaline was already pumping through him, elevating his heart rate. Andy took one look at him and his expression changed.

"What's happened?"

"A possible shooting at Chatswood Elementary."

Andy set his coffee cup down and headed toward the locker room, Tom close behind him. As if the thought had only just occurred to him, Andy came to a sudden halt and swung around. "Isn't that where Lily—?"

Tom's response was short. "Yes."

Andy nodded once, his expression grim. "Right."

"They're vague on details. They don't know if there are any injuries," Tom added, aware that he was trying to convince himself as much as his partner.

"Right. Of course. I'm sure she's fine."

Andy continued on his direct course toward the locker room. Tom followed on his heels and sent up a silent, desperate prayer that his partner was right.

Tom and Andy stood outside the high fenced perimeter

that surrounded a number of unappealing red brick buildings that made up Chatswood Elementary School. A half dozen uniformed officers were also on the scene. On a normal day, the silence that greeted them wouldn't have seemed out of place—it was class time, after all. But knowing that something dreadful had gone down made the lack of noise and activity in the school yard eerie. It was almost as if everyone knew there was something very wrong at Chatswood Elementary. Tom thought of his wife and the hair stood up on the back of his neck.

A sense of urgency held him taut. He had to get in there and find out what was going on. He had to get in there and find Lily. He'd tried her cell phone on the way over, but it had gone straight to voicemail. He tried not to read anything into that. She often had her phone switched off, especially when she was teaching. He took a deep breath and forced his pulse rate down.

The school was currently in lockdown, with nobody but emergency personnel allowed in or out. It was standard procedure during any kind of threat that the occupants of the building remained in their classes, sitting or lying down on the floor, as far away from the door as possible and no movement was allowed. Looking around at the crowd of police officers and other emergency personnel, he located the officer in charge of the scene and strode over to him.

Upon closer inspection, Tom recognized Detective Senior Sergeant Lane Black from the State Crime Command based in Chatswood and offered him a muted greeting.

"Lane, what do we know?"

Lane glanced up and gave Tom a brief nod of greeting. "Tom. At this stage, we believe it's a single shooter. An eleven-year-old kid in the fifth grade. He's holding his class of about twenty-four students and a teacher hostage."

Tom swallowed and did his best to keep the panic at bay. Lily taught the fifth grade. "Do we know who the staff member is?" he asked in a voice as steady as he could manage.

"Nope. We're trying to track down the deputy. Apparently the principal is away at an inservice."

"What about the shooter? Any word on him?"

"Only what we got second hand from some kid who was walking past the classroom, so nothing's been confirmed. He told my partner the boy's name is Brady something or other." Lane looked up and called out to another plainclothes detective who stood a short distance away.

"Hey, Jett. Give us a sec, would you?"

A fit, young detective with dark hair and bright intelligent eyes moved closer to Lane. He nodded a greeting to Tom and then turned to Lane. "What is it, mate?"

"This is Detective Senior Sergeant Tom Munro. He and Andy Warwick are negotiators based at North Sydney. Tell Tom what you got from our witness."

Jett turned to face Tom, an expression of curiosity on his face. "Munro? Any relation to Clayton Munro?"

Tom nodded. "Yes, he's one of my brothers. I have a few of them."

Lane issued the slightest of smiles. "You can say that again. Jett and I were part of the investigation team that tracked down Clayton's daughter, Olivia, when she was kidnapped earlier in the year. We've gotten to know him quite well since then. We've become friends."

Tom nodded and recalled Clay mentioning the name of the lead detective and his partner. His brother had been impressed with Lane's investigative skills and Clay was beyond grateful to have his daughter returned to him unharmed.

Andy edged closer and Tom understood the impatience in his partner's eyes. "Give us what you have," he said.

Jett drew in a breath and began to relate the course of events as best he knew them. "Ten-year-old Travis Church is in the fifth grade and is a member of the class that has been taken hostage. He was on his way back from the bathroom when he saw a boy he identified as Brady Sutton through the little viewing window in the door. Sutton was shouting and brandishing some kind of rifle. According to Church, everyone looked scared."

Tom frowned. "Sutton? Isn't that the name of the deputy?"

Lane nodded. "You're right. Hannah Sutton is the deputy principal. We're still trying to make contact with her."

"I think that's her now," Jett interrupted and Tom turned to see a woman in her mid-thirties with soft brown hair pulled back in a bun hurrying toward them. She was pale and wore a grave expression. He stepped forward to greet her. Lane followed suit.

"Oh, my goodness, officers. I'm so relieved to see you. I'm sorry. I was on the other side of the school, in a meeting. I've only just been informed. I understand one of the children is armed with a rifle. He's threatening to shoot. We-we have the school in lockdown. Is there anything else I can do?"

"Are you Ms Sutton?" Lane asked.

She nodded and extended her hand. "Yes, I'm Hannah Sutton, the Deputy Principal."

She turned to Tom and he shook her proffered hand. He guessed she was acting on auto pilot.

"Tom Munro. We've met before. I'm Lily's husband."

Color flared in her pale cheeks and she looked away. "Tom, of course. I'm sorry. I'm a little..."

She flapped her hands in a distracted manner and shook her head. Tom could understand her preoccupation.

"We understand the boy is holding a class of students and a teacher hostage with a rifle," he said.

"Yes, that's what I've been told. My-my assistant relayed the information to me."

Lane cleared his throat. "We've spoken to a boy by the name of Travis Church. Right now, he's waiting in a police cruiser for his mom to arrive. Apparently, he was out of the room when it happened and saw the shooter through the glass panel in the door. He told us the boy with the rifle is a child by the name of Brady Sutton."

Any color that was in the deputy's cheeks vanished the same instant she heard the child's name. She went so white, Tom thought she was going to collapse. She wobbled on her feet and reached out for Lane's sleeve, her movements jerky.

"D-did you say B-Brady Sutton?"

"Yes," Lane replied. "I assume he's a student here."

"Y-yes. He's...he's my son."

Tom sucked in a breath and tried to hide his shock. All of a sudden, he hoped to God their witness got it wrong. He couldn't imagine what this woman would go through if it were true. Her *son?*

"Christ," Lane murmured under his breath and Tom knew exactly how he felt.

"I-I need to talk to Travis," Hannah pleaded. "Please, let me talk to Travis. I need to ask him. I need to—"

"Hannah, with all due respect, we have to get into that classroom. You need to get hold of yourself and take us there, or at least point us in the right direction. Whether your son's involved or not, there are at least twenty other people in that classroom. We need to ensure their safety. And the safety of your son," Tom added.

His harsh words, tinged with urgency, seemed to penetrate the panic that had taken hold of her. She stopped short and took in a deep, shuddering breath. She put a shaky hand up to her mouth, then seemed to collect herself.

"Of course, Tom. I'll do everything I can. I believe this time of day that class is in the music room with Mrs Munro..."

The rest of what the deputy said was blocked by a roaring sound in Tom's ears. Dread and fear twisted inside him, turning his gut inside out. *Lily was in the classroom.* His wife was in the classroom with a kid who had a rifle. A roaring sounded in his head.

"Tom, Tom! What the hell? We have to get in there!" Lane yelled at him, but Tom barely heard over the noise in his head and the blood that rushed through his veins. He had to find Lily. He had to find her...

Andy appeared in his periphery and then gripped him hard by the arms. "Snap out of it, Tom. We need you. Lily needs you."

"What's going on?" Lane asked, confusion plain on his face.

"It's the teacher. Lily Munro," Andy explained. "She's Tom's wife."

"Fuck." The word fell with quiet force from Lane's tongue. Tom nodded, in an agony of fear and indecision. He wanted to get inside and find Lily. He needed to keep her safe. But he didn't know if he'd be of use or merely a hindrance. Lane made up Tom's mind.

"Here's what we're going to do." He pointed to Tom. "You're going to stay right here and wait for us to come out."

An instinctive protest rose up in Tom's chest. "But—"

Lane stared at him with hard eyes. Tom stared right back. The tense moment was broken when Andy stepped forward and drew Tom slightly to one side.

"Tom, listen to Lane. You need to stay out here, mate. It's for the best. You're too close. You won't be able to think straight. It's not what Lily needs right now. She needs the best we have."

Tom listened and nodded reluctantly. Andy was right. There were teams of highly trained officers, including a team of negotiators, waiting to go in. None of them had the added emotional burden of being related to a potential victim. Lily needed the best. She needed a team that was cool and calm and focused. He was everything but.

"Okay, I'll stay. I promise." He stared hard at Andy and then grabbed hold of his sleeve. "Find her for me Andy. Bring her to me. I need to have her here, by my side. I need to know she's safe."

Andy held his gaze, his eyes bright with the intensity of the moment. "I will, Tom. I promise. I will."

"Okay, people, gather close," Lane called. "We're going in."

Chapter 2

Chatswood Elementary School, Sydney—present day

Brady wiped the sweat out of his eyes with the back of one hand, careful to keep the gun aimed as best he could on the members of his class. His gaze darted wildly from face to face, searching for the one he sought.

Where was he? He should be here. He was always here. And yet, Brady couldn't see him. With another swipe at the perspiration that slid into his eyes, he walked between the rows of desks, searching for Ian Little.

Kids shrank away from him, their eyes wide and wild with fear. He chuckled. They should be scared. He was a hunter on the prowl. They didn't know which one of them was in his sights.

"Ian Little!" he shouted, becoming impatient. "Show your gutless face right now. I know you're here. You're always here. You've been here every day of your miserable life. I should know. You've done all you could to make my life miserable, too. I'm here to tell you it's over. You're not going to bully or tease or fight me again. Got it?" he roared, spinning around and cursing loudly when his nemesis failed to appear.

"Show yourself, you gutless cocksucker. Don't force me to choose someone else. You're the fucker I'm after. Have some balls and show your fucking face." He could see from the look on the faces of the other kids that they were shocked by his cursing. He'd be shocked, too, if he were them.

But somehow, after a month of almost daily exposure to the obscenities freely uttered in *GTA*, the profanity felt good, the mere utterance of the words empowered him: He was all that mattered. Right here, right now, it was all about Brady Sutton. His cursing and fuck-you attitude had certainly had the desired effect—the kids looked more terrified than ever. Even Mrs Munro had gone pale.

Brady swung around to face her, the gun steady in his hands. She flinched and moved away, placing the large teacher's desk between them. He lowered the gun a little and tried to make her see she wasn't the one he hunted. He liked Mrs Munro. She'd done nothing but treat him with kindness. Besides, she was his mom's friend. He had no gripe against her.

"Brady, honey. Put down the gun. Let's talk about it. You're looking for Ian. I take it he's made you angry?"

Brady stared at his teacher like she was talking in tongues. "Angry? Of course he's made me angry. For every single day I've spent here, he's made my life a living hell. I'm here to even the score. It's only fair, don't you think?"

"Of course, Brady. I understand exactly how you feel, but hurting Ian won't help anyone. How about you put down the gun and we can talk about it. I'll help you come up with an agreeable solution."

Rage ignited inside him and despite the fact it was Mrs Munro trying to help him, he lashed out.

"I don't need your fucking help! I've found an agreeable solution! I have a gun! I'm going to blow his fucking head off. Boom! His brains are going to splatter all over the place, like a watermelon dropped from a three-storey building. I've seen what happens when someone takes a bullet to the head. It isn't pretty."

A heightened level of fear now shadowed Mrs Munro's eyes. Brady compressed his lips in a moment of regret. He hadn't gone out of his way to scare her, but the fact was, he was there for just one purpose and nothing she said or did was going to deter him.

"Ian!" he screamed. Get your fucking, chicken-livered, gutless self out here right now! In a moment, I'm going to start shooting and it will be your fault if anyone dies."

A second passed and then another. Brady looked wildly about. No one looked at him, no one moved. And then he saw it—or more accurately, saw *him*. Ian Little.

The gutless wonder was on the floor, crawling on his hands and knees between the desks, doing his best to escape undetected. Brady scoffed. *As if*. There was only one way Ian Little was leaving this room and it wasn't on his hands and knees.

With long strides, Brady ate up the distance between him and the boy he hated above all others. Mrs Munro cried out to him, trying to get him to stop. He ignored her pleas and the screaming of the class. His vision narrowed to Ian. The cocksucker was a matter of feet away from the door.

Brady halted and looked down the scope of the rifle and then carefully took aim. His heart thudded hard. It was like a movie playing out in slow motion. The moment he'd dreamed of had arrived and he would savor every second of it. This was the moment Ian would pay for every insult, every blow he'd ever inflicted. Let him feel the pain for a change and the uncertainty of what was yet to come. Yes, Brady might toy with him a bit then deliver the final blow. It was do or die, just like on *GTA*.

As if sensing the game was up, Ian turned around and faced him. Spying the barrel of the rifle only inches away from his head, Brady's lifelong enemy screamed and scrambled and stumbled, trying hard to get out of the way. He slithered and slipped and stumbled until he'd almost made it to Mrs Munro's desk.

Brady advanced upon him, knowing how this was all going to end. There was no escape. Ian should know that. The end was close. So close. He took aim again. *This was it.*

His finger squeezed the trigger just as Mrs Munro threw herself in front of the gun. She reached out for it and dislodged it, knocking it out of his hands. At the same time, a puff of smoke came from the end of the barrel and a bright red stain appeared low on his teacher's front. The fear on her face turned to shock and then she slowly slid to the floor.

The classroom erupted into screaming and kids knocked him this way and that in their haste to get out of the way. He stared at Mrs Munro. Just like when he played *GTA*, she lay still and silent in a pool of blood. The gun lay abandoned on the floor.

He bit his lip against the tears that threatened to choke him when he realized what he'd done. A howling started way down deep inside him and a moment later, his own cries of distress and disbelief joined the chaos in the room. He slid to his knees beside his teacher and used his hand to try and stem the blood. It oozed, warm and sticky, between his fingers. It felt nothing like he expected.

Shouting and the pounding of feet from outside in the corridor drew his attention and it was like he was in the middle of a PlayStation game when a barrage of officers dressed in combat gear poured in through the door. With guns drawn, they screamed at him to put his hands in the air. Trembling violently now, he did his best to comply.

With his gaze lowered, he stared past his teacher and then spied the figure of Ian Little. The boy was huddled beneath Mrs Munro's desk, shaking from the force of his tears. An overwhelming sense of failure surged through him and he moaned. It had all been for nothing. He hadn't shot Ian at all. Ian was alive and well. It was Mrs Munro who lay so still and pale, bleeding all over the floor and just like in *GTA*, the game had come to an end.

Lily tried to put her hand over the hole in her stomach and stem the flow of blood. Fire raged through her, radiating from the center of her wound. *She'd been shot.* She couldn't believe it. The pain was like nothing she'd ever felt before. Not even the agony of childbirth could compare to this torment. She only hoped the paramedics arrived before it was too late.

Blood seeped through her fingers, staining her skin red. She looked at it distantly, as if observing it from afar. In some part of her mind, she registered the slow and steady seepage with relief. It wasn't spurting out. The bullet hadn't hit an artery. That was good.

She was still at a complete loss to explain what had happened. One minute she'd been going through the C major scale on the electric keyboard with her fifth grade music class and the next, all hell had broken loose. Brady Sutton had appeared in the doorway brandishing some kind of rifle.

The wooden stock was old and worn, but had been polished to a high sheen. Someone had taken care of it over the years. The long barrel was black and also shiny. She registered these minute details in the seconds it took to realize her eleven-year-old student had walked into the classroom with a gun. A moment later, it became clear he wasn't bringing it in for show-and-tell.

His eyes were wild and unfocused. He was sweating like he'd just run a mile. And then he started shouting obscenities and screaming for Ian Little. Shocked and more than a little concerned, Lily had done her best to distract Brady. She'd known Ian was in the class. She'd called the roll not more than twenty minutes earlier, but she didn't know where he was at that exact moment and she hoped Brady didn't either.

And then, he'd spied him, crawling low across the floor. Lily still couldn't believe how Brady had turned on Ian and hunted him down, like a wild animal scenting its prey. The memory of it shocked her, almost as much as the knowledge she'd taken a bullet.

A swarm of police officers dressed in combat gear, and two paramedics wearing dark blue overalls, suddenly surrounded her and she breathed a sigh of relief. Help had arrived. She'd be okay. She was sure of it. As if to confirm it, a female paramedic reached over and put an oxygen mask over Lily's face.

"You're going to be all right, okay? Just hold on and we'll get you to the hospital. You've lost a little blood, but we're going to get you to the hospital very soon. Do you understand?"

Lily nodded.

"We're going to give you something for the pain, okay? Just sit tight. It won't be long."

The other paramedic moved Lily's arm off her stomach and unbuttoned the buttons on her blouse. Lily looked down and grimaced. She'd probably never get the stain out of it. Scrap that, the blouse had a bullet hole in it. It was fit for nothing but the trash. What a waste. It was one of her favorites.

The irrational thoughts went back and forth in her head while she did her best to breathe through the pain. A wad of padding was pressed against her wound and then bandaged tightly around her stomach. She closed her eyes, exhausted. She wanted nothing more than to drift into sleep.

"Lily? Lily, can you hear me?"

Lily frowned and opened her eyes. It was one of the paramedics. She forced herself to nod through the haze of pain and narcotics.

"We're going to move you now, Lily. We're going to lift you onto the stretcher and get you into the ambulance. We're taking you to the Royal North Shore Hospital."

It was the female paramedic who spoke to her again and Lily thought she acknowledged the woman's words with a nod, but in the end, she couldn't be sure. The morphine they'd given her was taking effect. She could barely keep her eyes open.

"She's losing consciousness. Quick, we need to get her to the hospital."

The words echoed across the vastness of Lily's brain. She fought against the blackness with everything she had, but still it wasn't enough. The murmur of voices above her receded.

Tom. She had to tell Tom. He'd have heard it over the police radio. He'd be worried sick. He'd know straight away she could be involved, even injured. She had to talk to him. She had to make sure he knew she was okay.

And Cassie and Joe. She didn't want them finding out on Facebook. Cassie was always watching live news feeds on her phone. It fascinated her that she could be watching a drama unfolding in real time. Lily found it a little unsettling, if she was honest.

Another hospital mask came down over her face, replacing the first one. It smelled different. She tried to struggle against it, but it was useless. Her limbs were leaden, her head was dull.

And there was Tom. She breathed a sigh of relief, but then realized it wasn't the Tom she'd kissed good-bye that morning. *Had it really only been that morning?*

It was Tom as he was when she'd first met him, more than seventeen years ago. His hair was thick and blond and curling up a little across the back of his neck. He'd worn it longer in those days. Not that he still didn't look hot. He'd always looked hot. From the moment she'd spied him across the room at that party, he'd had the ability to weaken her knees...

She smiled at the memory, suddenly yearning to have him close. She needed him to reassure her that everything was going to be all right, to give her a wink and to toss her a cheeky grin. But more than anything, she needed him to hold her hand and keep the fear at bay. She needed to tell him she loved him. She needed to hear it from him, too. She needed... And then, there was nothing.

The paramedics hurried across the front of the school yard, pushing a gurney. Tom could see a woman strapped to it. The patient was tall, but petite and sported a sleek crop of golden blond hair. His heart lurched in an agony of disbelief. He howled in shock and despair.

It was Lily. Even from a distance, he could tell it was her. The fact that she was the first one brought out was also telling. The most urgent cases were always treated first. As the paramedics moved closer, he could make out the large patch of blood that stained the front of his wife's shirt.

Oh, Christ. She'd been shot. She'd been *shot!* His heart stopped cold and then took off faster than the speed of light. She was hurt. She could even be dead.

No, not dead. The urgency in every motion of the paramedics' bodies and the tension on their faces gave him confidence that she was still alive. No one rushed for a corpse. It was just the way it was.

As they drew nearer, he raced toward them and then growled out his frustration when two of his colleagues held him back.

"Give them some space, Tom," Andy muttered close to Tom's ear. "Let them do their job. You know how it works."

"But, it's Lily! She's hurt. I need to be with her."

"Of course you do and you will be, but just give them a minute, okay? They need to do their stuff. I'll go and have a word with them and let them know you're here, all right?"

Andy stared hard at him, his eyes just inches away. A moment later, with a heavy sigh, Tom's shoulders slumped and the tension left his body.

"You're right, I'll let them do what they need to do." He snatched at Andy's sleeve. "But tell them I'm here, all right? Tell them as soon as they're finished, I need to see her. She's my wife. She's... She's my everything..."

His voice cracked and he had to turn away, embarrassed to have his colleagues witness him in such bad shape. The Tom Munro they knew was cool and calm and collected. Never did he let the drama and tension of a high stakes situation get the better of him. It's what made him one of the best negotiators in the state.

But with Lily, it was different. She was his wife, the love of his life, the mother of his children. He couldn't lose her. He couldn't.

"Tom, I've just had a word with the paramedics. She's

injured pretty badly mate. They need to get her to the hospital ASAP."

Andy's words came to him from a distance, through the wall of panic in his brain. Finally, they registered and with it his panic flew into overdrive. He grabbed Andy with both arms and shook him.

"What are you trying to say? Is she alive? Please fucking Christ don't tell me she's not alive..."

Andy drew in a deep breath and eased it out. His expression more grave than Tom had ever seen it.

"She's alive, Tom, but only just. She was shot in the abdomen. She's lost a lot of blood. The bullet seems to have missed the arteries, but they don't know what kind of damage it's done inside. They need to get her to the hospital as soon as possible."

"I need to see her." Tom didn't wait for Andy's response. Instead, he pushed away from his partner and ran to the ambulance. Two paramedics worked over his wife, their expressions grim. Tom stared at Lily, so still and silent and pale on the gurney.

"Lily, please, babe, hang in there. You've gotta hang in there. Please don't die on me. Please."

One of the paramedics glanced over at him and her lips compressed with understanding.

"Tom, is it? I'm Crystal and my partner here is Bob. Your wife's been seriously injured. She's lost a lot of blood. She's going to need a transfusion. Do you know what her blood type is?"

Tom gulped in a breath and nodded. "Yes, it's O positive."

"You're sure?"

"Yes. I remember from when she gave birth to Joe, fourteen years ago. It was a long and difficult labor. He was a big baby and in the wrong position. She-she hemorrhaged afterwards. She needed a transfusion then, too."

"Where did that happen, Tom? What hospital was she at?"

"The Royal North Shore. It's where both of our children were born."

The paramedic nodded in relief. "Great. That means her records will be easy to locate. We're taking her there now. Would you like to ride with her?"

Tom nodded, still in a daze and then turned to look at Andy who hovered nearby.

"It's fine. Go with her, mate and when she wakes up, tell her we're all here barracking for her," Andy urged. "Call me, okay?"

Tom nodded and then closed his eyes and drew in a deep breath before slowly blowing the air out again. He needed to be strong and calm for Lily. It wouldn't do for her to see him looking so stressed when she woke. *When*, not if. He had to stay positive. The alternative was just too much to bear.

He glanced around him and his heart fell. He'd been oblivious to the growing number of cars that had parked along the road outside the school fence, but now that he took the time to look around him, he noticed the swelling crowd. Word had gotten out.

Lane's partner Jett and a couple of uniforms were holding them back from the school gates. So far, most of them were no more than a little anxious, but that could change in an instant.

Some of them held phones with the cameras pointed toward the ambulance. Anger surged through him, but he forced himself to keep it in check. What was the point in shouting at them? He'd only give them something more to film. It would make their thirty seconds of YouTube fame even more exciting to have a decorated Sydney police officer and the husband of the victim spewing forth tirades at the curious spectators. He wouldn't give them the satisfaction.

Instead, he turned his back on them and climbed up into the ambulance. He sat down on a seat beside the gurney and reached out for his wife's hand. It was cool and limp and lifeless and sudden tears burned behind his eyes.

He thought of their kids and then glanced at his watch. It was ten o'clock. Soon, they'd be coming out for their morning break. If he was lucky, it hadn't yet made the pages of social media. If he wasn't and they read something...

Both of them were enrolled in a local high school only a few miles away. He needed to call someone to collect them and tell them what was going on. He pulled out his phone and dialed Brandon. As briefly as he could manage, he filled his brother in on the recent events and asked if he'd collect the kids. Finally, the doors of the van closed, blocking the outside world and he sighed raggedly with relief.

Hannah Sutton pressed her hand against her mouth in an effort to contain her cry of distress. Two heavily armed officers dressed in full combat gear stood on either side of her son and marched him down the corridor toward her office at the front of the school. His hands were fastened behind his back with handcuffs. Another officer followed behind them, carrying what looked like her husband's old gun.

They were still a few yards away from her when she ran toward them, unable to contain her anguish a second longer.

"Brady! Oh, my goodness! Brady! Honey, what have you *done*?" She took hold of the lapels of his shirt and tried to draw him close. It was then that she noticed the blood. A fine spattering of it covered his clothes and a little of it was on his bare arms. Shock rendered her mute.

He'd shot someone! He'd actually *shot* someone! The thought spun madly around in her head, but she refused to comprehend its meaning. It couldn't be true. He couldn't have shot a real person. It was ludicrous to even think it. There must be some mistake. There must be some other explanation.

"I'm sorry, Ms Sutton, you're going to have to stand back from the prisoner."

A detective who had introduced himself earlier as Lane Black spoke to her, his expression grave. She spied a flash of sympathy in his eyes, but a moment later, it was gone.

"P-prisoner? But... But he's my son!"

The same officer spoke again. "So you said, but right now, he's under arrest for the attempted murder of Lily Munro. We're taking him back to Chatswood Police Station. I suggest you meet us there."

Tom paced up and down the corridor outside the operating theaters and waited for news of his wife. She'd been rushed to surgery upon their arrival and he had yet to talk to whoever it was who now held her life in their hands. It had been more than four hours since she'd been whisked away and still there was no news. The waiting and not knowing was killing him. He'd never felt more helpless. He spun on his heel and began another lap of the corridor.

"Can I get you a coffee, Tom? Or a Coke?"

Tom looked across at his brother Clayton and shook his head. Brandon sat up from where he was slouched across the hard plastic seats.

"I'll have a coffee, if you're doing a run," Brandon said.

Clayton acknowledged Brandon with a nod. "Anyone else?"

Tom looked around at the members of his family, who had gathered at the hospital *en masse*. Clayton's wife, Ellie, also sat in the row of seats. His brother Declan had called from Canberra and Clayton's twin, Riley, had called from work. He was the local area commander up in the country, six or seven hours' drive away.

Tom's parents had also telephoned and expressed their concern. They'd given him their love and had asked him to pass it on to Lily. He was a little overwhelmed by the love and support of the Munro clan, but he was glad for it. He had no idea how Lily was faring and he was barely holding onto his panic. He needed all the support he could get.

"Where are Cassie and Joe?" he asked in an effort to distract himself.

"I called Alex and told her what was going on. She offered to go to their school and has taken them home," Brandon replied. "She'll stay with them until we know what's going on."

Tom gave a brief nod of acknowledgement. "What did she tell them?"

"Not much, just that there had been an accident and their mom had been taken to hospital. She thought that was for the best. No sense in worrying them unnecessarily. Besides, we don't know much ourselves. There's nothing any of us can do at the moment but wait."

"And pray," Clayton murmured.

Tom grimaced and once again, forced his panic down. Lily would be fine. She was in surgery right as they spoke. They were going to fix her, stop the bleeding and make her better. She was going to be fine.

He looked around at Clayton and Ellie and Brandon. Knowing Brandon's wife, Alex was with Tom's kids, a sudden thought occurred to him. He turned to his family.

"What about all your kids? Where are they?"

"Sam's going to a friend's house straight after school and Bella and Justin are in day care," Brandon offered. "It doesn't close until six."

"What time is it now?" Tom asked.

"A quarter to three," Brandon said.

"What about Olivia and the boys?" Tom directed his question to Clayton, but it was his wife who replied.

"The older two are at school and Damon's at my mother's," Ellie said. "She'll collect Olivia and Mitchell from school in an hour or so. Don't worry, they'll be fine. We're here for as long as you need us," she reassured him.

Tom breathed out a sigh of relief, grateful once again for the show of support. His family meant everything to him. Next to his wife and kids, they were the most important people in the world. There was nothing he wouldn't do for them. It was comforting to know the feeling was reciprocated.

"Mom called again while you were in the bathroom, Tom. She and Dad are taking the next flight out of Grafton. They should be here late this evening," Brandon said.

"They don't have to—"

"They know they don't have to, Tom. They want to. Besides, you'll need someone to help out with Cassie and Joe. They might be teenagers, but they still need someone at home, especially at a time like this. I figure you're going to be here with Lily for the next few days, at least."

Tom sighed again and nodded. "You're right. Thanks. I-I didn't give it any thought. I want to be here when she gets out so I can get some answers from the doctors about her condition and the extent of her injuries. I want to be holding her hand when she wakes up and tells me hello."

For a brief moment his mind wandered in another direction... *What if she didn't make it out, what if the doctors had nothing to tell him other than they'd tried their best? What if he never heard her voice again?* Christ, he wasn't ready to go down that road.

As if sensing his fragile emotions, Brandon stood and walked over to where Tom stood propped against the wall. He patted his brother on the shoulder.

"It's okay, mate. We understand. It wasn't that long ago when I was sitting at Alex's bedside."

Clayton listened and nodded, as if remembering. Tom compressed his lips. No one needed to be reminded of how serious it had been. Alex was also a police officer and had spent a week in the intensive care unit after being shot in the line of duty. For a while, they'd been scared she wouldn't make it.

"She's going to be okay, Tom," Brandon murmured, his voice firm with reassurance.

Tom blinked back tears and nodded. "Yeah, of course she is." The stress of the last few hours was taking its toll. A burning sensation radiated below his ribs on the left side near his sternum, up through his chest and down over his shoulder. He instinctively went to rub the area hoping it would bring him some relief. His hand brushed up against the lump below his left nipple.

He'd found it more than a year ago and had managed to ignore it for just as long. Over the months, he'd made at least two doctor's appointments, but hadn't managed to keep either of them. Before he knew it, the anniversary of the day he'd discovered the lump came and went and he was reminded he still hadn't done anything about it.

After his father's brush with death from a ruptured brain aneurysm last Christmas, Tom had finally resolved to do something about it, but he'd gotten busy at work and there was always something going on with the kids. Time slid by. More weeks went by before he finally made another appointment.

It was scheduled for three days away. Yet again, it looked like another appointment would be missed. Now, it seemed so less important than being by his wife's side. They'd known each other for more than seventeen years. A lifetime. And yet, it felt like it was only yesterday...

CHAPTER 3

Seventeen years earlier

It was late into the night and Tom was well into his cups. Despite being at a party, he was feeling a long way from cheerful. He'd been drinking steadily for the past few hours in an effort to obliterate his day. To call it shitty was putting it too mildly. He was twenty-two years old and a junior constable stationed in Sydney's outer west, and even though he'd undergone rigorous training and numerous psychological tests while at the Academy, nothing had prepared him for the discovery of the bodies of the man and his three children in the garage attached to a lonely farmhouse on the edge of town.

It was the kids who haunted him.

Seven, three and six months old, they'd died of carbon monoxide poisoning. Their father lay slumped over the steering wheel of the family SUV. A bullet had ravished most of his head. What was left of his face was barely identifiable.

To make matters worse, the late spring weather out west had been unseasonably hot and humid, reminding everyone summer wasn't far away. The bodies of the father and his children were green and bloated and oozing putrid body fluids. The stench when Tom wrenched open the passenger door would stay with him forever. Later, the forensic pathologist who carried out the autopsies would estimate the deaths occurred up to three days earlier. It was the estranged wife of the man, the mother of the children, who'd finally alerted police.

According to the officer who had interviewed the wife, she'd become concerned when her husband hadn't returned the children after a scheduled access visit. She wasn't immediately alarmed when she couldn't reach him by phone. Cell phone coverage was sporadic at best at the farmhouse and he'd never given her any reason to panic.

Knowing how it had all gone down, Tom shuddered and took another swig from the bottle of rum in his hand. He wondered a little dazedly when he'd made the switch from a glass. His mind was fuzzy, but still clear enough that he could see those poor children... According to his colleague, even the wife had been at a loss to explain.

The front door of the apartment swung open and brought with it a gust of cool night air. Tom lifted his head and tried to focus on the newcomers. The party had been in full swing for hours. It was odd for a guest to be arriving so late. The host was Charlie Allen, a fellow officer from his station. They were celebrating the man's recent promotion.

It was then that he saw her.

The noise from the music and the crowd of partygoers around him receded and there was nothing and nobody but her. She'd come in with another man and had her back to Tom while she hung up her jacket on the coat rack near the front door. Her long blond hair bounced off her shoulders in a silky wave that shimmered beneath the lights shining down from overhead. His fingers itched to touch its softness. She turned around and laughed at something the man she'd arrived with said and Tom's breath caught.

She was beautiful. No, she was more than beautiful. She was perfection. She was sunshine and laughter and sleepy Sunday mornings. She was quiet walks on the beach...

She moved slightly and the glow from a nearby lamp caught the sheen of her skin. He sucked in another breath. She looked like fine spun crystal, delicate and ethereal. He could almost believe if he reached out and touched her she'd shatter, and yet he sensed a strength deep inside her that seemed to make a lie of his observations.

All of this he managed to ascertain in a handful of seconds. He simply couldn't drag his gaze away. He took a step toward her and then stumbled and reached out blindly for the wall.

"Hey, Tom old boy, you might want to ease up on that stuff." Lionel Skinner, a fellow officer who worked at the same station, laughed and thumped Tom on the back and then continued on his way.

Tom took a moment to draw in a deep breath. He made an effort to steady the pounding of his heart. He looked back toward the front door, but the vision was gone. He blinked.

Had he imagined her? Surely he wasn't that drunk? She couldn't have been a figment of his imagination. He was sure she'd been right there.

With a surge of disappointment, he turned, almost convinced that in his inebriated state, his imagination had conjured her up. He lifted the bottle of rum to his lips and then lowered it without taking a drink. Lionel was right. He'd probably had enough. In fact, he probably should call it a night and head off home to bed. It was lucky he was rostered off the next day. No doubt he'd wake with a stinker of a headache.

With a resigned shrug, he set the bottle of rum on a nearby table and looked around for his host. He'd find Charlie and make his farewells and then call a cab. He'd been stupid to think he could erase the horror of the day's events with alcohol. Now, he'd pay the price.

Shouldering his way through the crowd, he nodded good-byes and acknowledgements to his friends and colleagues. Most of the partygoers were police officers. They tended to socialize together. Not many people outside the force understood the kind of situations they were confronted with day in, day out, and somehow, it was easier to stick with your own people.

None of his colleagues expected him to talk about his

day, but if he volunteered information, there was always a sympathetic ear. He'd barely been out of the Academy two years, but already he'd learned there was plenty about the job that he just didn't feel like talking about.

He stumbled into the hall that led toward the other rooms in the house and continued in search of his host. He wondered again at the angel he'd spied at the front door. Frowning, he entered the kitchen.

The full-throated sound of a woman's laughter stirred something totally foreign and unexpected in his gut. He peered over the heads of a few partygoers that filled the modest space and headed in the direction of the sound. She was surrounded by male officers, all of them hanging off her every word. He couldn't decipher her words, but it was obvious the men were enthralled—or maybe they were just enthralled with *her*. He could well understand their fascination.

He pushed his way through the crowd until he'd joined the group that surrounded her. She leaned back against the kitchen counter, her eyes sparkling with good humor. Up close, she was even more beautiful. And young. She barely looked older than his twin brothers and Clayton and Riley were only seventeen.

He narrowed his gaze and wondered who she was and what she was doing with such a dissolute group. Perhaps she was Charlie's sister or the relative of one of the other guests? Or perhaps she was someone's girlfriend? She'd arrived in the company of a man, after all.

His mind shied away from the thought, not wanting to consider the possibility. He found a position with a clear view of her and leaned back against the wall.

He let out a quiet sigh. It was late. He was tired. He'd had a shit of a day. A day he was glad to put behind him. Closing his eyes, he let the music of her voice wash over him.

———

Lily Strickland looked up from the group of men who surrounded her and noticed the good-looking stranger saunter near. She'd noticed him earlier, when she'd first arrived with David, but she hadn't had a chance to enquire about him. Now he was standing less than three yards away and her heart skipped a beat.

Aware of the men around her eagerly waiting for her to finish her story, she took a breath and forced herself to concentrate. From the corner of her eye, she saw the tall stranger get comfortable against the wall. A moment later, he closed his eyes and appeared to drift off to sleep. Right beneath her nose.

She frowned in consternation. She wasn't used to being ignored. Surely, he wasn't *really* asleep?

And then she heard it. A snore. Soft and muffled and utterly gentlemanlike, but a snore just the same. She halted mid-sentence and stared at him, completely taken aback. He looked like a Greek God, an Adonis with his dark blond hair, thick and mussed. A sun-bleached hank of it hung over his forehead and partially obscured his eyes—eyes, she recalled from moments ago, that were as blue as the summer sky.

She'd lost herself in their depths for the few seconds he'd stared at her and her breath had caught from their impact. And then he'd frowned and squinted, as if trying to bring her into focus and the moment had been lost. But not the memory.

Never in her nineteen years had a man stirred her like he had and they hadn't even exchanged so much as a greeting. *How could that be possible?* This wasn't a Hollywood chick flick where the girl saw the guy and the cameras slowed and the music built and the girl fell instantly and deeply in love. That kind of idiocy only happened in the movies, not in real life. *Never* in real life.

And yet, she couldn't deny that he'd triggered something way down deep inside her and she yearned to know more about the handsome stranger who'd captured her attention like no other. Except now, the man in question was snoring.

It would be a little damaging to any girl's ego and she had to admit, she was slightly miffed. While the men around her hung on her every word, the only one that interested her was sleeping in the corner. She smiled wryly, in good humor. The scenario was more than a little bit comical.

Vowing to forget about him like he'd evidently forgotten about her, she turned back to the men she'd been entertaining with an amusing tale from a day in the life of a college student and continued on with her story. She was about to deliver the punch line when there was the sound of a thud, and a grunt, followed quickly by a curse.

"Fuck!"

The men around Lily turned in unison and stared at the man on the floor. A chuckle built up in Lily's chest and burst out before she could stop it. She laughed and gasped and held her hand over her mouth in an effort to contain her mirth. The stranger stared balefully up at her from his place on the hard floor. His eyes narrowed dangerously.

Lily should have taken his dark look as her cue to stop, but her laughter continued to sound. He looked so surprised to find himself flat on his butt on the floor. Now, she simply *had* to know who he was.

———————

Tom heaved himself up off the floor and surreptitiously rubbed his sore ass. One minute he'd been listening to the angel regale the men near her with tales of college shenanigans and the next he was coming into contact with the very hard, wooden floor. The least Charlie could have done was find an apartment that had carpet. Tom's bum would be bruised for a week.

Not that anyone cared, from the looks of amusement on their faces. Even the angel thought it was funny. In fact, from the way she was splitting her sides laughing, she found it downright hysterical.

He shot her an intimidating look that would make most

people go weak with fear, but it didn't have the same effect on her. She looked like she had no intention of stopping. How could he have found her so desirable? She was a heartless, little witch. At last, Charlie appeared in the doorway, looking concerned.

"Tom, are you all right? What happened? Someone said you fell over. Did you hurt yourself?"

Knowing the angel could hear every word that was said and not wanting to embarrass himself further, Tom shrugged his shoulders in response and remained silent. If he were honest, his pride was damaged far worse than his ass.

Had he really fallen asleep? Christ, he must have been more exhausted than he'd thought. He was at a party and he'd fallen asleep, right after locking eyes with the most beautiful girl in the world. And now she was laughing at him.

He snuck another glance in her direction and was relieved to find she'd sobered and was looking suitably concerned. She pushed her way through the crowd of men and came up to Tom with her hand extended.

It was pale and slender and her fingers were long. It was all Tom had time to comprehend before her soft, slim hand was in his. Her handshake was firm and sure and reminded him of the hidden strength he'd sensed in her earlier. She was made of sterner stuff than she looked. Her eyes, a bright, clear blue now sparkled with intelligence tinged with humor.

"Lily Strickland. Nice to meet you."

"T-Tom. Tom Munro. It's... It's nice to meet you, too."

"Really? A moment ago you were snoring. I was sure I'd bored you to sleep." She grinned and then offered him a wink.

A fresh wave of embarrassment swept over his cheeks, but her teasing went right through him. It unsettled his gut and suddenly it felt like a swarm of butterflies had been let loose inside him. He swallowed and tried to get his tongue to work so he would appear somewhat in control of his faculties. At the same time, he silently cursed the rum that clouded his brain.

He wanted to be sharp and witty and clever for this vision in front of him who still couldn't help but grin. He opened his mouth and waited for some brilliant repartee to come pouring forth.

"I don't snore."

He clamped his mouth shut in horror, unable to believe he'd come out with such a lame line. Here was the chance of a lifetime and all he could do was dispute her powers of observation. She'd more than likely turn away and never speak to him again.

He almost didn't dare to look up again, lest she'd done exactly that, but to his relief, she laughed again—that beautiful, full-throated sound.

"Oh, yes you do and I have a number of witnesses to prove it. What's more, given that you were asleep while it was happening, the odds aren't great that you'll disprove it!"

Charlie watched the exchange in amusement. "She's got you there, Tom."

Tom grimaced, but tempered it with a rueful grin. "Thanks for your support, mate."

"Anytime." He held his arms out wide. "What are friends for?"

Tom chuckled and then wished he hadn't. Already the effects of his overindulgence were making themselves felt in his belly and in his head. As much as he now wanted to stay, if he wanted to leave the angel with even a modicum of a good impression, he best make his departure now. It was only going to get ugly from this point on.

He turned back to her and did his best to keep her in focus. "Lily, it was lovely to meet you."

She smiled. "You already told me that."

"And I'm telling you again. Surely, there's no harm in that?"

"You're right. There's no harm in it at all. It was lovely to meet you, too, Tom Munro."

"Christ, you're beautiful. Will you give me your number?" he blurted out and then groaned inwardly at his lack of finesse.

"I don't think so, Tom, but it was nice of you to ask."

Tom stared beseechingly at her for a moment longer and then sighed. "You're right. It was nice. I guess I'd better get going. All of a sudden, I don't feel so well. In fact, I think I'm going to—" He bolted in the direction of Charlie's bathroom and only just made it there in time.

CHAPTER 4

Roseville, Sydney—present day

Brady Sutton flipped over onto his side for the hundredth time and tried to get comfortable on his bed. He'd been interviewed by the police in the presence of his mom and the lawyer she'd arranged and after several hours had been charged with attempted murder. He'd been fingerprinted, photographed and taken before the judge where he'd been granted conditional bail. He'd then been allowed to return home with his mom until the next court appearance.

Lawyer; charges; judge; bail. The unfamiliar words crashed around inside his brain and he shook his head at the enormity of what had happened. It was never that way when he went hunting on *GTA V*.

He thought of Mrs Munro and bit down hard on a cry of pain. How had it gone so wrong? She'd wrestled with the gun right at the moment he'd pulled the trigger. It wasn't supposed to happen that way. It was Ian Little who should be dead, not Mrs Munro.

Not that she was dead—yet. The police were quick to inform him with their hard, narrow-eyed stares that if her condition deteriorated and she died, his charges would be upgraded to murder.

Murder. The very word was incomprehensible. He wasn't

a murderer. All he'd wanted to do was to even the playing field; set the record straight; stand up for himself, like his mom was always encouraging him to do; rid himself once and for all of the agony and torture at the hands of the school yard bullies.

But it hadn't turned out that way and now his life was over. Ian and his buddies would go on their merry way, teasing and tormenting. His mom looked like she'd aged a decade. She could barely bring herself to look at him. She kept blaming his father over and over again. Brady couldn't bear the thought of what she'd say to his dad.

It wasn't his father's fault. Okay, he'd given Brady the gun to look after, but he'd never encouraged him to use it. He'd never even shown him how to load it. He'd given him *GTA V*, but the game hadn't caused Brady any grief. It was Ian who shouldered the responsibility for working him up to such an extent that fatal violence seemed to be the only solution.

But it was Brady, not Ian, who was now in big trouble. Until today, he'd never been inside the belly of a police station. Even when his mom had woken him in the middle of the night to file a police report against his father, he'd been left in the care of another officer out in the reception area.

The interview rooms were located way in the back, not far from the steel barred cells. Brady had been marched right past them when they'd entered the station from the rear through an access not open to the public. It was probably built that way on purpose, to put fear into the baddies. It had certainly worked on him.

After being handcuffed and dragged out of the school grounds, he'd been tossed into the back of a police wagon. His mother had protested on a loud cry, but the officers had paid her little heed. He'd been taken to the station by the same two officers who had arrested him. They hadn't seemed to mind that he was thrown from side to side when they took the corners too fast.

His mom had been forced to wait out front until they went and got her. Brady had been given plenty of time to contemplate the state of his life. He'd barely been able to hold back the tears when his mom had finally been allowed to join him.

After one of the arresting officers had explained what was going to happen, his mom had been given a chance to call a lawyer. Brady didn't even know she knew a lawyer, but nearly an hour later, a man a little older than his father, wearing a dark pinstripe suit turned up at the station and introduced himself.

The rest of the interview had passed in a blur. He could remember his lawyer cautioning him against answering many of their questions, but Brady had nothing to hide. He'd gone to school with the intention of eradicating a vermin from society, or at least a vermin from the school yard. Assholes like Ian Little had no place in this world, no right to be a part of it.

The fact that Mrs Munro had gotten injured was nothing more than an accident. Surely, they would see that? But despite his pleas that he hadn't meant to hurt her, the police went ahead and charged him.

His mother had burst into tears.

A doctor appeared in the corridor that led to the operating theaters and headed toward the group of people gathered in the waiting room. Tom was the first to spot him and leaped to his feet, his heart taking off at a gallop. He prayed the news was good.

The fatigue etched into the doctor's face spoke volumes. Night had fallen. He'd been in the theater all day.

"I'm looking for the family of Lily Munro. Are you her relatives?" the doctor asked in a weary voice.

Tom stepped forward and wiped his palms on his police overalls. "I'm Tom Munro, Lily's husband," he said and offered the doctor his hand.

"Tom, I'm Matthew Reeves, one of the surgeons here. My team and I operated on your wife."

Tom could barely breathe past the lump that had lodged itself in his throat, but he forced himself to voice the question.

"H-how is she?" The doctor sighed and Tom's pulse leaped into a higher gear.

"Please, doctor, tell me. Is she…is she alive?"

The doctor nodded and Tom breathed out on a heavy sigh of relief. It was short lived. A moment later, Doctor Reeves spoke again.

"Yes, she's still alive, but I'm afraid she's in bad shape. The bullet passed through her abdomen and exited out through her lower back. While it missed all of the major arteries, it caused a lot of internal damage. We've repaired a tear in her spleen and two in her liver. The lining of her stomach was also torn. Part of her large intestine was damaged beyond repair. Three ribs were also fractured, but that's the least of our concerns." He paused and then continued.

"I need to warn you that not many people take a bullet through the stomach and live to tell the tale—and if they do survive, it's usually with lifelong afflictions. We removed part of her large intestine and we've managed to repair the rest of the damage. The bleeding's stopped, but she's lost a lot of blood. We gave her a blood transfusion and for now we just have to wait and see."

Tom struggled to take it all in. He stumbled and leaned on Brandon for support. "So, what are you saying? That there's still a possibility she'll die?"

"The next twenty-four to forty-eight hours will be crucial," the doctor replied. "We'll keep a close eye on her in the ICU. I'm sorry, I wish I could give you more hope."

This time, Tom's legs buckled and he would have gone down if not for the strength and support of Brandon's arm. Clayton and Ellie moved closer, shock and concern shadowing their eyes.

"She's going to be okay, mate. You'll see," Brandon muttered.

Tom wanted to shake his head in denial, but even that simple action was beyond him. Brandon couldn't give him reassurances like that. Not even the doctor offered that much hope. Feeling suddenly detached and far removed from the reality of the situation, Tom saw Brandon reach for the doctor's hand and give it a firm shake. It all seemed to play out in slow motion.

"Thank you, doctor. Please keep us informed. We'll be here, waiting."

The doctor nodded somberly and then quirked an eyebrow. "You look a little familiar. I seem to remember operating on *your* wife a few years back. If I recall, she was also the victim of a gunshot wound."

Brandon slowly nodded. "You're right. Doctor Reeves. Now I remember. It was four years ago. Alex is her name. You saved her life."

The doctor's lips compressed, but his eyes reflected his silent acceptance of Brandon's praise and gratitude. "I hope she's doing well."

"More than well," Brandon assured him. "We owe it all to you."

"Thank you, but I was merely doing my job."

"Well, we appreciate your efforts all the same," Brandon murmured.

The doctor nodded. "I just hope we have as good an outcome with Lily. Her injuries are so much more severe... It's hard to tell."

"When can I see her?" Tom asked, needing desperately to be close to the woman he loved more than life itself. His heart was silently shattering and it was tearing him apart.

"She's not long left the operating theater. She'll be in recovery for a little while longer, but the nurse will give you a call when they have her settled. They'll take her up to the ICU. You'll be allowed to see her there, but please keep in mind she's gravely ill. We ask that you restrict your visits to one family member at a time and keep your visits brief. Ten minutes or so at the most."

"Is she conscious?" Brandon asked quietly.

Doctor Reeves shook his head. "Not yet. At this stage, it's hard to tell how long she might remain that way. I promise I'll keep you regularly informed of her progress."

The black hole of despair and disbelief sucked Tom in deeper. His jaw ached with the effort it took to refrain from voicing his pain. It wasn't fair. Not his Lily. He couldn't bear the thought of how he might be forced to go on without her.

Lily fought against the thick, dark current that held her down, preventing her from opening her eyes. She couldn't ever remember being in so much pain. Everything hurt. Her chest, her side, her back, her belly... It even hurt to breathe. The memory of what had happened came back to her in a rush and she was filled with despair and disbelief.

Tom. She needed to see him. She didn't know if he'd been at the school, but she was sure he was at the hospital. Being a police officer stationed near the crime scene, he would have been one of the first people to find out that she was involved and he would have made certain he was by her side. He was probably pacing the corridor right now, waiting impatiently to be allowed in to see her.

She still couldn't believe Brady had shot her, albeit by accident. If she hadn't thrown herself in the path of the bullet, Ian would have been hit and the outcome might have been fatal. *Or perhaps it had been fatal? Perhaps she was already dead?* No, she wasn't dead. She hurt far too much to be dead.

Her thoughts switched to Hannah and she bit her lip against another surge of despair. She couldn't imagine what her friend was thinking. She'd be blaming herself, questioning everything, wondering how the hell it had happened. Her son...

Hannah had been doing it tough ever since the breakdown of her marriage and lately, perhaps she hadn't been quite as attentive to Brady's needs as she normally was. She'd been dealing with a lot with Colin and the stress of a new school term beginning and everything else she juggled in her daily life. Lily knew firsthand how overwhelmed

Hannah had begun to feel and now she couldn't help but sympathize with the agony her friend must be enduring over her son.

All of a sudden, the weight of her thoughts and the heaviness deep in her heart was too much to bear. The smooth, cool darkness beckoned to her, promising relief from the tragic reality that faced her. On a soft sigh, she succumbed once again to the deep...

CHAPTER 5

Seventeen years earlier

More than a week had passed since the party at Charlie Allen's apartment, but Lily could remember it like it happened yesterday, or more particularly, she could remember every second in time she'd spent with the man who had haunted her thoughts ever since. She'd been invited to attend the party with her roommate and although she'd been reluctant at first, David had finally convinced her to go.

"Come on, it will be fun. The host is a cop friend of mine. There will be plenty of hot single guys in uniform to choose from." He'd wiggled his brows suggestively and she'd burst out laughing.

"I thought you said it was a party? I'm pretty sure they're not going to turn up in uniform," she giggled.

David grinned, unabashed. "Okay, so maybe they won't be in uniform, but have you ever seen an ugly cop? Those broad shoulders, those tight buns. It's from all that running after criminals that keeps them in such good shape."

Lily rolled her eyes and shook her head, but had eventually agreed to accompany him. She'd been bogged down in study for her end-of-year exams and could do with a break.

She and David had been sharing an apartment since

their second semester at college. Like her, he was in his first year and also studying to be a teacher. They'd met on campus and discovered they shared many of the same classes. Pretty soon were comparing notes about their professor. David's outrageous sense of humor and flamboyant ways had drawn her and they'd quickly become friends.

She'd suspected right from the beginning that he was gay and wasn't at all surprised when he came out to her the first month after they'd arrived at college. Blinking back tears, he confessed quietly that she was the only person who knew. It was almost as if the freedom and anonymity that came from living in a big city had given him the courage to finally stop pretending.

Glancing at the clock on the kitchen wall, she grimaced, remembering her mother and stepfather were expected to visit later that day. There were dirty dishes in the sink from breakfast and the carpet hadn't been hoovered for a week. The stereotype that all gay men were clean and tidy was simply not true. At least, not the gay man she shared an apartment with. David might have been fastidious about his appearance, but the state of his home was entirely another matter.

With a sigh of resignation, she began collecting old newspapers and junk mail off the coffee table and dropped them into the trash. Next, she grabbed a cleaning cloth and disinfectant and headed into the bathroom. Her mother and Tony weren't staying the night, but the chances that at least one of them would use the bathroom were high. It wouldn't do for her mother to find it less than sanitary and by that, Fiona Gibbons meant *sparkling*.

Lily shook her head and her lips tugged upwards in a rueful smile. She shouldn't be too harsh on her mother. Lily's life would have been a whole lot different if her mother hadn't loved her enough to find the courage to walk out on Lily's abusive father.

Before the depressing memories of her childhood took hold, Lily dampened the cloth in the bathroom sink and sprayed disinfectant around the toilet. She thought again of the hot police officer from the party and smiled. She wouldn't have wanted to wake up with the headache she was sure had greeted him the next morning, nor the mess that had no doubt been splattered all over the toilet.

Her smile slowly faded. It was obvious the guy had been drunk. More than drunk. Plastered, was probably a better word. He'd fallen asleep standing up. That told her more than enough.

She shook her head, her heart slowly filling with regret. It was a shame. He was cute enough to send her heart fluttering like a brightly colored banner in the wind. It was a pity he was a drinker. She didn't do drunks. Period.

Chapter 6

Royal North Shore Hospital—present day

Tom stared down at his wife's pale form where she lay against the pristine white sheets that covered the steel hospital bed and tightened his grip on her hand. The nurse had reassured him Lily's vital signs were good and she was resting comfortably, even though she had yet to regain consciousness.

"She'll wake up when she's ready," the kindly woman with the gray hair and tired eyes added and then patted him lightly on the arm before moving away to attend to another patient.

Tom tried hard to believe her, to force some of her optimism deep into his heart, but his body resisted his efforts and the blackness continued to weigh him down. His wife looked so small and defenseless amongst the tubes and monitors in and around her bed. He silently cursed the boy whose stupidity had reduced her to this state of fragility, her life held in the balance. Lily didn't deserve this pain. She'd always been so committed to her students. He couldn't fathom why someone would want to hurt her in this way.

An IV cannula carried essential fluids through her veins and another tube protruded from under the sheets. Tom guessed it was some kind of drain. It was attached to a large glass bottle that stood on the floor beneath her bed. From the look of the dark colored liquid that emptied into it, the tube was draining blood. He shuddered and turned away.

It wasn't like he'd never seen a person in trauma before. Christ, he'd lost count of the number of victims he'd dealt with over his years on the force, but it was different when it was Lily. She was his wife, the woman that he loved. She wasn't some faceless stranger from whom he could remain detached.

The sight and sounds of so much medical equipment sent cold dread shivering through his veins. He hadn't been inside an ICU since his father's ruptured aneurysm the year before, but he hadn't forgotten the rows of motionless patients, silent except for the sound of their breathing machines and the beeping of their monitors. Lily was now one of them.

Tom leaned over in his chair beside her bed and pressed a soft kiss against her hand. Despite the fact that it had been hours and hours since the shooting, tension still held him tightly in its grip. His phone vibrated against his hip and he pulled it off his belt clip and glanced at the screen. It was a text message from Brandon.

Alex has arrived with Cassie and Joe. They're in the waiting room. The kids are asking to see their mom.

Tom bit his lip and scrunched his eyes tight and tried to find the courage to face his children. He didn't know what they'd been told, but they weren't stupid. No one was put in the ICU unless it was life threatening. He prayed he'd find the words to tell them what they needed to know without causing them unnecessary fear or alarm.

He made an impatient sound in the back of his throat. *Unnecessary fear or alarm?* Who the hell was he kidding? They'd be scared stiff and thinking the worst. He owed it to them to tell the truth.

Pushing back from the chair, he leaned over and kissed his wife on the cheek. Despite her pallor, she was warm to the touch and for that at least, he was grateful. She might look like death, but she *felt* very much alive. He had to keep clinging to that fact. Swallowing a sigh, he made his way out of the ICU and headed down toward the visitors' waiting room.

A television murmured low sounds in the background, but nobody in the room appeared interested in what was on the screen. Tom caught sight of his daughter and son. Brandon and Alex were close by. With eyes downcast, they were all seated in the mismatch of chairs that filled the modest room. He cleared his throat.

"Hi, guys."

Cassie twisted in her chair and jumped to her feet. A moment later, she launched herself at him. His arms came around her and held her close. "Cassie, how are you, honey?"

"How's Mom?" she gasped, tears gathering in her eyes.

"She's doing fine, sweetheart. The doctors operated on her earlier today and she's holding her own."

"What does that mean? Is she awake? Can I see her?" his daughter pleaded.

"Um...sure. But she's still unconscious. I don't want to frighten you. There's a heap of equipment around her bed. It looks pretty scary. Are you sure you're up to it?"

"Dad, I'm seventeen. I'm not a baby. I want to see her. I want to know she's going to be okay."

"How come she's not awake?" Joe asked, his expression solemn.

Tom's heart broke a little at the shadow of fear in his son's eyes. Releasing Cassie, he greeted Joe with a hard hug and then stepped back.

"She's been given some pretty strong medication to help with the pain, buddy. She's sleeping right now, but she's okay. She came through the operation and the doctors are keeping an eye on her for the next little while. Don't worry, she's in good hands."

Tom heard the words that fell from his mouth and knew they were said as much to convince himself as they were to reassure his children. He was glad Alex had brought them by, but all he really wanted was to ignore everyone and everything and head straight back to Lily's bedside. He wanted to hold tightly to his wife's warm hand and never let go.

Joe pulled away and returned to his seat. Brandon stepped forward and shook Tom's hand.

"How is she?" he asked quietly, keeping his back to his niece and nephew.

"No change, so I guess that's a good thing. At least, that's what the nurses keep telling me. I just want her to wake up and speak."

"I'm sure they're right, mate. They do this for a living, remember? You have to trust that they know what they're doing."

"Yeah, but watching her lying there with all those tubes and machines and a heap of other junk keeping her alive—it's killing me, Bran."

Brandon held Tom's gaze. "She's made of stronger stuff, mate. Remember how she was when Cassie was taken? And even before that. The crap she went through when Alex and I split up—she's as tough and resilient as anyone I know. It all worked out in the end. She's going to pull through, Tom. I'm sure of it."

Tom stared at Brandon and his chest grew tight. He was grateful for Brandon's reassurances, even though his brother knew no more about Lily's chances than he did.

"Thanks for bringing Cass and Joe by, Bran." His gaze encompassed Alex who stood and moved over to where they were. "I really appreciate it," he added.

"That's okay," Alex replied. They've been bugging me all evening to be allowed over here. It was wearing on them. I don't know how many times I explained to them that their mom's visitors were restricted in the ICU, but they wanted to be here."

She smiled softly and Tom's lips lifted in response. The simple action felt good. It had been awhile since he'd smiled.

"I can understand how they feel. I want to be here every minute of every hour, despite the fact she doesn't even know I'm here."

"It's natural to feel like that, Tom," Brandon said quietly, "but you've been here most of the day and it's now going on for ten. You need to take a break." He looked at Tom's kids who'd returned to their seats, looking without interest toward the TV.

"It's late. Why don't you take your kids home and get a good night's rest? You won't do Lily any good if you crash in a heap. When Mom and Dad arrive, I'll send them over to your place. That way, they can take over and you can come back here first thing in the morning."

Tom grimaced. A moment later, he did his best to hide a yawn. "You're right, Bran, but I can't leave her on her own. I just can't."

"I've arranged to have a few days' leave. I'm happy to stay tonight."

Tom looked at Brandon in surprise. "Really? You'd do that for me?"

"Will you go home if I don't?"

Tom shook his head. "Nope."

"That's why I've offered to stay. I rested up this afternoon especially, in preparation for the night shift."

Tom choked up and hugged his brother hard. When he spoke, his voice was gruff with emotion.

"Thanks, Bran. I really appreciate it." He sighed and rubbed a hand across his forehead. "Chanel called me earlier. She also urged me to get some rest. She said it's unlikely Lily will regain consciousness tonight. She also explained a bit about comas. I'd heard some of it before, of course, when Dad was sick, but with her medical background, it was nice to have someone to explain it in plain English."

"I know what you mean. Now, how about you take these kids to visit their mom and then go home? I have everything under control."

"Call me if anything changes?"

"I will. I promise."

"I don't care what time of night it is. If something happens, if Lily wakes up...or deteriorates...I want to know."

Brandon nodded, his expression solemn. "Of course. I'll call if anything happens. I swear."

Tom felt a rush of affection for his brother. With a hug good-bye and another one for Alex, he put his arms around his children and with measured footsteps, led them in the direction of the ICU.

CHAPTER 7

Seventeen years earlier

It took Tom over a week to find the courage to phone Lily Strickland. After calling Charlie the day after the party to apologize for his unseemly behavior, he'd casually enquired about the blond angel who went by the name of Lily. Charlie ribbed him about his interest and told him she was way out of his league.

Lily Strickland was the stepdaughter of Tony Gibbons, a very successful, prestigious car dealer on Sydney's lower north shore. She'd been educated in the city's most exclusive girls' school and was now attending Sydney University, not far from the city. Tony, it seemed, had done very well in the car business and his stepdaughter wanted for nothing.

It explained the posh accent and cultured ways that had immediately drawn him. Tom might not have come from a privileged background, but his father's job as a criminal defense lawyer and later, a District Court judge, had given him a comfortable life. He'd attended public school, lacked nothing and there had always been an abundance of love—that for him, was far more important than money.

He didn't know how his angel felt about the material advantages she enjoyed, but he was intrigued enough to find out. While Charlie didn't have her phone number, he did know how to contact her roommate. Tom was relieved to discover the man she'd arrived with at the party was no more than a friend and immediately his heart leaped with hope.

Could it be that she was between relationships? Could he really be that lucky?

It took Charlie more than a week to come back to him and having found the courage to call her, Tom chafed at the enforced delay. They were the longest days of his life. Finally, he received the news he'd been waiting for: Charlie had spoken to David who'd talked to Lily and yes, she was willing to give Tom her number.

He'd punched the air with excitement and then immediately felt sick to his gut. *What if she only wanted to speak to him in order to chew him out?* He was mortified over his behavior at the party. He could only assume she'd heard him being sick. Charlie had been more than happy to tell him he'd made so much noise, there hadn't been a single soul at the party who hadn't heard Tom Munro emptying his guts.

At least he'd made it to the toilet in time. He couldn't imagine the humiliation of having to ask for a mop and bucket...

Pushing the revolting thought aside, he concentrated on the positive. Lily had given him her number. It was better progress than he'd made the night they'd met. She wanted him to call. *Surely, that was a good sign?* He was determined to believe that it was.

Lily pulled her long hair back into a ponytail and secured it with a band. Choosing a pale pink lipstick, she applied it to her lips. Moving back from the bathroom mirror, she stared at her reflection and sighed. Her heart was racing at the thought of seeing Tom Munro again, but was she being fair? To either of them?

When David told her that Tom had asked about her and wanted to give her a call, she'd been both excited and nervous. She recalled how she felt when she spied him from across the room; how everyone and everything had simply faded away. The moment was surreal. It was the most romantic moment of her life. But then, she'd gotten closer to him and had realized he was drunk.

His Hollywood looks had immediately lost a lot of their appeal. She remembered feeling disappointed. After the nightmare of her childhood, she'd vowed never to get involved with a drinker. It was the reason she'd refused to give him her number at the party. Now, she had to admit he'd been almost constantly on her mind.

She was nineteen and had nearly finished the first year of her teaching degree. She'd dated a string of men, though none of them had made a lasting impression. One thing her dates had in common was that none of them, not a single one, drank.

Most of the time, she vetted them before they went out. She simply asked them straight up if they drank. Those that said yes never made it to the first date. There were still plenty of men who refrained from alcohol. Okay, maybe she had to search a little harder, especially on a college campus, but it was possible to find them and she'd enjoyed their company.

It was just that none of them had reached into her soul and touched her like Tom Munro had. It depressed her and saddened her and maddened her all at once. Finally, she'd found a man who touched her so deeply, she was sure she wouldn't find it with anyone else. There was just one problem: He was a drinker. And that fact was insurmountable.

Not only did he drink, but he drank until he fell down. The thought of having any kind of relationship with him went against every promise she'd ever made to herself. And yet, here she was, primping and preening in preparation for his arrival and doing her best to contain her excitement.

Perhaps he wasn't much of a drinker at all? Perhaps it was

his first time? Maybe that was the reason he hadn't handled his liquor? Or perhaps someone had spiked his drink?

She shook her head at the list of excuses and smiled ruefully at her reflection in the mirror. She was being ridiculous. She barely knew the guy. Besides, he'd been holding a bottle of rum. It was only because he'd managed, without even a word, to touch something deep inside her and despite her reservations, she was intrigued enough to want to spend a little more time with him.

The doorbell to her apartment chimed and her nerves kicked up a gear. With a hand that wasn't quite steady, she applied another coat of lipstick and then dropped it into her evening bag. She could hear the murmur of voices and was pleased David was home to break the ice. He'd made her promise to tell him all about her date when she got home later that night.

With a deep breath, she squared her shoulders and then eased the air out on a gentle sigh. For better or worse, she was ready—ready to give him a chance.

Tom stared at the woman who came toward him, a vision in a short crimson dress. It was made from some kind of flimsy material that floated around her slim thighs. The top of it was secured around her neck and left her shoulders bare. Her skin glowed golden in the soft light of the living room.

She leaned over and pecked him on the cheek and his nose was filled with her scent—something sweet and feminine and floral. Her nearness sent blood surging straight to his groin. He swallowed a groan and wondered how the hell he was going to get through the next few hours. He'd arranged for them to go to dinner at one of the city's most exclusive restaurants and was thinking they'd hit a nightclub afterwards, but right at that moment, he wasn't sure he could withstand the pressure of being so close to her and not being allowed to touch.

He wished they were over that awkward first-or-second-date stage when neither of them knew the rules. Did she want him to kiss her or just hold her hand? Maybe she didn't want either. It was a minefield of possible hits and misses and it made him nervous just thinking about it. He wished he could go back to being drunk, when he hadn't felt quite so inhibited—not drunk enough to fall asleep and then disgrace himself in the bathroom—just a slight buzz to take the edge off.

His throat was suddenly parched and he longed for an ice cold beer: Just a glass or two to settle his nerves. The polite chitchat he'd engaged in with Lily's roommate wasn't nearly enough. Suddenly, he couldn't get to the restaurant and its promise of alcoholic relief quick enough.

He glanced around the living room and noted the tidy, but mismatched furniture. Colorful cushions added interest to a brown sofa that had seen better days. A small kitchen that was also neat and tidy, stood off to the left. Behind him, a corridor led to what he assumed were the bathroom and bedrooms. At least, he hoped there were two bedrooms.

"You look beautiful, Lily. Are you ready to go?"

She blinked and he realized he'd spoken a little fast. Wiping his sweaty palms against his dark dress pants, he tried again.

"It's lovely to meet you again and thank you for accepting my invitation. We didn't really get a chance to talk at Charlie's party."

"Well, if you hadn't been getting up close and personal with the porcelain, you might have," David quipped with a cheeky grin.

Tom's cheeks exploded with heat and he cursed David silently beneath his breath, but there was nothing he could do but accept the jibe with as much grace as he could manage. After all, the man was only speaking the truth. Tom offered a wry grin and nodded.

"Yep, you're right about that. It'll teach me to drink half a bottle of rum on an empty stomach. My dad would be appalled. I can hear him even now telling me I'm old enough to know better."

David laughed, but Lily's smile was strained and Tom wondered briefly about its cause. He could only imagine she found the topic a little distasteful. He could hardly blame her. Most people found the thought of someone vomiting a little distasteful, let alone resurrecting memories of the sound. Keen to get their date back on a proper footing, he turned back to her.

"So, how do you two know each other?"

David threw an arm around Lily's shoulders and pulled her close to his side. "We met at college," he said. "We're both studying teaching and we have a number of classes together. I'm hopeless at reading a map. I was trying to find the English Literature lecture theater, but was on the wrong side of the campus. Lily came across me wandering around lost and confused and took pity on me. We've been friends ever since."

Lily smiled at him and Tom couldn't help the stab of jealousy that pierced his insides. He had no right to be jealous. Charlie had told him they were friends. Good friends. There was nothing wrong with that.

"I take it you're a better map reader than he is?" Tom said, making an effort to keep his voice light.

Lily nodded and this time, the smile she turned on him seem to come more naturally. "I guess you can say that. I manage to get us to where we need to go most of the time." She turned back to David who still had his arm around her shoulders. "Don't I?"

David smiled down at her fondly. "Yep, I don't know where I'd be without you."

"Lost, that's where." They shared another mutual look of contentment and understanding and Tom was suddenly envious of their closeness. Whether there was more to their relationship than they were saying, he had yet to discover, but there was no denying they shared a special bond.

"How long have you been in college?" he asked, keen to discover how long they'd known each other.

"We're coming up to the end of our first year," Lily replied.

"I went to college straight out of high school. David took a gap year."

Tom digested that information in silence. No wonder she looked so young. She was probably eighteen or nineteen. Much younger than the girls he usually dated. As the oldest of seven children, Tom had matured early and had always had a finely honed sense of responsibility. He could still remember coming home after school and having to watch over his younger siblings until his mom came home. Sometimes it was an hour or two later, depending on what she'd been doing.

Marguerite Munro had worked as a nurse during the early years of her marriage. After the children arrived, whilst she gave up her career, she became heavily involved in charity work and often didn't arrive back home until well after they'd climbed off the school bus.

Still, what was in an age? Tom had dated girls his age and even older who lacked common sense and know-how. Age didn't always equate to maturity. Just like youth didn't necessarily mean stupidity.

Eighteen or nineteen—what did it matter? Somehow, some way, she'd touched him way down deep inside. He'd never felt that way with anyone and he owed it to himself to see if she felt the same.

He looked at her and David again and while her roommate still had his arm around her shoulders, there was nothing possessive in his embrace—more like a protective, older brother. Tom could relate to that and he was absolutely fine with it. In fact, the more he thought about it, the more he was pleased she had someone looking out for her.

A renewed surge of confidence flooded through him and he turned to shake David's hand in farewell.

"It was nice to meet you, David. I guess I'll see you later."

David winked at him and then threw Lily a teasing smile. "You can bet on it. Have a nice time."

Tom opened the door to the glitzy restaurant that overlooked Sydney Harbor and Lily was once again impressed with his old-fashioned manners. He'd opened the door for her when she'd climbed into and out of his car and now, was ushering her up the stairs. She held onto the balustrade to steady herself and found Tom's hand right there at her elbow.

"Are you okay?" he enquired in his deep, sexy voice that sent her pulse into overdrive.

"Yes, thanks, I'm…I'm fine. My sandals are…a tad high. They're slipping a little on the parquet floor."

He glanced down and nodded, at once understanding her dilemma. The highly polished tiles were a beautiful chestnut color and gleamed golden in the restaurant's soft lighting, but it also looked hazardous to anyone wearing four-inch heels.

"I don't know how you walk in those things at any time, let alone over a polished floor," Tom teased.

Lily smiled. When he smiled back—a slow, sexy you're-the-most-important-girl-in-the-world smile—her heart skipped a beat. She couldn't believe how quickly she was falling for him and despite all her silent promises not to get involved with a man who liked to drink, everything else she'd seen so far impressed the hell out of her.

That was the problem. She wasn't thinking with her head. He was funny and sexy and considerate and polite and she was letting those admirable qualities override her knowledge of his fondness for a drink. She needed to be a little more circumspect and find out exactly what had happened that night at Charlie's party. In the meantime, she was going to enjoy being taken to one of her mother's favorite restaurants.

They made it to the top of the stairs and Tom guided her over to the maître'd, his hand still warm on her elbow. She should have taken offense at the proprietary feel of that, but the truth was, she liked it. The boys she'd dated in high school and even the ones she'd gone out with in college had the attitude that a girl could fend for herself and even though Lily was a feminist, she also liked to have her femininity appreciated.

"Miss Lily! I didn't know you were dining with us tonight!"

Lily smiled fondly at the maître'd and gave him a warm hug. "Manny, how are you? It's been ages! How are Mona and all of those grandkids? Still keeping you busy, no doubt."

Manny nodded, his face wreathed in a smile.

"Max's twins turned thirteen the other day." He shook his head. "Where does the time go?"

Lily smiled again. "You're telling me. I'm almost finished my first year at college."

"No, bambina. It can't be so. It only seems like yesterday your Mama and stepfather were bringing you up those stairs in pigtails and cotton socks."

"Ah, hm." Tom cleared his throat and Lily suddenly remembered her manners.

"I'm sorry, Tom, I'd like you to meet Manny Antonopoulos. Manny, this is Tom Munro." She turned back to Tom. "Manny has been the maître'd here since I was a little girl."

Tom shook Manny's hand and then turned to Lily.

"I didn't realize you'd been here before. I wanted to take you somewhere special."

"Don't worry, this *is* somewhere special. Watsons by the Sea is my mother's favorite restaurant and it's also one of mine. My stepfather brings us here quite often. They do a fantastic pecan pie and the ice cream is to die for."

Tom's eyes glimmered with amusement. "I take it you have a sweet tooth."

Lily shot him a wry smile. "I'm not a big eater. Sometimes I don't have room for dessert and that's the best part of all." She shrugged. "So, I start at the other end. If I don't have room for an entrée, it doesn't matter."

Tom laughed outright. It was the kind of joyous rumble that came from deep inside him and people couldn't help but respond to. Lily noticed a few of the other diners turn to look in their direction and smile. Even Manny chuckled. Tom directed his attention toward the maître'd.

"Is it true, Manny? Does she really skip the main meal and head straight for the dessert?"

Manny's lips twitched, but he managed to keep a sober face. "Oh, yes, it's true Mr Munro. Most of our chef's expertise is wasted on this one. It's always been that way."

"I guess that means she's a cheap date, then?" He winked, his expression telling her he was teasing.

"Oh, no, Mr Munro, there's nothing cheap about our Lily. She's top shelf all the way."

Tom's gaze gave her a slow once-over that had Lily curling her toes. Heat followed in a trail behind him and centered in her core. Her nipples hardened under his inspection and she silently cursed the clingy material that exposed her reaction to his gaze. From the way his eyes deepened to cobalt when they once again met hers, she could tell he'd missed nothing.

What did she expect? He was a police officer, after all. Clearing her throat of sudden nerves, she urged Manny to show them to their table. A few moments later, they were ensconced in a cosy corner overlooking the harbor.

Manny went to pull out her chair, but Tom beat him to it. Lily murmured her thanks. His warm hands skimmed across her bare shoulders and she shivered from the heat left in their wake.

This was ridiculous! How could she be so turned on by a man she'd only just met? But no matter how much she tried to tell herself it was madness, her reaction to his nearness couldn't be denied.

He took a seat and pulled his chair closer into the table. His knee brushed against hers and once again, her pulse quickened. She wished for an instant that she could gulp down some wine in order to steady her nerves. Her friends had often told her alcohol was good for that.

Having vowed never to get involved with a man who drank, she'd also sworn off alcohol. It would be the worst kind of hypocrisy to indulge when she expected her man to exercise restraint—and a hypocrite she wasn't.

A waiter appeared with a wine list and a menu and then asked, "Can I get you something to drink?"

Lily opened her mouth, but Tom beat her to it.

"I'll have a Corona, thanks."

Lily's jaw clicked shut and she stared at Tom in disappointment. Her reaction was ridiculous. She knew he drank. She'd seen him drunk. Somehow, she'd convinced herself there was another explanation; that his actions at the party were completely out of character. In fact, that he wasn't himself at all that night. She couldn't believe how much she'd set her heart on that hope.

"And you, madam?"

Lily blinked and realized the waiter was still waiting to take her order.

"Um, I-I'll just have a Diet Coke, thank you."

The waiter nodded and silently disappeared. Tom grinned and quirked an eyebrow. "I'm the driver, remember? I'm the responsible one tonight. Feel free to let your hair down. What's your poison? Red or white? Or maybe you're a cocktail kind of girl?"

Lily was shaking her head long before he'd finished. "No, thank you. I-I'm good. The soda will be fine. I-I don't drink."

Tom's eyes widened in surprise and this time he laughed aloud. "A college student who doesn't drink? That has to be a first."

She should have taken offense, but the teasing glint in his eyes took the edge off his words.

She shrugged and offered him a self-conscious smile. "We do exist. In small numbers, I will concede, but that only makes us more unique."

"Hey, I'm all for unique." His voice dropped to a husky growl that sent her pulse rate soaring. "You can be my unique any day."

His gaze moved over her face and then dropped lower to pause on her rapidly rising chest. Heat flared in his eyes and bloomed across his cheeks. Lily squirmed in her chair, feeling her response to his gaze way down deep.

Before she could come up with a suitable reply, the

waiter reappeared with their drinks. Lily stared at the bottle of beer that was placed near Tom's hand, a wedge of lemon clinging to the top. The glass was icy and left imprints from his fingers as he picked it up and brought it to his lips.

With dread that warred with fascination, she watched as his strong, tanned throat moved in time with his mouth. One swallow. Two. Hell, he was going for a third. Panic tightened its grip. She clenched her hands into fists.

Tom set the bottle back down on the table and sighed in satisfaction. "Damn, that was good. Just what I nee—"

As if only just noticing her reticence, he stopped in mid-sentence and frowned. "Lily, are you all right? You've gone as white as the tablecloth. What's the matter? Are you feeling okay? Hell..."

He looked around for a waiter and Lily hurried to reassure him. Reaching out, she took hold of his hand and squeezed. It was the first thing she thought of. Tom stilled and turned back to face her, all of his attention narrowed on her and their fingers.

"I-I'm fine. Please, don't make a fuss. I... It's just..." She shrugged helplessly, suddenly unable to find the words. She couldn't just tell him she didn't date drinkers. She'd come off sounding holier than thou. He'd want an explanation and he probably deserved one. The problem was, she didn't know if she was willing to give him one.

Apart from her mother and Tony, the only other person who knew about her childhood was David. They'd shared their pasts over tears and chocolate. It was the night he told her he was gay. She'd urged him to tell his parents, sure that they would understand. She felt every second of his agony a few months later when his father proved her wrong.

And so, while David stressed that not all men who drank were abusive alcoholics and had urged her not to let her father dictate how she lived her life, after the experience he'd had with his parents, she buried the tiny sliver of hope his words had kindled and refused to ever again consider the possibility of dating a drinker.

She wouldn't drink and she wouldn't get involved with a man who did. It was as simple as that.

Well, it was supposed to be simple. From the look on the face of the man who sat across from her, it was going to be anything but. His expression was filled with such concern and kindness, it nearly undid her. All of a sudden, she wanted to tell him everything. She wanted to tell him the truth.

"I don't date men who drink." There, she'd said it. Now she'd wait for him to bluff and bluster and pepper her with increasingly aggressive questions that usually turned into accusations and then, what was supposed to be a perfect evening would come to a sudden halt. She'd gather her purse and quietly excuse herself and they'd never see each other again.

"Why?"

The breath she hadn't realized she'd been holding poured out of her mouth in a rush. She stared at him, searching for signs of hostility and found none. What she did find was kindness and gentleness and a quiet curiosity.

"Why do I steer clear of men who drink?"

"Yes. Most men like a beer or two, especially when they go out. You must have a good reason why you're against it."

She looked away, her thoughts in turmoil. She couldn't remember ever being asked for a reason. Most guys went straight on the defensive. She should have known Tom would be different. The knowledge warmed her.

"I-I guess I just don't," she said lamely, cursing her cowardice.

A flicker of impatience flashed through his eyes, but his tone remained low and mild. "What happened to make you so afraid of alcohol?"

She closed her eyes and shivered against the sudden tightness in her chest. For all of her desire a few moments ago to be honest with him, she didn't know if she was ready. *Could she find the courage to tell him?* Could she handle the repercussions when she did? He was a drinker. There's no way he'd understand how it made her feel.

Tom reached out and took one of her hands and held it. "Talk to me, Lily. You're shaking. Don't tell me it's nothing. I deserve better than that. We hardly know each other, but it doesn't seem to matter. At least, not to me. I-I feel something so strong for you... I can't even describe it."

He dragged in a breath and then kept going, as if determined to lay everything on the line before he lost his courage.

"I've never felt this way with anyone and it scares me half to death, but I need to see where it's going, if you feel anything for me. Please, Lily, tell me what's going on. There's something very wrong and I don't believe it's me."

A flash of anger at his arrogance surged through her and then just as quickly died away. She wasn't angry at him. After all, he was only telling the truth. It wasn't him, it was all men—or at least, the ones who enjoyed a drink. She thought of what David had said and was suddenly filled with determination and then she focused on what else Tom had said.

He felt the same connection that she did. He'd just said as much. A tiny flame of hope flickered to life inside her. Something told her she could trust him with her secrets. She'd tell Tom the truth and see where it left them. She only hoped it wouldn't end in disaster, like David's confession had.

Forcing the awful memories from her mind, she drew in a deep breath and squeezed Tom's hand. Out of the corner of her eye, she saw the waiter approach, but Tom waved him away.

"Talk to me, Lily. Please."

His quiet words and the sincerity in his blue-eyed gaze gave her the courage she needed. She took a quick gulp of her soda and then told him.

"My father was an abusive alcoholic. When I was six, my mother finally left him. We stole away one morning, right after he left for work. By the time he arrived back home that evening, we were long gone. I was allowed to pack one suitcase of my favorite clothes and toys. We could only take what we could carry. Everything else was left behind. I cried for days over the dolls and books and dresses that hadn't fit in. The suitcase had been bursting as it was. And it was heavy. My mom carried it, along with hers, most of the way."

Tom's hand tightened on hers, but he remained silent and let her speak. She shot him a look of gratitude and drew in another deep breath.

"For the next few months, we lived in hiding, moving frequently from one rental house to another. I got used to changing schools and meeting new friends on a regular basis. I guess it's one of the reasons I'm comfortable socializing with perfect strangers." She shot him a small, wry smile. "I've had a lot of practice over the years.

"We moved around a lot. It was hard for Mom to find work. She could only take on jobs that allowed her to work school hours and of course, she needed the holidays off. She was an only child and I'd never heard her talk about her parents. There wasn't enough money for childcare, so Mom had to make sure she was home when school got out. When I was nine, she met Tony."

"Your stepfather," Tom guessed.

Without conscious thought, Lily's voice softened. "Yes, my stepfather and a more kind and generous man you'll never meet."

"You love him."

"Yes, I do and he loves me. What's even better, he loves my mom with all his heart. I'll love him forever for that alone. He saved her from a difficult life. He taught her to love again and he gave her back her self-esteem."

She sighed quietly. "I was too young to even know what that was when she was with my dad. It was only much later, when I was older, that I could appreciate and understand the horror of what she'd been through and how deep her scars ran."

"I take it your mom and Tony are both still alive?"

"Absolutely. They've been married now for ten years and though they've had their ups and downs, they still love each other."

"So you believe in love, then?"

Tom's gaze grew warm with intensity and she couldn't look away. Her heart skipped a beat and then accelerated. She caught herself from pressing a hand against her chest.

How could they be talking about love? They'd only just met. But somehow, with Tom it didn't matter. She nodded.

"Yes, I do. I absolutely believe in love." She paused and then grabbed hold of her courage and the next few words came out in a rush. "How about you?"

Tom picked up his beer. The bottle was halfway to his lips when his progress halted and he set the drink aside. Lily swallowed her surprise.

"My mom and dad have been married for more than twenty years. They still kiss, they still hold hands. In fact, I'd say they're more in love than ever. They have a quiet respect and understanding of each other that transcends even time. It's special to watch and be a part of. It's something I've always yearned for myself and I'm not prepared to settle until I have it."

His expression was open and vulnerable and she felt his hunger all the way through to her heart. And then he blinked and shook his head as if to clear it and his lips quirked upwards in a self-deprecating grin.

"I'm sorry. I probably just gave you way too much information. We're still getting to know each other, right? To give you the short answer, yes, I believe in love and I'm prepared to wait until I find it."

Lily slowly withdrew her hand from his. For all of their revelations, nothing changed the fact that he was a man who liked to drink and she didn't fall for drinkers. As if he could read her thoughts, he spoke quietly again.

"The night of Charlie's party, I'd had a pretty difficult day. Hell, what am I saying? It was the worst day of my life. I've been a cop for two years and I'd never before seen what I did that day." He shook his head and then added in a whisper, "And I pray to God I never see it again."

"What happened?" she asked softly.

"We were called to a suspected murder-suicide. I'd been

to a couple of suicides before, so I braced myself for what we were likely to find. No one warned us that three of the victims were kids."

Shock ricocheted through Lily. Her hands flew to her mouth and she couldn't hold back a gasp.

"Oh, Tom! No!"

He nodded, his eyes dark with remembered pain. "It was a father and his three children. He'd gassed them in the family car. He made sure the deed was done by putting a shotgun in his mouth. It wasn't a pretty sight."

Lily shook her head slowly back and forth, still trying to come to terms with the horror he'd endured.

"You poor, poor man. How on earth did you deal with it?"

His short burst of laughter sounded more like a bark and held none of his trademark humor.

"Who says I dealt with it? What I did was got myself good and drunk. So drunk, that I fell over and then entertained the guests by vomiting in the bathroom, but for a little while that night, I forgot the faces of those children." He shrugged apologetically. "Don't get me wrong, there's nothing courageous about drinking yourself into oblivion, but it was all I could think of to do."

"Have they offered you any counseling?"

"Of course and I've attended the mandatory sessions, but nothing's going to change what happened or erase my memories. It's just something I'm going to have to learn to live with. It's part of the job."

He grimaced. "And as much as I hate to say it, there'll be other times like this. It won't be the last suicide or murder I see and sometimes, they'll involve kids. Next time, I'll remember to ask a few more questions beforehand, so I can be better prepared."

Lily's heart filled to overflowing with respect and admiration for this special man. All of a sudden, the fact that he was drunk at the party didn't matter so much. After what he'd been through that day, she could understand his need to forget, if even for a little while.

His explanation, while not eradicating her lifelong vow not

to get involved with a drinker, helped to soften it a little, until it wasn't a black and white, non-negotiable instrument, but something blurred and much closer to gray—and now, she didn't have a clue what to do.

Tom filled the silence by reaching once again for her hand. Taking it between his two large ones, he held it firmly. When he spoke, his voice was full of such quiet sincerity that tears burned behind her eyes.

"Knowing about your childhood, I get why you don't like alcohol, or more specifically, men who like to drink. But not everyone is like your father. My dad enjoys a beer every now and then. Hell, occasionally he even gets drunk. But he doesn't come home and belt my mom and he doesn't punch holes in the wall. He doesn't yell at his kids or kick the dog. He doesn't do any of those things. It's possible to drink and not be abusive." He grinned ruefully. "It's possible to drink and just fall down."

She stared at him, her heart in her throat. His smile slowly faded away. When he spoke again, his voice was little more than a murmur.

"A few drinks here and there don't have to end in fear and violence."

Lily gave up on trying to keep her tears at bay. They slid down her cheeks, one after the other, a silent witness to her pain. She bit back a sob and tried to explain.

"I know there are men out there who can drink without turning into a monster. My stepfather's one of them. While he doesn't drink in my presence, I know he enjoys a glass of wine with his meal. He even has a beer or two, if he's at a party or is entertaining guests. But the thing is, I've been terrified for so long at the thought of getting close to someone like my wretched dad. I don't know if I can even think about setting that fear aside and even if I wanted to, I don't know how."

Her voice cracked with emotion and her tears now fell with a vengeance. She was conscious of the other diners, but too upset to care. To her relief, Tom didn't seem to care, either.

Instead of looking embarrassed, his expression was filled with pain—as if he hurt for her as much as she hurt for herself and he wanted desperately to fix it. He pushed back his chair and came around to her side and then slowly drew her up into his arms. She leaned into his strong, broad chest and sighed.

Home. It felt like she was home.

CHAPTER 8

Chatswood, Sydney—present day

Tom took a sip of his coffee and sighed in gratitude. "Thanks, Mom. You don't know how much I needed that."

His mother smiled fondly at him from her place across the breakfast table. Marguerite Munro was in her mid-sixties, but looked at least a decade younger. She glowed with health and vitality, which was a comfort to Tom after the health scare they'd endured with his dad the previous Christmas.

She and his father had arrived late last night from where they lived in the city of Grafton in northern New South Wales and had caught a taxi from the airport. They'd stopped in to see Lily at the hospital and then continued on to Tom and Lily's comfortable, two-storey house in Chatswood.

Outside the wide bay window that framed the modern kitchen, the day dawned bright and sunny. It was the kind of day that could lift anyone's spirits and would have lifted Tom's if his wife wasn't gravely ill in the hospital. He'd already called Brandon, who'd maintained his vigil by Lily's side throughout the night. There had been no change. Lily was still unconscious.

Tom tried not to let Brandon's words affect him, but he couldn't help the fear that tightened his gut like a vise. *What if she never woke up? What if this was as good as it was going to get?*

With a muttered curse, he forced the negative thoughts aside. There was no reason to think like that. The doctors and everyone surrounding her were still talking positively. There had been no mention that she might remain in a coma forever. He had to believe she was going to wake up again and offer him her usual sunny smile. The alternative was unthinkable and with steely determination, he refused to allow his thoughts to wander down that path again.

"What time are you leaving for the hospital?"

His mother's question intruded into his thoughts and he welcomed the distraction. "As soon as I've finished my coffee, if that's all right with you?"

"Of course," his father answered, making his way into the room. "We're here for as long as you need us, son, and don't worry about the kids. We'll make sure they have everything they need."

Tom threw his father a heartfelt look of relief. "Thanks, Dad. And you too, Mom. I'm so grateful to both of you for being here. I don't know what I'd do without you."

His mom pushed back her chair and came around to his side of the table. She patted him on the shoulder in a sign of comfort, like she used to when he was a kid.

"Nonsense, Tom. You'd cope, just like you always do. Or one of your siblings would come to your rescue. You know how much they look up to you." She shrugged. "You're their oldest brother. They'd do anything for you."

Tom cleared his throat of the lump of emotion that threatened to choke him. "Yeah, well, thanks anyway. I-I really appreciate your help."

"Do you think Cassie and Joe will want to attend school today?" his dad asked.

Tom frowned. "Let's leave the decision up to them. They might prefer to stay at home, at least for the next day or so. Hopefully we'll have good news about Lily by then."

"I'm sure you're right, son. It wasn't that long ago when I was the one lying in the ICU and everything turned out all right. These things take time. Leave it to the experts. They know what they're doing."

Tom nodded agreement. "It's funny, the doctor who operated on Lily yesterday was the same one who treated Alex when she was shot. How's that for coincidence?"

His mother frowned. "I thought she was treated at the Prince of Wales Hospital in Randwick?"

"Yeah, you're right," Tom replied, remembering. "He must have transferred to the North Shore. I guess it was four years ago. People change jobs, get promotions."

"Well, he did good work on Alex. Let's hope he has a similar result with Lily," his mom said.

"Yeah," Tom murmured, wanting desperately to believe it. "Let's hope."

Cassie listened to the murmur of voices that drifted up from the kitchen to her bedroom second from the right at the end of the stairs, and tried not to think about why her grandparents had hopped on a plane overnight from Grafton. The knowledge that her mother had been shot by some weirdo fifth-grader at her mom's school and now lay seriously injured in the hospital scared her to death. It just went to show how perilous life could be. Right when you thought everything was cruising along and life was back on track, it went and self-combusted and completely derailed itself again.

It was four years since she'd been stalked online by a child predator and eventually kidnapped and terrorized by him and despite countless hours of intensive therapy, the memories were still there. The sheer panic and mind-numbing terror every time she thought about it had eased, but she could never forget what happened—or that the perpetrator had been someone close to her family. Her mother's stepbrother, James Gibbons, was now serving a ten-year sentence. She'd been duped by him online into believing he was a cute teenager. That would never leave her.

She shuddered to think about how many other innocent young girls would be taken in by the lies of online predators. Kids were so trusting. Her dad was a police officer. She'd been cautioned many times about the dangers of the Internet and still she'd become a victim.

It had cured her penchant for surfing the Internet and dropping into online chatrooms. She didn't even have a Facebook or Twitter account and Instagram and Snapchat had never been given a chance. Her therapist encouraged her to join at least one social media network, just to prove to herself that it was possible to be part of the Internet world without falling prey to a monster, but so far, she hadn't found the courage to take that step, no matter how much not doing it limited her and her ability to socialize with her friends.

Everyone was on Facebook. There were always stories about funny photos posted on Instagram, but still she resisted. If that isolated her from her peers, then so be it. She wasn't prepared to take the risk of becoming a victim yet again.

Her parents understood and were supportive, but even they had weighed in on the issue not long after she'd turned seventeen. Being online was now a part of life. She couldn't do any of her school assignments without logging on and using the Internet to research.

Her mom explained gently how it might be best for Cassie to ease her way back into the online world while she was still at home, under the support and guidance of her parents. If she moved out to attend college or even later, when she was old enough to secure a full time job, she'd need to be computer-savvy. There wasn't a job Cassie would be interested in that wouldn't require her to be on the computer.

Cassie understood where her mom was coming from, but still it didn't help ease the fear that once online, she'd become a victim of an evil monster again. On some level, she knew her fears were silly and irrational, but she couldn't seem to rid herself of them. And now with her mom dying in hospital at the hands of some crazy kid, it was obvious the world was as unpredictable as it was unsafe.

She bet her mom hadn't thought for an instant when she woke for work yesterday morning that she'd be shot by a boy from her class and yet, it had happened. One moment she was a teacher doing her job and the next, she had a bullet through her belly. Her life had changed in an instant, just like Cassie's had four years earlier.

It was the unpredictability of it that terrified her. *What if she was the next target in life's sights?* What if she was thrown another unexpected curve ball? It might not mean being preyed upon again by a pedophile. It could be something as simple and random as being run down by a bus. But that's what life was like. It chewed you up and spat you out without care or concern for the consequences and there was nothing you could do about it. It was like she stopped really living four years ago on that fateful day when James Gibbons destroyed her life.

Her heart rate thudded against her chest and she made an effort to slow it down, but even the deep-breathing exercises her therapist had shown her didn't make an impact. The truth was, life and everything it entailed, now scared her to death. She didn't know when the next disaster might happen. Everything around her was out of her control and she didn't know what to do about it.

Reaching underneath her bed, she felt for the shoebox she had stored there and sighed in relief when her fingers closed around it. She pulled it out and removed the cover and reached in for the bottle of rum. Unscrewing the lid, she gulped down a mouthful, two, and then another. The alcohol burned her esophagus and slid down into her belly. Within moments, she was enveloped in a warm glow.

Her mother wasn't a drinker and it was only on the odd occasion her father indulged. Even then, it was only a beer or two. She'd never seen him drunk. There was never any hard liquor in the house and she'd relied upon one of the older boys at school to buy her the bottle of rum. She'd heard from some of her friends that it was a good way to chill out and forget about the world and they were right. It interfered with her ability to concentrate and her grades were beginning to suffer, but that was a small price to pay for oblivion as far as she was concerned.

Staring at the bottle, she debated about taking another gulp. The liquor seemed to beckon to her. Supplied so conveniently, it was her escape from the world, her life line and she clung to it like a drowning person desperately holding onto a life preserver.

A gentle tap on her door made her heart skip a beat. With flustered fingers, she screwed the cap back on the bottle and tossed it under her bed. Arranging the bedclothes around her, she sleepily asked for the visitor to enter. Her dad stepped into the room.

Cassie's gaze ran over his tired appearance. Though his hair was still wet from the shower, his clothes were already rumpled and he appeared weighed down with fatigue. She knew he was concerned for her mom and he had spent much of the evening at her mom's bedside. A low ache formed deep in the pit of her belly and she had to blink back sudden tears. No wonder she was turning to alcohol as a means to blot out the pain.

"Hey, baby," her dad murmured and attempted a half-hearted smile. "How're you doing?"

Cassie's return smile was just as weak as his. "I'm okay, Dad. How's Mom?"

"She's doing all right. I spoke to Uncle Brandon a little while ago. He spent the night at the hospital."

"Has she woken up yet? I really want to talk to her."

"Me, too, sweetheart. Me, too."

"How long is it going to take, Dad? What if she never wakes up?" Cassie's voice broke on the last few words and she bit down hard on another surge of emotion. Tears burned behind her eyelids. To her alarm, her dad moved closer and perched on the edge of her bed. He reached over and gently smoothed the hair out of her eyes.

"I'm not sure, honey. The doctors are doing all they can. She's holding in there. All we can do is pray."

"I want to see her again."

"Of course. How about I pick you and Joe up after school? Who knows? She might even be awake by then."

"I don't want to go to school."

Her dad nodded. "That's okay. I think a day off under these circumstances is perfectly understandable. I've called work. I'm going to be take the next few days off. At least until Mom's out of the ICU. I'm heading over there now to see how she's doing."

He leaned over and kissed her on the cheek. Cassie froze, hoping he wouldn't smell the alcohol on her breath. A moment later, he pulled back and stood and made his way to the door.

"I'll call and let you know how Mom is and come back and get you and your brother a little later, if you like. Grandma and Grandpa are downstairs. Grandma's got breakfast ready."

Cassie turned over onto her side and tugged up the bedclothes around her shoulders. "I don't feel like breakfast."

A shadow of concern passed across her dad's blue eyes and he compressed his lips and sighed. To her relief, he merely offered a brief nod of acceptance and then quietly left the room.

Cassie blew her breath out on a heavy sigh. She hated to deceive him, to pretend there was nothing wrong. He thought her reluctance to face the day had everything to do with the fact her mom was in the hospital. He had no idea her anguish and distress were rooted in that fateful afternoon on the netball ovals when her life had come crashing down.

Everyone talked about how lucky she was to have escaped without being sexually assaulted, and she was thankful to have been spared that pain, but most days she didn't feel lucky. The fact that James Gibbons hadn't entered her body was a blessing, but in fact, he'd done far worse by entering her mind. More often than she could count, she had nightmares of being teased and taunted by her mother's stepbrother and still all these years later, she broke out in a cold sweat every time she thought about him and what had happened.

Oh, but she was lucky, remember?

Tom made his way back down the stairs, his thoughts troubled. Even before Lily was shot, he'd been growing increasingly concerned about their daughter. He didn't expect her to be the Cassie she was before the attack, but it was more than four years and countless hours of therapy later. He expected her to be on a gradual incline of improvement.

Instead, it seemed like she'd made a little improvement in the short term, but now had slumped back into depression. She used to be a bright, little ray of sunshine—the happiest, cheeriest kid he knew. It was useless wishing for the happy-go-lucky child she used to be, but he'd give anything to have her back—even a part of the old Cassie.

When he'd leaned in to give her a kiss, he could have sworn he'd smelled alcohol. The very idea was ludicrous. Lily wasn't a drinker and Tom rarely had more than a couple of beers. It was only if they were having people over that they ever stocked the bar fridge. He must have imagined the smell of it. There wasn't any other explanation.

With a sigh, he headed back into the kitchen and made his farewells to his parents. Joe was seated at the breakfast table, half-heartedly spooning cereal into his mouth. Tom crouched down beside him.

"Hey, buddy. How're you doing?" Joe shrugged and continued eating.

"I spoke to Uncle Brandon a short time ago. He said Mom had a good night. I'm on my way over there to see her now."

"Yeah, Grandma told me."

Tom looked across at his son's stoic face and bit his lip. The trauma with Lily was tough on *him*, let alone a fourteen-year-old.

"Would you like to come back to the hospital and see her again? I told Cassie it's okay if you want to take the day off school."

Another shrug and then Joe's gaze slid to his. "Is she awake, yet? I don't want to go back and see her asleep like that with all those tubes hanging out of her."

Tom drew in a deep breath and eased it out. "Uncle Brandon said she's still sleeping, but she's doing okay. I understand if you don't want to see her in the ICU. It's a scary place, all right. How about I call you after I've been in to see her and let you know how she is? I'm sure they'll move her to another ward as soon as the danger's passed."

Joe looked immediately alarmed. "Danger? What—like you think she might still die? I thought you said she was doing okay?"

"I did and she is, but the bullet did some damage to her insides. They worked hard at repairing it, but I guess there's always a slight risk something might go wrong."

Joe closed his eyes and shook his head back and forth with increasing vehemence. When he opened them again, he stared at Tom with anger and defiance.

"She's going to be *fine*, Dad. She's going to be fine. Just you wait and see."

Tom stood and pulled Joe hard against him, the action made awkward by Joe's seated position.

"You're right, Joe. She *is* going to be fine. I love you, son." He pressed a kiss against the softness of Joe's short hair and then released him.

Tom looked across at his parents who sat on the opposite side of the table. His mom averted her gaze and swiped at her eyes with the back of her hand. Tom caught his father's gaze and held it.

"She's going to be fine, isn't she?" he said, his voice strong and sure.

"Of course she is," Duncan Munro replied.

His mother's response was slower in coming, but her voice was just as confident. "She'll be back home laughing and joking before you know it."

A lump of emotion clogged up the back of Tom's throat. It was all he could do to nod in agreement. He turned and collected his wallet and car keys and headed for the door.

Cassie heard the front door open and close and breathed a sigh of relief. Her dad had left. At least now she could get back to what she'd been doing before he'd stopped in to check on her. Reaching under the bed, she once again dragged out the bottle of rum. It was already a quarter down. Funny, she didn't remember drinking that much.

Now that she didn't have to go to school, she was free to overindulge. Her grandparents would leave her alone. They assumed she was in her room resting and coming to terms with the shooting.

Her mother had been shot! What kind of family were they? First Cassie, and now her mom! Most kids she knew had never been touched by crime. *Why her family?* It wasn't fair!

Okay, Rodney Ling's home had been broken into six months ago, but they weren't even home when it happened. A break and enter didn't compare to what her family had endured. *Why?* Why did it keep happening? What was wrong with this world? Why did bad things keep happening to good people—and to them, most of all?

She struggled to sit up and then unscrewed the lid of the bottle she held in her hand. Bringing it up to her mouth, she gulped down as much as she could bear. It tasted revolting, but it did the trick. Stowing it back under her bed, she slid down under the covers and closed her eyes. Slowly, the alcohol worked its magic and she relaxed and floated away.

CHAPTER 9

Seventeen years earlier

Tom glanced up at the clock on the wall and his heart skipped a beat. There was less than half an hour before his shift ended and he could rush home and get ready for his date with Lily.

Lily. Her name rolled off his tongue in a lilt so lovely it almost brought tears to his eyes. He couldn't believe his luck when she agreed to see him again. He was sure he'd blown it by admitting he didn't mind a drink or two with his friends. When she told him the story behind her fear of men who drank alcohol, he not only understood, but he vowed never to give her any cause for concern. In fact, he'd gladly give up the drink altogether if it meant he could have her.

They'd been out three times in the week since their date at Watsons by the Sea and each time, he'd been determined to steer clear of anything other than soda. While he missed the taste of an ice cold beer, he found he didn't have to drink alcohol in order to have a good time, especially not when he was with Lily.

She was all he'd ever dreamed of in a woman: beautiful, intelligent, compassionate and thoughtful. She loved school and was doing well. In between classes, she volunteered at a women's shelter. She also squeezed in story time once a week for the kids at her local library. She was perfect and Tom had fallen head over heels in love with her.

His mates would have roared with laughter if he'd shared his inner thoughts. He'd met the woman less than a month earlier and already he knew he wanted her for his wife. If he hadn't experienced a stable and loving upbringing where, even after more than twenty years of marriage, his parents still loved and adored each other, he might have been just as cynical as his friends were about his devotion to a girl he barely knew.

His parents were his yardstick. They'd taught him through their words and their deeds that true love was more than a figment of some romance novelist's vivid imagination. Love that would stand the test of time existed, was possible…if you found the right person.

He could still recall his dad telling him a few years ago how he'd known the instant he set eyes on Tom's mom that she was the woman he was going to marry. At the time, his dad urged caution in matters of the heart. Tom was eighteen and had just finished high school and was eager and ready to take on life and all the possibilities that it offered him. While he'd mucked around a little with girls in his senior years and had lost his virginity the night of his seventeenth birthday to Marcia Adams in the backseat of his dad's VS Holden Statesman, there had never been anyone really special.

Now that he'd met Lily, his dad's words came back to him and he understood exactly what his dad had meant. She filled him with so much yearning, it nearly took his breath away. It was more than just a desire to hold her in his arms and keep her close, but a deep-seated need to call her his.

She was young—they both were—but it didn't seem to matter. At least, not to him. He wasn't sure how Lily felt. Each time they'd gone out, she'd been eager to spend time with him and share with him things from her present and her past. She hadn't had the secure childhood he had, but she wasn't closed to love. Tom was sure he had her stepfather to thank for that and he looked forward to the day when he could meet Tony Gibbons and voice his sincere gratitude.

Tom's thoughts turned to the last time he and Lily were together and his body tightened at the memory. Though it had only been two days, he missed her every moment they were apart. They'd gone down to the beach at Bondi and had splashed in the water and played on the sand. Lily had asked him to rub sunscreen into her back and had then returned the favor.

The feel of her long, slim fingers against his skin had been torture and he'd been relieved he was wearing boardshorts. Knowing his erection wasn't going to subside on its own, he'd forced himself back into the water. The cold surf had worked to assuage the pressure in his cock, but it did nothing to cool the heat in his veins or the need deep in his heart.

Later, they'd walked hand in hand along the promenade, licking ice creams and enjoying their time together. Their silence was companionable; it felt like he'd known her forever.

When he dropped her off at her apartment, the sun had been low in the sky. He'd leaned across the seat of his Ford pickup truck and kissed her, no longer able to resist. After a moment's hesitation, she'd returned his kiss with a wave of sweetness and heat. It had been all Tom could do not to drag her into his arms and make her his.

His hand had stolen down and cupped the softness of her breast. Her nipple had pebbled beneath his fingers. They'd both been breathless when he finally pulled away. His heart had pounded so hard, he was sure she could hear it, but she'd done nothing but offer him a smile that was so soft and beautiful, it had stolen away what little breath remained.

That had been two nights ago. His mouth went dry at the possibility of what a night out at the ice skating rink might bring. He'd asked her earlier if she could skate and she'd laughed.

"Of course! Doesn't everyone know how to skate?"

Now, he hoped she needed a little coaching. He'd enjoy the chance to guide her with his hands.

The phone at his elbow rang and he swallowed a sigh. He had ten minutes before his shift ended. The last thing he needed was an emergency. Grimly, he picked up the handset.

"Hey there, big brother! What are you up to this fine and sunny afternoon?"

Tom grinned into phone. "Declan! It's good to hear from you, mate. How's the Academy treating you?"

"Yeah, yeah. You know how it is. All work and no play."

"It doesn't sound like the Academy I know. I've only been out two years. I can't imagine it's changed that much," Tom replied in a dry voice.

"Hey, what can I say? You're a party animal. I prefer to sit in my room and study."

"You're so full of shit, Declan Munro." Tom grinned, pleased to hear from his brother. There were a couple of years between them, but they'd grown up close and it was always nice to catch up.

"Hey, you know me better than anyone, bro. It's not my fault if the boys drag me out to the bar more nights than not. What's a man supposed to do?"

Tom chuckled and shook his head. Declan had never been any different. Tall and broad-shouldered with looks the girls went wild for, he'd always had his fair share of women. Tom had lost count of the girlfriends Declan had brought home, not to mention the ones he hadn't.

Tom was happy for him. Each man to his own, that's what he always said. Declan was happy to play the field. He had no intention of settling down and that was fine with Tom.

"When are you coming back to Sydney?" Tom asked. "It's been awhile since we had a night out on the town." With the words barely out of his mouth, he thought of Lily.

If he told her he wouldn't drink again, did it apply when he was out with his mates? He frowned, unsure of the answer and even more uncertain of his response. It was one thing not to drink in her presence, but did it have to mean no drinking, period? Like, never ever again? He wasn't sure if he was comfortable with the possibility and uncertainty swirled in his gut.

"I'm in the middle of end of year exams, Tom, so I'm not going to be able to get out of here until they're over. What are you up to for Christmas? Are you going home?"

Tom forced the somber thoughts from his mind and focused on his brother's question. "I'm not sure, yet. The boss hasn't done up the rosters that far ahead. I had last Christmas off, so the chances of being rostered on this year are pretty high."

"Crap. Oh, well. I guess I'll have to keep the single, young women of Grafton entertained. It'll be a tough job, but someone has to do it."

Tom laughed and the feel of it lightened his mood. It was good to catch up with his brother and it was even better knowing in a few short hours, he'd be once again spending an evening with Lily. He glanced at the clock and noticed the time. A surge of anticipation went through him.

"Listen, Dec. I have to go. It's nearly time to clock off and I have a few things to do."

"No worries, bro. Have a good one. I'll speak with you soon."

Tom hung up the receiver and then pushed away from his desk. With excitement and anticipation dogging his footsteps, he strode to the locker room and collected his belongings. Waving good-bye to his colleagues on his way out, he left the building and headed straight for his car.

Lily's pulse went into overdrive at the sound of Tom's knock on the door. David was spending the night at a friend's house, so answering it had been left up to her. Not that she minded. Over the ensuing week, she'd gotten to know Tom Munro better and better and she couldn't wait to see him again.

Swiping pink lip gloss across her lips, she ran the brush

quickly through her ponytail before hurrying to open the door. She stood back and did her best to catch her breath. He looked so good in his fitted T-shirt and jeans.

As if reading her thoughts, Tom's gaze traveled from her hair down to her toes. Despite the warm afternoon, she'd dressed in leggings and a loose sweater. It was always cold on the ice.

"Hi, beautiful. It's great to see you."

Lily silently cursed the blush that stole across her cheeks, but smiled back at him. "Hi. It's great to see you too and I love your T-shirt, but aren't you going to be a little cold?"

Tom shook his head and then pulled at his shirt. "I didn't know you were a fan of Keith Urban."

"I think fan is putting it too lightly. My mother calls me a groupie. I've been to all of his concerts from about the age of fourteen. I haven't missed one yet."

Tom quirked an eyebrow and his face broke into a grin. "Well, what do you know? I was at Keith's concert earlier in the year. I was sitting in the first row of elevated seats back from the floor."

Lily looked at him sheepishly. "I was *on* the floor. Or more precisely, in the mosh pit."

"Boy, your mother was right. You *are* a groupie."

"No, just an avid fan. He has so many great songs, not to mention a very cute ass."

Tom laughed. "Ah, now we're getting to the truth of it. Admit it, your interest in the country singer has nothing to do with his songs and everything to do with the way he fills out his jeans."

Lily grinned. "Maybe. I'm not going to deny he looks hot in a tight T-shirt and denims that cling to him in all the right places." She dropped her gaze and ran it over his well-muscled chest and then dropped lower to his jean-clad thighs. She lingered on his zipper and her heart picked up its pace. "He looks just about as good as you do."

The air between them was suddenly charged with delicious heat and want and need. Lily remembered they were there alone and her excitement and nerves ratcheted up another notch. The sexual tension between them had been there right from the beginning, but until now, they'd done little more than kiss.

And what a kiss it had been. She could still feel the warm pressure of his lips on hers and the heat that had spread through her body until every nerve ending was on fire. She'd yearned for more and more and more and had been powerless to stop.

But, Tom had pulled away and though disappointed, she'd been gratified to see the same level of desire reflected in his eyes. He wanted it as much as she did. A part of her was pleased he was prepared to take things slow.

Now, as the heat in his gaze drew her inexorably closer, she shut her eyes in anticipation. A moment later, his lips were on hers and she breathed a sigh of relief. His kiss was every bit as wonderful as she remembered and she gave as much as she took. While she hadn't yet gone all the way with a guy, she'd perfected the art of kissing.

Freddie Barclay was probably still gnashing his teeth over the fact that she'd refused to sleep with him in high school, but she'd learned a lot from him about kissing and for that, she was grateful. From the feel of Tom's rock-hard erection that pressed insistently against her stomach, he was more than pleased with her performance.

Once again, Tom was the first one to pull away and Lily couldn't help feeling bereft. With her breath coming fast, she grinned at him. "We have to stop doing this."

Tom grinned back at her and ran a hand through his hair, knocking the thick waves askew. "Yeah. Any more of that and we won't be going anywhere. Ice skating, be damned."

Lily stared at him and her heart hammered at the thought of what she was about to say. She drew in a breath and laid a hand on his chest, pleased to feel his heart thumped just as madly as hers.

"Who says we have to go anywhere? I haven't told you. David is out."

Tom's eyebrows lifted and a smile played around his lips. "He's out?"

"*Mm hm.* All night, in fact. He's staying over at a friend's house."

This time, Tom's eyes flared with heat and his lips parted on a sudden intake of breath. He reached out to Lily and drew her in close against him. She wrapped her arms around his neck and drew his head down for another kiss.

"Wait." Tom lifted his head and stared down at her. "Are you sure?"

She nodded and swallowed the sudden lump of nerves. "Very sure."

"I want our first time to be special."

"It will be. Make love to me, Tom."

As if her words were enough for him to throw caution to the wind, Tom groaned and dragged her in tightly against him. His lips found hers and he kissed her like a man starving. She knew exactly how he felt.

Pressed against him, she arched her back and kissed him like they had mere moments to live. A moment later, Tom bent and lifted her in his arms and then cradled her securely against his chest.

"Which way?" he murmured, his mouth buried in the curve of her neck.

"Second door on the left, past the bathroom."

Within moments, he found her room and kicked the door shut behind them. Depositing her onto her double bed, he quickly followed her down. Reaching for her sweater, he dragged it over her head. Her fingers worked just as frantically on his shirt. He pulled off the T-shirt she wore underneath and then caught his breath at the sight of her in her white lacy bra. She blushed and looked down, suddenly shy and embarrassed.

"You're so beautiful," he whispered in a voice that was husky with emotion.

Lily looked up at him. His eyes blazed with sincerity and heat and all of a sudden, she felt as beautiful as he described. With a hand that wasn't quite steady, he reached out and caressed her, his fingers skimming over the top of her bra. She shivered from the deliciousness of it and goose flesh peppered her skin.

Tom reached behind her and undid the clasp. Her breasts sprang free and he stared at her with delight and wonder in his eyes. Unable to stand his scrutiny any longer, Lily lay her palm on his chest and tangled her fingers in his light smattering of dark hair.

Her fingers grazed one of his nipples and his breath hitched. He stilled her hand's explorations and then turned her until she lay flat on her back. Straddling her hips, he started from the top and pressed heated kisses against her skin. He sipped at her lips and nibbled his way to her ear. His tongue traced the delicate whorls and the indescribable magic of it sent shivers of desire coursing through her.

He moved lower and buried his face against her neck and then he moved lower still. He kissed her until she could take no more. When his mouth closed over one of her nipples, she nearly came off the bed.

"Tom!" she gasped and tried to twist away.

He lifted his head. "What's the matter? Don't you like it?"

"No! Yes! I mean... I don't know what I mean. It feels amazing, but I don't know how much more of it I can take." She squirmed uncomfortably.

"We've got all night, remember? There isn't any need to rush. It feels like I've waited a lifetime for this. I'm going to make it last." He grinned ruefully. "Well, as long as I can, anyway. It's been awhile for me. My self-control is going to get a workout."

Heat spread across Lily's cheeks and she wondered if this was the best time to tell him she was a virgin. He probably assumed she wasn't. She was nineteen and at college, living in the twentieth century. It was natural for him to think she was sexually active.

She wondered if it would make a difference to him if he knew she'd never had sex. He was such a traditional guy, it was possible he wouldn't go through with it if he knew. She determined then and there not to tell him. She wanted him to be the first. She was already a little in love with him and was pretty sure he felt the same way.

Tom eased her leggings down her hips. Unexpectedly, his tongue dipped into her bellybutton and she gave another gasp. He was an amazing, attentive lover and even though she didn't have any hands-on experience, she'd read enough and had listened enough to the other college girls to know it often wasn't like this. Want and need spiraled way down deep inside her, leaving her tingling and desperate for more.

At last, when she didn't think she could bear it a moment longer, he raised his head and slid back up until once again, his lips claimed hers. The frenzy had eased and this time, he kissed her slowly, lovingly, tasting her, savoring her, like a connoisseur of fine wine.

Lily wound her arms around his neck and held his head still while she kissed him back. The smell of his spicy cologne tickled her nose. She reveled in the feel of his bare chest against hers and the scrape of his hair against the sensitive peaks of her breasts and knew life couldn't get any better.

This was what she'd read about in the pages of the romance novels she'd pilfered off her mother's bookshelves. This was what they meant when they'd described the woman melting in her lover's arms. It's exactly what was happening. She was weightless, floating on a cloud far above the earth—all of the trite phrases that up until now had been nothing more than words. And they weren't even completely naked...

As if reading her mind, Tom shifted and moved until he could tug off his jeans. His boxers quickly followed. Lily stared at the magnificence of him, all manly taut muscle and wildly aroused. Nerves fluttered inside her, but she was determined to push them away. He looked so huge, but she was sure they would fit. She'd never heard of one that didn't.

Tom returned to her side and pressed another kiss against her mouth. His lips were soft and full and the gentleness of his kiss liquefied her bones. Desire flared once again to life inside her and she clung to him with renewed urgency.

He moved lower, pressing kisses as he went. This time, when he got to her leggings, he tugged them all the way down. Her panties came with them and a moment later, she was naked. Tom stared at her, his eyes wide. They were on top of the bedclothes, which made pulling the sheet or blanket around her a little awkward. She squirmed a little and wished she had something to cover herself. As if sensing her discomfort, he leaned over her and kissed her.

"You're so perfect. Please, let me look at you." He held her gaze. His eyes darkened to cobalt. The glint of desire gave her the confidence she needed to let him look his fill.

His lips met hers in yet another searing kiss and her inhibitions melted away. With her arms around his neck, she clung to him and returned his passion with fire.

"Do you have a condom?" he murmured against the soft skin of her neck.

Lily shook her head, mortified. She hadn't even thought of protection.

"It's okay," he smiled. "I have one in my wallet."

He moved away and reached over the side of the bed and tugged out his wallet from the back pocket of his jeans. A moment later, he tore open the packet and fitted the condom over his erection.

Lily watched with interest. Apart from the sex education talk she'd received in high school where the nurse put a condom over a banana, she'd never seen how it worked in real life. Within seconds it was done and Tom returned to her side. Gathering her up in his arms, he stared into her eyes.

"Are you sure you want to do this?"

Lily gazed back at him, loving him for asking again. She nodded and kissed him hard on the mouth.

"Yes. I want you so much I can't find the words. It's like I'm combusting from the inside out. Does that sound strange?"

Tom's answering smile was so slow and sexy, it took her breath away. Her heart pounded so loudly, she was sure he could hear it. She yearned to feel the fullness of him inside her.

"No, that doesn't sound at all strange. I feel the same

way. I've never been with anyone like you. I've never felt so connected. It's like we're one already." He looked away and Lily could tell he was embarrassed, but it only made her love him more.

"Make love to me, Tom," she whispered, gazing into his eyes.

He groaned and then shifted until she was underneath him. His impressive erection pressed into her belly and she suffered another flutter of nerves. He parted her knees with his leg and then settled between her thighs. His cock nudged her entrance and she braced herself against the pain. She'd heard it always hurt the first time.

Tom eased further inside her and she clung to his broad shoulders. She could feel her inner muscles stretching to accommodate him. He pushed harder and came up against a barrier. She cried out a little against the pain.

Tom froze. He stared down at her, confusion flooding his face. "Lily, have you... Have you ever done this before?"

Embarrassment set fire to her cheeks. She hadn't realized he'd know. She thought she'd be able to bluff it out and pretend she was as experienced as he assumed.

"Um..."

His confusion cleared and was replaced with a look of wonder. "This is your first time?"

The heat in her cheeks intensified. She averted her gaze and nodded.

Tom closed his eyes and drew in a deep breath and then lay down by her side, gathering her close. "Why didn't you tell me?"

She bit her lip against the gentle curiosity in his voice. *Couldn't they just do it? What did it matter if she was a virgin?* She kept her mouth shut.

"Lily. Talk to me."

"What is there to say?" she muttered. "I'm a virgin. Big deal. Can we please just have sex?"

Tom took her by the chin and gently forced her head around until she faced him. Lily caught her breath at the emotion in his eyes.

"It *is* a big deal and you think so too, or you wouldn't have waited until now. Losing your virginity is a moment in time you remember for the rest of your life. I'm way more than flattered you chose me, but are you really, *really* sure?"

She reached up and cupped her hand around his cheek and stared into his magical eyes. "I'm really, really sure. I...I think I've fallen in love with you. I want you to be the first."

Tom's face lit up with wonder and more than a hint of disbelief. "You *love* me? Are you sure? I mean, we've haven't even known each other a month. Not that I put any stock in time. My parents fell in love the moment they met and they've been together more than two decades. They still look at each other with love in their eyes. Sometimes it makes me cringe."

His hands cradled her head, forcing her to look at him. Her heart skipped a beat at the intensity in his eyes.

"That's how I feel about you, Lily. I fell in love with you the instant I spotted you from across the room. You arrived at Charlie's party with David and I was instantly jealous. I didn't know if you were together, but I feared you were. I was desperate to find out the truth. You drew me from clear across the room and you didn't even say a word. Did you feel it? Did you feel it that night, too?"

Lily bit her lip and blinked back happy tears. "Yes! Yes, I felt it. It scared me half to death, but I couldn't deny it was there."

Tom whooped and pressed his lips hard down against hers. "I love you, Lily Strickland."

"Oh, Tom. I love you, too."

They kissed with all the love and passion that had built up inside them until both of them were out of breath. Tom kissed his way back down her body until he was once again poised between her legs. Lily tingled with anticipation and need. Once again, Tom's erection probed at her entrance.

"We'll take it slowly, I promise," he whispered. "It might hurt just a little, but then it will feel right. So damn right."

He groaned and eased into her another inch and Lily

rejoiced in their coupling. She loved him and he loved her. She was overwhelmed with the magic of it.

Tom slid a little further inside her and once again came up against the barrier. This time, he pushed a little harder and Lily bit her lip. Pain splintered inside her and she dug her fingernails into Tom's back.

"It's okay, sweetheart. Just relax. Soon the pain will be over and we get to enjoy the good stuff."

She listened to his words of comfort and did her best to relax against him. He pushed his cock in further, another inch and then another.

"Oh, Christ, Lily. You feel so good."

He pushed further still and then with a surge of his hips, he buried himself inside her. She cried out against the pain and Tom captured it in his mouth. He kissed her and crooned to her and all the time, his cock moved slowly in and out.

The pain eased and Lily concentrated on the rhythm of his movements. Hesitantly, she lifted her hips and met his slow thrusts. He groaned in her ear and she wondered if she'd done something wrong, but his rhythm continued without interruption and she relaxed back against him again.

Time and time again, he slid in and out of her body. Need built deep in her core and she clung to him, seeking relief.

"That's it, Lily. Christ, you feel so good. Relax and go with it. I can see how close you are. Close your eyes and feel me. I'm buried way deep inside you. It feels beyond fantastic. I don't know how much longer I'm going to last."

Tom's thrusts became harder, more frantic and Lily held on for the ride. The need inside her reached fever pitch and all of a sudden, she reached the peak and was falling. Her muscles tightened around him, pulsing out their relief. Tom's groan was almost guttural with need and he pounded his hips into her.

One thrust, two and he cried out in exultation. A moment later, he collapsed on top of her, his breath harsh in her ear. It seemed a lifetime passed before he moved his weight off her and propped himself up on one elbow.

"That was amazing," he whispered, his eyes full of wonder.

Lily smiled shyly and nodded.

"It was pretty amazing for me, too." She looked away and then found the courage to ask the question she'd been dying to ask. "Is it... Is it always like that?"

Tom shook his head. He rolled onto his side, taking her with him and tucked her up under his chin.

"Not that I've had a lot of experience, but it's never been like that before. Maybe it's because we care for each other. Maybe that's why it's different?"

She smiled again and snuggled up beside him and drifted off to sleep.

Tom listened as Lily's breathing deepened and traced a finger across the petal-softness of her naked skin and then skimmed his palm down the length of her spine. He wondered if life could get any sweeter. His fingers tangled gently in the silkiness of her long hair and he turned his head to breathe in its intoxicating scent.

Reluctantly, he moved away and pulled the condom off his cock. A droplet of liquid hung off the end of the rubber. It took him a moment to realize what it was...and what it meant. He stared at it in shock and then cursed in alarm. The hole was tiny, but it was there. As real as the woman he'd just made love to. He shook his head in disbelief. They might as well have used no protection.

With the condom between his fingers, he stepped into the hall and through the doorway that led to the bathroom. Disposing of it in the trash, he wished he could get rid of the knowledge he now possessed and its implications just as easily. He cursed again. He had only himself to blame. The condom had been in his wallet for months. He should have known better than to trust that it would still perform at its peak.

It wasn't that he was against the thought of a baby—

he'd always intended to find a wife and raise a family—but they were both so young. Lily was only nineteen. She'd just finished her first year of college. She had her whole life in front of her and so did he. A baby wouldn't necessarily ruin everything, but it sure as hell hadn't been in his immediate plans.

They'd have to get married, of course. There was no way his baby was being born out of wedlock. Call him old-fashioned, but it was just the way he was. Besides, the way he felt about Lily, he'd be proud to call her his wife. He hadn't been lying when he'd told her he'd fallen in love with her on the night that they met.

He stared at himself in Lily's bathroom mirror and tried to think things through. *Perhaps the hole in the condom wouldn't matter? Perhaps it would be nothing more than a scare?* He could be worrying over nothing. Yes, that was it. He was worrying over nothing. The chances of Lily falling pregnant the very first time must be one in a million. Surely they couldn't be that unlucky?

Leaning over the sink, he splashed some water across his face and then dried it against a towel. With a sigh, he pushed his concerns to the back of his mind and returned to the bedroom. Lily was still sleeping and for that, he was guiltily relieved.

There was more than likely nothing to worry about. No sense in alarming her unnecessarily. It was her first time. She didn't need the burden of wondering if she was pregnant. Not now, when she was in the middle of her end-of-year exams.

With his mind made up, he pulled her unresisting form in close against him and fell asleep with his face buried in her shiny, blond hair.

CHAPTER 10

Tom stared down at his wife and wished he could believe she was just sleeping. She looked so young and beautiful, like she had when they'd first met. The age lines that had begun to creep around her eyes had been smoothed away in sleep. Her lashes were dark and as thick as they'd always been. They cast shadows on her pallid cheeks. Her lips, while still full and luscious, were now also pale, almost lifeless.

No! His heart rebelled against the thought. Not lifeless. He refused to think that way for even an instant. The steady rise and fall of her chest reassured him, even if it was being regulated by a machine. She was alive and she'd get better. She'd come home and laugh and dance and sing again. They'd make love all night long. It *would* happen. He refused to contemplate any alternative.

The ICU ward was busy that morning, with all but one bed occupied. The lack of curtains in the open plan room meant that privacy was non-existent. Seeing as all of the patients were either unconscious or too sick to care, Tom guessed it wasn't an issue. Besides, it meant that the staff could monitor every patient at a glance from the centrally located nurses' station. He could see how such a thing would be an advantage.

The phone on his belt clip vibrated and he glanced down and frowned at the unfamiliar number. The last thing he wanted to do was speak to someone who didn't know what had happened. He couldn't bear to pretend all was well in his life when the truth was, his world was falling apart.

The fact was he didn't want to talk to anyone. The only voice he wanted to hear was that of his wife's but for the moment, all that confronted him was the repetitive humming and beeping of the machines.

The phone fell silent and he breathed a sigh of relief. A moment later, it began vibrating again. The Caller ID displayed the same number. Tom cursed under his breath. *Why couldn't they just leave a message and leave him the hell alone?*

Again, the phone fell silent and once again, it began vibrating not a minute after Tom sighed in relief. Momentarily forgetting his surroundings, he exploded.

"Oh, for fuck's sake! You've got to be kidding!"

A nurse appeared a few seconds later and frowned at him. "I'm sorry, Mr Munro, but you'll have to switch that off. We don't allow cell phones in here."

Tom nodded and mumbled an apology. Stowing the phone in his pocket, he leaned over Lily's bed and pressed a soft kiss against her lips.

"I'll be back in a minute, sweetheart. Don't go anywhere." He tried to summon a smile at his lame joke, but failed miserably. With a sigh, he turned and headed out of the ward.

Once outside the ICU, Tom pulled out his phone and stared at the screen. *Three missed calls from an unfamiliar number.* He supposed there was nothing to do but to return the call. With a deep breath, he dialed the number and waited for it to connect.

"Doctor Slee's rooms, may I help you?"

It took Tom a moment to register the name and another to remember who she was. Doctor Mary Slee was an oncology specialist his local doctor had referred him to. He'd been trying to see her for more than a year. It was no wonder she was growing impatient with him. He'd made three different appointments and had canceled two. His third was due in two days. With Lily fighting for her life in hospital, it would be yet another appointment he couldn't keep.

"Oh, hi. It's Tom Munro. Someone from your office called me. I assume it's about my upcoming appointment." He opened his mouth to advise the receptionist that he was going to have to reschedule again and then he closed it.

What if Lily died, or stayed in a coma forever? He'd be the only parent his kids had left. He absently fingered the lump in his breast and came to a decision. He had to keep this appointment and deal with whatever it threw up at him. For the sake of Cassie and Joe, he owed it to them to investigate.

"Oh, yes, Mr Munro. It's Judith, here. I'm Doctor Slee's receptionist. I was calling to confirm your appointment the day after tomorrow. Doctor Slee's concerned you have already canceled twice. Are you seeking care from another specialist?"

Tom's face heated. "Um...no. I-I've been busy. I haven't had time to have it checked out."

"I understand, Mr Munro, but these things are better treated sooner rather than later. Who knows, you might not have anything to worry about?"

Tom grimaced and rubbed at the lump again. "Yes, you're right, of course. I-I'll see you in a couple of days."

"Do you know where we are?"

"Yes, in the medical center next door to Royal North Shore Hospital, right?"

"That's right. Suite twenty-nine, level three."

"Thanks."

"We'll see you then."

"I guess so."

Tom ended the call and clipped the phone back onto his belt. The truth was, he'd forgotten all about the appointment. With everything that had happened, his lump was the last thing on his mind, but with Lily gravely ill and his children still very much dependent upon him, he had to face the situation head on and deal with it, once and for all.

With a bit of luck, it would turn out to be nothing and he could forget about it. In the meantime, he'd pray for his wife's speedy recovery.

Brady Sutton stared at the plastic case that held his *GTA V* game. The picture on the cover depicted a lifetime of fun and adventure. A mad ride from one crazy mission to another, where nothing was taken seriously and nothing ever went wrong. The worst that could happen was that you were killed in a shootout or blown up by a stray grenade. You'd hit "reset" and then press "play" and start all over again.

But things hadn't worked out that way for him. Reality was far harsher than he'd anticipated. He'd been charged with attempted murder and was now out on bail. His mom had put up their house as collateral. *Collateral.* He hadn't even known what the word meant until his mom had explained it to him.

His father called and had been horrified, unable to believe what his son had done. Brady shook his head slowly and his lip curled up in a sneer. He didn't care what his father thought. It was his father who had given him the gun. It wasn't all Brady's fault that he'd used it.

Okay, so his dad hadn't shown him how to load it and probably didn't expect him to know how, but anyone who thought giving a kid a gun and a box of ammunition was a good idea was just plain dumb. The cops thought so, too. He'd heard his mom talking to someone on the phone. His dad had been charged, too. Something about an unsecured firearm and leaving a gun in the possession of a minor.

It wasn't as if his dad even cared that much about him anymore. The last he'd heard, his dad had moved on with another woman and she was going to have his kid. Apparently, it was a girl. What use was a rough-and-tumble son amongst all that softness and pink? It would be only a matter of time before his dad forgot all about him and now that he was headed for jail, he'd become nothing more than a distant memory, a topic of conversation avoided around the dinner table, a constant reminder of how his mom and dad had failed as parents.

The shooting had happened more than twenty-four hours ago, but he hadn't returned to school. How could he? The last time he'd shown up, he'd been brandishing a gun intending to shoot Ian Little. Despite his mom's position in the school, it didn't take a genius to work out he wouldn't be allowed back at Chatswood Elementary.

There was a brief knock on the door and then his mom appeared in the opening. Her face was drawn and pale and she looked like she'd been doing more crying. Brady closed his eyes and turned on his side, away from her.

"Can I come in? We need to talk."

Brady shrugged and remained silent. It was the first time she'd mentioned the "talk" word since it happened. Dread stirred in his gut. This wasn't going to be good.

"Please, Brady. I'm trying to understand. What happened? How did it come to this? Is this about me and your dad? The fact that we've split up?" She sighed quietly before continuing.

"Unfortunately, it takes time to sort things out when a marriage falls apart. It can't have been easy on you, having to front up to the court time and time again to talk about our life. It hasn't been easy on any of us. I wish—"

He rolled over to face her and lashed out angrily. "It's got nothing to do with you and Dad Why do you always think it has something to do with you? The world doesn't revolve around you." He ignored the hurt on his mother's face and his anger ratcheted up another gear. He clenched his fists and shot her an accusing stare.

"I *told* you about those bullies. I told you how they were giving me a hard time. I begged you to switch my classes, so

I didn't have to face Ian Little every day. Every second of my life was a living hell and you didn't want to know. You told me to ignore them, not to give them the time of day. To walk away, to avoid them.

"Well, guess what, Mom? It didn't work. It didn't matter what I did, they found me anyway. They'd spill my soda and force me to drink it up from the floor. They'd call me gay boy and insinuated that Dad had left because he couldn't stand the sight of me. As if that wasn't bad enough, they'd corner me in the bathroom and piss all over me. I couldn't take it anymore, Mom: the stares, the laughter, the name calling. 'Brady Sutton has a weenie like a button, does he like girls, does he like boys, he cries like a baby when you take his toys.' Ian Little was the ringleader, but the others were almost as bad."

He drew in a ragged breath, gasping from the strength of his anger and pain. "I *tried* to talk to you about it, Mom, I did, but you didn't want to know."

"*No!*" His mom shook her head. Tears streamed down her face.

"*Yes!*" he shouted. "In the end, I had no choice. Not even my mother would help me. My own mother couldn't make them stop and she was the deputy principal." He dragged in another breath and all at once, felt calmer. "The only one who could make them stop was me."

His mother gasped on a sob. "But you didn't, Brady! You didn't make them stop! Cory James wasn't even there that day and Ian Little was thankfully left unharmed. Mrs Munro threw herself in front of him and now she's lying in the ICU. An innocent woman, Brady. A teacher, a mother and a friend. How could you do it?"

Grief and despair rushed through him and he blinked back a flood of hopeless tears. He pleaded with his eyes for his mom to understand. When he found the strength to reply, his voice was cracked and broken.

"How could I not, Mom? How could I *not*?"

———

Lily struggled to breathe through the fire in her stomach. The pain was almost unbearable. Surely she was in a hospital? Where were the doctors and nurses? Anybody? Why wasn't her pain being managed? Her belly felt like it had been attacked with a thousand heated knives. There wasn't a part of her that didn't hurt.

She blinked and tried to open her eyes. She could tell from the feel of the mattress beneath her that she was lying on a bed and the sharp smell of antiseptic filled the air. She must be in hospital. There was nowhere else she could be. She just wished they'd increase her pain medication. Right now, it felt like she was existing on nothing.

She tried once again to open her eyes and this time, managed to lift her lids enough so that she could make out the shape of a man beside her.

Tom. It was Tom. He was stretched out in a chair and his eyes were closed. His head had tilted forward until his chin nearly rested on his chest. It looked like he hadn't shaved for a couple of days and his clothes and hair were rumpled. She'd never seen him looking so unkempt.

Tom. Her husband, the love of her life. He was here, watching over her, protecting her. Like he always did. Her heart swelled with love and her eyes flooded with tears. She was alive and the man that she loved was beside her. With a soft sigh, she drifted back to sleep.

Chapter 11

Seventeen years earlier

Lily rolled over and draped her arms around Tom's neck. She tilted her head and pressed a kiss against his hair. He continued to nuzzle her neck and her shoulders and she shivered from the heat of it. They'd been together for six weeks, spending every available minute together and yet, her body still craved his touch. It was probably like an ice hit was to a drug addict. She'd been on a high since their first night together. Every minute of every day would have been perfect, if her period wasn't late.

She was only three weeks overdue, which wasn't that long, but it felt like a lifetime. She'd been late before, but usually only a day or two. Never more than a week. She didn't want to admit it, but she was beginning to worry.

She told herself she was being silly. They'd used protection every time. There was no way she could be pregnant. But in the dark hours before dawn when she woke and couldn't get back to sleep, she wondered if she was wrong. Her breasts were more tender than usual and she was feeling way past tired.

She put the fatigue down to the last month or two, when she'd been up late studying for her exams and then partying down the end of the year. Her grades wouldn't be as good as she hoped, but she didn't regret a single moment she'd spent with the most beautiful man in the world. A man that was even now driving her crazy with his mouth.

Finding his lips, Lily kissed him with all the love and passion she held deep inside. She was the luckiest girl in the universe to have found him. Okay, he'd been falling-down drunk when they'd first met, but he'd more than made up for the aberration in his behavior. In all the time they'd spent together since, he hadn't once taken an alcoholic drink. While they hadn't spoken about it, the thought that he'd given it up for her made her feel special beyond any words.

Relishing the feel of his hands on her body, she pressed herself hard against him. She swiped her tongue across his lips and then licked her way inside his mouth. Her hand caressed his muscled chest and then teased his nipples into hard nubs. He caught his breath and she smiled in pure female pleasure. She was still such a novice in the game of lovemaking that the fact she could bring him to such a point of desire still surprised her.

"You're a wicked woman," he muttered against her lips. "You're driving me crazy."

His words filled her once again with pleasure and she vowed to increase her efforts. Pushing him down until he lay on his back, she straddled his hips. With single-minded purpose, she kissed her way across his chest and then all the way down to his stomach. It was washboard flat and tense with anticipation. Like he'd done with her in the past, she paused to dip her tongue into his bellybutton and was rewarded with a moan of appreciation.

"Like I said, you're a wicked woman."

"I'm only just getting started," she teased. "You haven't seen anything yet." He groaned again and she chuckled in delight, more than pleased with his reaction.

His erection lay thick and hard against the nest of hair below his abdomen and she reached for it with eagerness mixed with nerves. It was the first time she'd found the courage to go down on him and she was a little worried her inexperience would show. Still, she wanted to experience all that there was with the man she was in love with and with that thought in mind, she reached for him and closed her hand around his hardness.

His gasp of pleasure gave her the confidence she needed to open her mouth around his cock. His skin was warm and silky and yet so very firm to the touch. It was an interesting combination and liquid heat stole down to her core. She raised and lowered her mouth over him and with her free hand, cupped his balls.

Tom groaned again and stared at her with desire-filled eyes. "You're killing me, Lily. I've died and been catapulted off to heaven."

Smiling, she renewed her efforts and added her other hand to the mix. She sucked and squeezed his thick cock and fondled his heavy balls.

All at once, he pulled away from her and reached down to drag her up his body. The feel of his erection against the softness of her belly elicited a gasp of her own.

"Two can play at this game," he murmured and she shivered with anticipation at the roguish glint in his eyes.

He kissed her thoroughly on the mouth, taking what he wanted without pause. Her heart pounded from need. Releasing her mouth, his lips skimmed over her breasts and then moved lower over her stomach. One hand fondled a breast and the other delved lower into the warmth and liquid softness between her legs.

His finger slid over her silky folds and probed between the slick flesh. A moment later, he pressed inside her. One finger and then two stroked her in a rhythm that drove her wild. She squirmed then bucked under his attention. She voiced her need.

"Tom, please..."

"Please, what?" he murmured, his fingers continuing their sensual attack.

"I-I can't take anymore."

Tom's smile was full of male pride and confidence. "Oh, but you will, babe. Much, much more."

With that, he moved lower and his mouth and tongue

replaced his fingers. Lily's hips came off the bed in shock and delight. She clutched at the sheets and rolled her head from side to side, almost unable to stand the sheer pleasure he aroused inside her. When he raised his head at last, she was taut with need.

"Please," she gasped.

"Please, what?"

"I-I want you. I want to feel you inside me."

As if he needed no further encouragement, Tom rose from his position between her legs and moved up her body. His thick cock pressed against her entrance and her knees fell open in eagerness.

He reached across her to the nightstand where she now kept a supply of condoms and quickly sheathed himself. A moment later, he entered her and she gasped from the impact. His strokes were smooth and sure and powerful and she clung to him, riding the wave of excruciating pleasure until at last, she toppled over the other side and found her release. She gasped in relief.

Tom cried out and shuddered inside her and then collapsed upon her, spent. Lily slowed her breathing and enjoyed the feel of Tom, heavy and lethargic, on top of her. As if becoming aware of his weight on her, he rolled away and dragged her with him until she was snuggled up against his side. He pressed a tender kiss against her hair.

"I love you, Lily."

Warmth and happiness flooded through her. She twisted a little and reached up to leave a soft kiss on his lips. "I love you, too."

"Everything's so perfect, I feel like it's only a matter of time before something's going to go wrong. It's not right to feel so content."

Lily thought once again of the possibility that she might be pregnant, but offered Tom a smile. "Don't we deserve to be happy?"

"Of course. I just feel... I don't know... Guilty or something. It's like we have more than our fair share, you know? Our cup's overflowing and all that kind of stuff." A shadow passed through his eyes and then he blinked and it was gone. His arms tightened around her. "I don't want to do anything to jinx it—jinx *us*."

Lily laughed, but it felt forced. She waved his comment away. "Don't be silly. Stuff like that only happens in the movies and that's because they have to make the story last beyond the first thirty minutes. How boring would it be if the girl meets the guy, they fall in love and live happily ever after? That storyline doesn't make for good entertainment or a ninety-minute plus movie."

Tom chuckled. "Yeah, you're right. Real life is often much more tedious."

"Oh, so I'm tedious now, am I?" she said in mock annoyance.

Tom growled low in his throat and began to tickle her without mercy. She laughed and screamed and tried hard to get away from him, but he pinned her to the mattress and continued to wreak havoc on her body. Gasping, she begged him to stop.

"You need to be punished for your cheekiness, Miss Strickland," he teased.

"Okay, okay! I need to be punished. It's done. Please, stop. I-I can't breathe."

At last he relented and Lily gasped in relief. Tom bent his head and kissed her softly on the mouth.

"I'm happy to do tedious with you any day, Lily."

She smiled and could have floated away on a cloud of happiness if it wasn't for the nagging dread in her belly that things might be about to go way off course. No matter how happy or in love with each other they might be, she'd never let him stay with her for the sake of a baby. She'd seen firsthand with her parents how that had worked out.

Her father might have thrown alcohol and violence into the mix, but she'd never forget the number of times he'd screamed at her mother that he'd never have married her if she hadn't been pregnant. Tom Munro was good and kind and well mannered. He was nothing like her father—yet. She couldn't imagine her father had been the way she'd known him when he and her mother first met. They'd never have gotten together, if that were the case.

No, being trapped into marriage with an unplanned pregnancy changed people and men were affected most of all. If she were pregnant, Tom was just the kind of man to insist on them marrying and Lily simply refused to allow that to happen.

In time, they might come to the realization that they wanted to spend the rest of their lives together, but it had to happen without the added incentive of a baby. If Tom wanted to marry her, she wanted him to do it for her and her alone.

All of a sudden, Lily couldn't wait any longer to discover if her suspicions were correct. She vowed silently to purchase a pregnancy test first thing in the morning. She crossed her fingers and sent a little prayer heavenwards that her concerns would be for naught.

Tom pulled the door to Lily's apartment closed behind him and jogged down the short flight of stairs. The early morning sun caught him full in the face, warm and bright as it greeted the day. If he didn't hurry, he'd be late for work. She lived not far from the city, at least an hour's commute on a train to his station. It wouldn't do to be late the third day in a row.

He grinned ruefully and shook his head. It had been weeks since they'd first made love, but they still couldn't get enough of each other. In between his arduous shifts and the Christmas rush, they'd squeezed in whatever precious hours they could spend together and had enjoyed every minute of it. New Year's Eve had been beyond his wild imagination. He was thrilled Lily was still on her summer break.

He'd eventually taken her ice skating and she'd performed just like a pro. Even so, he'd taken every opportunity to put his arms around her and hold her close like he'd never let her go. They'd picnicked in Hyde Park and had gone sailing on Sydney Harbour. He'd even taken her to a quiet spot along the Parramatta River, where they'd thrown in a fishing line. It was something he'd enjoyed as a kid, living in Grafton on the Clarence River and he was delighted when Lily seemed to enjoy it, too. They hadn't managed to catch anything, but the anticipation was half the fun. Almost as much fun as making out with her on the river bank in the gentle summer dusk.

The only thing that kept him from being truly at peace with the world was the fact that he hadn't told her about the broken condom. Now, a month and a half later, he was guiltily relieved he hadn't said anything. Lily must have gotten her period by now and if she hadn't and suspected she might be pregnant, surely she would have said something? She might have been a virgin, but she wasn't completely naïve.

They'd been having sex whenever they could and although they'd continued using condoms, a missed period should be cause for concern. He wondered if he should ask her, if it was the right thing to do, but if her period had come as normal, she'd wonder why he wanted to know and then he'd have to tell her about the condom.

He was filled with another surge of guilt. Pregnant or not, he should have told her about the condom. It was just that, the longer he left it, the harder it got. He kept hoping there wasn't a need for concern, that if she wasn't pregnant, the incident wouldn't matter. He just wished he truly believed it.

With a glance at his watch, he picked up his pace and headed toward the nearest bus stop. Now wasn't the time to do anything. He had a twelve-hour shift ahead of him and he needed to clear his head of any thoughts that might distract him. Even so, he thought of how he'd left Lily still asleep and tangled naked in the sheets. His heart filled with emotion. Pregnant or not, he loved her and would look after her until the day he died.

———————

Lily read the instructions on the information leaflet contained in the pregnancy test box and did her best to absorb what it said. One line meant she wasn't pregnant, two meant she was. She drew in a deep breath and squared her shoulders.

"Okay, here we go."

Taking the stick to the toilet, she did her best to relax so that she could do what was required. She was pleased David had left to meet friends in the city. At least if things didn't turn out well, she wouldn't have anyone around to witness her distress. And distressed she would be.

It wasn't that she didn't like children; babies were definitely high on her list and Tom's babies would be something special. But the timing was all wrong. She was nineteen. She'd just started college. They'd known each other less than two months. A baby might have been in her vague plans in the future, but that future was a long way away. What was more, she didn't have a clue how Tom felt.

She knew how he'd feel if he thought she was pregnant, but his response would have everything to do with his honor and pride and the old-fashioned values he'd been raised with. She didn't even know if he wanted children.

No. She flat out refused to force his hand in that way. It wasn't fair and she'd be forever left to wonder if he'd married her out of no more than a sense of obligation. After the awful childhood she'd endured, she was never again going to be someone's obligation.

Still seated on the toilet and holding the stick in her hand, she forced herself to look at it.

Two pink lines.

Her heart skipped a beat and then thudded so hard she could feel it palpitating against the walls of her chest. Nerves mingled with dread and cemented themselves low in her belly. She swallowed on a sudden rush of nausea.

She was pregnant.

Oh, God. Panic welled up inside her and all of sudden, she knew she was going to be sick. Spinning around, she leaned over the toilet seat and emptied her breakfast into the bowl. Gasping for breath and with tears streaming down her cheeks, she wiped her mouth with toilet paper and then flushed the evidence of her distress away. Setting the stick down onto the washbasin, she rinsed her mouth and brushed her teeth and rinsed her mouth again.

With a shuddering breath, she buried her face into the soft comfort of a towel and dried her face. The stick lay on the washbasin, its presence a harsh reminder of the predicament she now found herself in. She wasn't sure how it happened—they'd been careful every time—but somehow, it had and now she had to deal with it.

There was no way she was getting rid of it. The thought of aborting their baby was abhorrent. Her mom and Tony would be supportive. She could rely on their love and protection, no matter what. The thought was comforting and with a deep breath, she squared her shoulders, collected the stick and tossed it into the trash.

She'd take a day or two to get her head around the idea that she was going to be a mom and then she'd tell them. David, she'd tell right away. He'd have to know. He shared an apartment with her. Besides, it would be nice to have someone know the truth. She hadn't even mentioned Tom to her mom and stepfather. Their relationship, if that's what they had, was still so new, she'd been keeping it to herself, waiting to see how it developed, how long it was going to last.

Now they'd be tied together, forever—if she told him. That was the question: *Did she tell him?* She thought about all the reasons she'd come up with why not telling him was the best thing to do, but she couldn't help the shaft of guilt that went through her when she thought of seeing it through.

A little voice inside her head needled her. *Surely he has the right to know he's a father? What right did she have to keep this from him? The baby was as much his as it was hers.*

Memories of her childhood crashed into her and she held her head in her hands and shook it in an effort to alleviate the pain.

'You used the oldest trick in the book to trap me.' 'I only ever married you because you were pregnant.' 'I'd have been long gone by now if it wasn't for your brat.'

Her father's ugly words pounded into her brain and she squeezed her eyes tight in an effort to escape his taunting. She could see her mother, standing in silent humiliation, her head bowed, accepting the torrent of abuse. Her refusal to defend herself told Lily everything she needed to know.

It was true. Her mother had gotten pregnant and her father had been forced to marry her. Never for an instant over the six years they were together did he let her forget the sacrifice he'd made and how much he regretted it.

Steely determination ran down Lily's spine. Her hands dropped away and she stood tall and proud. She wouldn't make the same mistake her mother made. She refused to let the father of her child treat her with such contempt. She'd take sole responsibility for the child that grew inside her and Tom Munro would never, ever know.

She had to come up with a plan that would remove him from her life. The thought of ending things with him simply broke her heart, but there was nothing else she could do. At the most, she was six weeks along, but in another month or two, the truth would be apparent for all to see.

She needed to convince him her feelings had cooled and that she was no longer interested in him. Over the coming weeks, she'd find less and less time for him until eventually, she'd tell him good-bye. It would be the hardest thing she'd ever done, but in her heart, she knew it was for the best.

With her mind made up, a measure of calmness descended upon her and she welcomed the modicum of peace. It wouldn't do the baby any good for its mom to be overwrought. She needed to think happy, calming thoughts. If not for her sake, then for the baby's.

She'd tell David the truth so that he could help her with her plan. He might not like it, but he'd accept her decision. Together, they would get through it and her wonderful, amazing snapshot of time with a man called Tom Munro would become nothing more than a fond memory.

David stared at her in shock, his mouth gaping open. "Pregnant? Wow, um... I don't know what to say!"

It was just after dinner and they were cleaning up. The lights from nearby houses and apartments glinted in the dark through the large kitchen window. The double glazing muted the sound of traffic and the *clickety-clack* of the passing trains.

Lily turned from the sink with a strained smile. "Congratulations, I guess. I'm going to have a baby."

Saying the words aloud for the first time suddenly made it real. She swallowed the bundle of nerves that threatened to choke her and forced herself to continue.

"It wasn't planned, of course, but there's no question I'm going to keep it. I'll take some time off school after the birth, but I'm hoping it won't be more than a semester. I'll pick up some online courses and keep my credits up. Hopefully it won't affect things too much."

David picked up a glass and wiped it, still looking dazed. "Wow, I still can't believe it. I guess that means you'll be moving out?"

Lily frowned and for an instant sudden fear stilled her heart. It hadn't occurred to her that David might want her to leave. She licked her dry lips and forced her tone lighter.

"Why would you say that? It's not the world's biggest apartment, but I promise, the baby won't take up too much room. It will sleep in my room and—"

"Hang on a minute. What are you talking about? I assumed you'd be moving in with Tom. It *is* his, isn't it?"

"Yes, of course it's Tom's, but things are a little...complicated."

"How?"

She closed her eyes briefly and then drew in a deep breath. "I'm not going to tell him."

"What?" David shouted and shook his head. "Are you insane? Who does that? Who falls pregnant and then doesn't inform the father? We're living in the twentieth century. He's just as responsible for this baby as you."

Tears filled Lily's eyes at his harsh words and she bit down hard on a sob. Ever since she'd found out, her emotions had been all over the place. Despite her determination earlier that morning, she'd spent the day at home vacillating between bouts of crying and frantic pep talks. She should have called her mom before she told David. Her mom would understand.

Seeing her distress, David's fierce gaze softened and his expression turned contrite. He put his arms around her and gave her a hug.

"I'm sorry, Lil. Please don't cry. I shouldn't have yelled at you like that. It's just that… You surprised the hell out of me. First the news that you're pregnant and then you tell me you're not going to inform the father. Tom loves you. I know he does. He's a good guy. He'll do the right thing by you."

"That's just it, David! I don't want him to do the right thing by me. I want him to be with me for *me*, not because of the baby."

"But he will be! Hell, what's the difference? Why does a baby change things? He loves you and wants to be with you. What's so complicated about that?"

"You don't understand," Lily wailed. "A baby changes everything. Okay, he loves me now, but we've only known each other two months. If we commit to each other for the sake of the baby, I'll never know if we were meant to be together or not. Most people give themselves months, even years to decide if it's going to work. I'm preempting his decision. I'm making him choose right now." She swiped at her tears and shook her head. "I won't do it."

David loosened his arms around her and moved slightly away. "I hear what you're saying, Lily, but it's not right. He's the father. He has a right to know. I'd be livid if something like this was kept from me."

A tiny grin lifted one corner of Lily's lips. "Yeah, like it's ever going to happen to you."

David smiled back at her and shrugged. "Okay, so I'm speaking hypothetically. You know what I mean."

Lily sobered and nodded. "Yes, I do and I feel bad about keeping it from Tom, but I don't have any other choice. After what my mother lived through…I refuse to take the risk that history might repeat itself."

"You're talking about your father?"

"Yes, dammit! Of course I'm talking about my dad! You know what he was, what he did to her, to us! He destroyed us! We were a family and he tore us apart. Don't get me wrong, I'm grateful my mother left him and found us a better, safer life, but she shouldn't have had to. I had a right to grow up with a mom and dad who loved me and loved each other. I had a right to feel safe and secure in my family home. He robbed me of that."

"He was an alcoholic, Lily and a nasty one at that. Selfish and self-absorbed. It's not fair to compare him to Tom. It just isn't."

Lily stared at him and tears burned in her eyes. What David said was true, but right here, right now, with her baby growing inside her, she couldn't find the courage to agree with him.

Tom guzzled on yet another beer and set the empty bottle on the coffee table in front of him. With bleary eyes, he scanned the mess of bottles, food wrappers and the remainder of a super supreme pizza that littered the table. His gaze lifted and he absently noted night had settled in outside his window.

It had been a week since Lily had dropped the bombshell: She was too young to settle down. She wanted to concentrate on her studies. She wanted to date other men. It was her last want that had hurt the most. He couldn't believe he'd misread her so badly. She'd been as crazy in love as he—or so he'd thought. Now he knew it had all been an elaborate façade. He wasn't the love of her life. He'd been the love of her life *for now*—and that had just come to an ugly, screaming end.

Not that he'd screamed at her. He'd held back the tears.

No matter that her words had devastated him, he'd maintained his dignity. For a wild moment, he'd wondered if there was something else behind her sudden change in heart. His thoughts had rested on the broken condom and he'd asked the question: 'Was there a chance she might be pregnant? Were crazy baby hormones responsible for all of this?'

She'd looked horrified when he'd posed the questions, as if the very thought of carrying his child was abhorrent. The memory angered him as much now as it had then and with a vicious oath, he swiped at the bottles and food detritus and took immense satisfaction in the sight and sound of glass smashing on the living room tiles and flying every which way across the floor.

He stared at the mess and tried to care, but once again the anger and pain he'd been drowning in ever since she'd called things off overtook him. Long pent-up tears burned behind his eyes and spilled over. With fists clenched, he gritted his teeth against the sob that built up in his chest, but the effort was beyond him. With a tortured gasp, he bent at the waist, and bellowed out his torment, oblivious to the carnage of mess and glass that surrounded him.

———————

Lily pressed herself up against the side of Tom's front window and put her hand up to her chest in an effort to still her pounding heart. The sight of the man she loved, drunk and angry in his apartment, frightened her. She'd seen him drunk once before, but never angry and the combination turned her blood to ice.

Memories of her father crashed into her from every direction and she held her hands up over her face and shook her head in an effort to chase them away. Tom wasn't her father, but right there in the shadows, the distinction didn't seem to matter. He was a drinker. She'd known that from the start. The fact that he'd made an effort not to drink in front of her didn't change anything. In his drunken state, he'd turned violent and it was a risk she couldn't take.

With her hand now protectively cradling the tiny life inside her, she pushed away from the window and picked her way through the haphazard garden bed that edged the tired scrap of front lawn. Tears ran silently down her cheeks, but she refused to pay them heed. Ever since she'd broken things off with him, she'd been drowning in her guilt, but after seeing him now, she knew she'd made the right decision. Once a drinker, always a drinker. It was safer for her and her baby to stay well away.

CHAPTER 12

Royal North Shore Medical Center—present day

Tom stared at the tan and navy geometric pattern that made up the carpet in Doctor Slee's waiting room and tried not to think about what the results of his biopsy might show. The fact that the doctor was concerned enough to even take a biopsy was enough to worry him. With Lily in a coma and Cassie acting out, the last thing he needed was another health crisis. Still, it was better that he deal with it now that he was here. If there were any nasties to be had, treating them sooner was better than later. Everyone knew that.

If his mom knew, she'd chew his ass, angry that he'd waited so long. Years earlier, she'd had a bout of breast cancer. The family was shocked and worried beyond belief, but she'd gotten treatment early and was lucky to be able to call herself a survivor. It didn't always turn out like that.

Tom pulled out his phone to check for messages. He'd turned it on silent while he was with the doctor and he wanted to make sure Lily's condition hadn't changed. The screen was comfortingly blank and he sighed softly and clipped it back on his belt. It had been three days since the shooting and still his wife remained unconscious.

The doctors had assured him earlier that morning as they had every morning that she was doing absolutely fine. The bleeding had stopped, her wounds were healing. So far, infection had been kept away. There was no reason not to expect a full recovery, but she'd do it in her own time. There was nothing they could do to speed the process.

Their words provided him with comfort, but he still longed to hear her voice. He wouldn't be completely reassured she was better until she opened her eyes and spoke to him—and smiled and laughed and teased him—just like the Lily of old.

"Mr Munro, Doctor Slee would like to see you again. She has your test results."

The receptionist's words suddenly registered and Tom blinked and focused on the woman behind the desk. It was the same one he'd spoken to on the phone. *Judith Bevan*. It was written on her name tag.

"Um...yes. All right. No problem." Tom stood and drew in a deep breath and braced himself for whatever was to come. *Perhaps he was worrying for nothing?* There was always that possibility. With the comforting thought uppermost in his mind, he strode across the carpet and knocked on the doctor's door.

"Come in."

While his heart pounded out a staccato against his ribcage, Tom schooled his expression into one of calm indifference, not sure which one of them he was trying to impress. Good news or bad, he'd hold his shit together. He was thirty-nine and a veteran police officer, for Christ's sake. Way old and experienced enough to handle a little bad news. If it *was* bad news.

"Mr Munro, please take a seat."

"Tom. Call me Tom," he mumbled and sat. Doctor Slee pushed back a strand of graying hair and then picked up the file in front of her.

"Okay, Tom. I have the results of your biopsy. I'm afraid it's not good news. The lump in your left breast is malignant. We're going to have to operate. The good news is that it hasn't yet spread to any of the lymph glands."

Tom's mouth went dry at the instant he discovered it was

cancer and now he licked his lips with a tongue that felt like sandpaper. His pulse thudded and the sound of blood rushed through his ears, almost drowning out the doctor's words.

"What... What happens now?" he managed through a voice he barely recognized.

"We need to operate and remove the lump. The sooner we do it, the better. In fact, I'd like to put you on my theater list for tomorrow morning. I hope that's okay with you?"

Tom nodded, his mind in a whirl at the speed with which things were happening. "Tomorrow morning? I-I guess that will work."

The doctor looked at him kindly through pale blue eyes that had seen her fair share of sadness. "It really is important that we remove the tumor as quickly as possible, before it has a chance to spread. I'm sure you understand how much more serious this becomes when it reaches the lymph nodes."

Tom nodded again. It was all he could manage.

"After the surgery, we'll retest you again. With a bit of luck, you won't need any other treatment."

"You mean, I won't need chemo?"

"Not at this stage. We may give you a short course of radiotherapy, just to make sure, but as I said, with the cancer contained to just the one area, more exhaustive treatment isn't necessary. You're very lucky you came to see me in time."

Tom compressed his lips and didn't answer, just grateful he hadn't left it too late. He couldn't imagine having to go back to his kids and tell them he was dying of cancer.

"Is there anyone you would like me to call, to explain what's going to happen?" Doctor Slee asked, her eyes dark with compassion.

"No, I'm fine. I-I'll let my family know."

"Good. Then I guess I'll see you at the hospital tomorrow. Have an early dinner and then nothing to eat or drink after seven tonight. I need you to fast for at least twelve hours before the operation."

She made a note in the file in front of her and then looked up at him again. "Do you have any other questions?"

"H-how long does the operation take?"

"If all goes well, not more than an hour or two. There'll be some time in recovery afterwards."

"Will I have to stay overnight?"

"Yes, we'd rather you stay in, at least the first night. If all looks fine, you can go home the day after. You'll feel a bit sore for a few days. Is there someone at home to look after you?"

Tom lowered his gaze and stared at her cherry walnut desk. "M-my parents are staying with me for a little while. I'm sure they'll be willing to help out. My...my wife's in the ICU. She was shot in the abdomen three days ago."

Doctor Slee lifted a hand to her mouth and her eyes went wide with shock. "Oh, my goodness. I'm so sorry. I-I didn't know. I heard about that school shooting on the news. I had no idea it was your wife."

"Yes, well, she...she's doing okay. I just want her to wake up." His voice cracked on the last word and he pinched the bridge of his nose in an effort to contain the emotion that burned behind his eyes.

The doctor didn't offer any well-meaning platitudes and for that, Tom was grateful. There was nothing she could say that Lily's doctors hadn't told him and he was sure she was more than aware of it. A few moments later, he dragged in a breath and blew it out on a heavy sigh.

"You've had more than your share of hardships lately, by the sound of it," the doctor murmured, her voice filled with sympathy.

"You can say that again." He offered her a wry grin and she smiled back at him, the action taking years off her face.

"Do you have any more questions, Tom?" she asked quietly.

He shook his head. "I don't think so. I'll be happy to have it over and done with and not have to worry about it anymore."

The doctor nodded and closed his file. "Good. Then I'll

see you in the morning. Don't forget—fasting from seven."

"No problem. See you then." With that, he let himself out and headed next door to the hospital and Lily. He wanted to spend as much time as possible beforehand with his wife. He could only pray that everything would work out all right—for both of them.

———

Brady Sutton scrolled through the pages of his Snapchat account with a growing sense of hopelessness. On every page, with every comment and picture, kids were talking about what he'd done. Most of them wrote about him with a snigger in their tone. There were too many comments to count that went something like this: 'How about that kid from Chatswood Elementary who came to school with a gun? What a dickhead.' The knowledge that he was a laughing stock made him shudder with despair.

It was one thing for his mom to be disappointed in him, even for his dad to yell and shout, but knowing the kids he went to school with, was bullied by, or played sport with, thought he was a joke was nearly too much to bear. The morning of the shooting, he'd gone into school sure in the knowledge that he was about to right a wrong. Good would prevail over evil. Justice would be done.

But it hadn't worked out that way. It hadn't worked out that way at all. From the very beginning, things hadn't gone to plan. First, he couldn't find Ian. Then Mrs Munro had gotten in the way. Now, the other kids were laughing at him. He'd never be able to show his face inside the schoolyard again. They'd have to move and probably to another part of Sydney, maybe even interstate. From what he'd seen on social media, word of his failure had spread to every kid who lived on the north shore.

It wasn't supposed to happen that way. He was supposed to come home victorious, just like on his PS4 games and on the shows he watched on television. The bad guys always got what they had coming. The good guy got the girl.

He flopped over onto his stomach and buried his face into the softness of his pillow. It was way past late. His mom had come in and wished him goodnight hours ago. But he couldn't sleep. He hadn't been able to sleep since it had happened. He didn't know if he'd ever be able to sleep again.

Everywhere he turned, there was disbelief and disappointment—in the eyes of his mom, in the voice of his dad. No one bothered to ask him how *he* was feeling. It was like they'd forgotten that he was disappointed, too. The asshole who had made his life a living hell from the day he'd started school was still walking the halls, a hero. He'd hidden like a girl beneath Mrs Munro's desk, but nobody cared about that. The fact is, he'd dodged a bullet. Overnight, he was king of the school.

The very thought of it sickened Brady. His stomach twisted up in knots. He squeezed his eyes so tightly together, lights spun behind his eyelids. He pushed his face even further into the pillow until he found it hard to breathe. He'd failed. He was a failure. A dickhead and a failure.

His mom could barely bring herself to look at him. Yesterday, she'd spoken to his lawyer on the phone. She'd come to tell him about the conversation and couldn't even lift her gaze from off the floor. Her eyes were always red and puffy, like she cried every minute of the day. He didn't know how much longer he could stand it. Surely, it would be better if he simply went away?

The thought took hold and gained strength in his mind until he knew what had to be done. A sense of righteousness and power flooded through him. *Yes, he knew what had to be done.*

———————

Tom stared at his parents across the dinner table and

waited for his words to sink in. His mother was the first to recover.

"How long have you known?"

"I went to the doctor today. She did a biopsy. I waited a couple of hours for the results." He shrugged. "She wants to operate tomorrow."

His father shook his head in disbelief, but managed a tight nod of acceptance. "At least you found out before it was too late. We can be grateful for that."

"How long have you known?" his mom repeated, her voice quiet, but firm.

Tom stared at her, knowing what she meant. "About the lump?" he asked, in an effort to buy time.

"Yes, son. About the lump. How long have you known?"

Tom dropped his gaze and his shoulders slumped. They were his parents. He owed them the truth. "A bit over a year."

Renewed shock turned both of them speechless and then anger flooded his mom's face.

"A *year*? You've known about a lump in your breast for a year and you've only now done something about it? How could you ignore something like that? After what I went through? I don't believe it. I simply don't believe it."

She pushed away from the table and stalked toward the kitchen. Tom felt her anger, but he accepted that her outburst was only because she cared. She'd gone through her own terrible battle with breast cancer. To discover her son had ignored a lump in his breast for more than twelve months was more than she could bear. He was just grateful the prognosis was so positive. He didn't know what he would have done if he'd been given news it was terminal.

"Your mother's just worried about you. She doesn't mean anything by it."

Tom shot his father a thankful smile, but it barely lifted his lips. Still, he appreciated his dad's attempt to smooth things over.

"Thanks, Dad. It wasn't my intention to upset her. I guess... After what happened to her, I was scared to find out what my lump meant. It was stupid, but..." He shrugged, helpless to explain any further.

"It's okay, son. You don't need to explain your actions to me. Go and talk to your mother. She needs you."

Tom compressed his lips and nodded. He stood and left his father alone at the table. Cassie and Joe had disappeared long ago—Joe to watch television in his room and Cassie begged off, talking about needing to study for exams.

He let both of them go without objection. Earlier, he'd made the decision not to tell his kids about his upcoming surgery. If all went to plan, he'd call them tomorrow from the hospital. They didn't need any extra stress in their lives. Tomorrow would be early enough, after he could give them the good news that he was in the clear. He found his mother in the kitchen, stacking the dishwasher.

"Hey, Mom."

She acknowledged his greeting with the briefest of nods and then rinsed a pile of utensils.

"I'm sorry I didn't tell you sooner, Mom and I'm sorry I didn't go to the doctor months ago."

"Does Lily know about it?"

"No. It's only small and I never said anything about it to anyone, apart from Dad."

She spun around, her hands still dripping. "Your father knew?"

"Yes, well, no. Not really. I talked to him when he was unconscious in the ICU last Christmas. I-I told him about the lump. It was the first time I'd mentioned it to anyone. I don't know if he remembered or if he even heard me."

His mom turned back to the sink without comment and continued to stack the dishwasher. Tom collected pots and pans off the stove and began scraping them off into the scrap bowl. He'd give them to the neighbor's dog after dinner.

In silence, his mom finished what she was doing and then dried her hands. With a soft sigh, she turned to face him. "I'm sorry for going off at you like that, Tom. It wasn't fair."

Tom set the pan he was holding on the side of the sink and went to her and hugged her hard. He towered over her and weighed more than double. It had been a long time since she'd seen the top of his head.

"Don't be sorry, Mom. You have nothing to be sorry about. I was an idiot to sit on it for so long. I should have taken myself off to the doctor the first time I found it. If I hadn't been such a coward, I would have."

Marguerite stared at him, her eyes full of love and understanding. "I know what you mean, son. I've been there, too. I wish I could tell you I went to the doctor the very next day after I found my lump, but the truth is, I didn't. I pretended for at least three or four weeks that it was nothing more than a cyst and it would go away all on its own."

Tom raised his eyebrows in surprise. He hadn't known that.

"See, I was scared, too. I thought I was better off living in hope there was nothing to worry about than knowing for certain there was. I didn't want to think of the possibilities if I was wrong."

She drew in a ragged breath and Tom suddenly realized that, even though the cancer scare had happened years earlier, the memory of it still had the power to affect her. He tightened his arms about her and pressed a kiss against her hair. She shuddered and then drew in a deep breath.

"Of course, when I finally told your father, he had me in the doctor's surgery the very next day. You know how things went from there."

She pulled away from Tom and offered him a shaky smile. "I waited longer than I should have. If I'd come in sooner, they could have caught it before it spread. I went through hell and back before I was done with it. I guess I was upset that, after seeing what I went through, you could have taken the same risk."

"I'm sorry, Mom. It was stupid. Like I said, I was an idiot to ignore it."

"Yes, well, let's be thankful it hasn't turned out like mine. They've caught yours in time and I'm glad." She swiped at her eyes with the back of her hand and then spoke to him again, her voice soft.

"What time is your surgery tomorrow?"

"I have to be at the hospital by six. I'm on the morning list. I don't know exactly what time."

"They'll keep you in overnight?"

"Yes, at least, the doctor said they would. If all goes well, I'll be discharged the day after."

"I'll get Dad to drive you to the hospital. Don't worry about the kids. I'm sure we can manage."

"Thanks, Mom. I-I haven't told the kids about the operation. I didn't think they needed to hear any more bad news right now."

"I think you've made the right decision, son. They can find out when everything is over and done with. When they ask about you in the morning, I'll tell them you're at the hospital."

Tom hugged his mom again and then set her gently aside. "I really appreciate you and Dad being here. I don't know what I would have done without you."

Marguerite stood on tiptoe and grazed his cheek with her lips. "You're very welcome, son. We both love you very much."

"I love you, too. I just want Lily to open her eyes and smile at me, Mom. Is that too much to ask?"

Tears sparkled in his mother's eyes and a lump lodged in Tom's throat. He missed his wife like he'd miss a limb. Losing her would be like losing a piece of himself. The very thought of it was unbearable. He missed her smile, he missed her laughter, he missed her soft body pressed up against him, holding him close, protecting him, loving him all through the night.

Sleeping in their bed alone had been hard enough, the emptiness shrouding him as he tried to fall asleep. He'd only done it for three nights so far, but already it felt like an eternity. He'd slept beside her for the best part of sixteen years. To suddenly be in their bed without her was the loneliest thing in the world.

"She's going to be all right, Tom. I know she is," his mom whispered.

He nodded, thankful for her attempt to reassure him, despite the fact that they both knew she wasn't in a position to make such a declaration. It was enough that she cared enough to want to.

"I-I think I might call it a night, Mom. I have to be up early in the morning."

Marguerite stood up on tiptoes and kissed him gently on the cheek. "Good night, son. I'll set an alarm for your dad and make sure he wakes up in time. When do you want to leave?"

"About five-thirty, I think. That will give us plenty of time to get there. At that time of morning, traffic should be light."

She nodded. "I hope you get some sleep. I'll see you in the morning."

Despite the fact Tom tossed and turned for most of the night in between dreams of him and Lily, he woke before his alarm. The house was still and quiet. Not even the sun had made an appearance. He glanced at his watch and saw he'd beaten the alarm by fifteen minutes. With a soft sigh, he struggled out of bed and headed to the shower.

Not eating anything, meant he didn't have to leave time for breakfast and he was just about to head down the hall in search of his dad when there was a soft knock on the front door. Frowning, he changed direction and descended the stairs. He walked into the entryway and opened the door. Brandon stood unsmiling on the other side.

"Bran! What the hell are you doing here this early? It's still dark out."

"Mom called me last night. Why the hell didn't you tell me about the cancer?"

Tom swallowed a groan. He so didn't feel like getting into this right now. "What do you want me to say, Bran? I'm sorry, all right? I should have told you, but I didn't. I don't have time for this. I'm on my way to the hospital."

"I know. Why do you think I'm here?" Brandon held up a set of car keys.

Tom frowned. "What? You're my ride? Is that what you're trying to say?"

Brandon shrugged. "Your ride, your buddy. Who else's going to laugh at your sad jokes and keep you occupied while you're waiting to go in? You could be sitting around for hours before your number comes up."

Tom blew out his breath on a sigh and his irritation melted away. He was only antsy from the thought of the upcoming surgery. He just wanted it over and done with. It had nothing to do with his brother.

In fact, he was secretly pleased to see him. Without Lily around to reassure him, he was at a loss. For all of their married life, they'd made important decisions together and had always had each other's backs. It felt completely wrong going through something like major surgery without her even knowing about it.

He shot Brandon a look of gratitude. "Thanks, Bran. I'm sorry for biting your head off. I guess I'm a little uptight. I appreciate your offer and I'm glad to have you along."

Brandon merely nodded and gave him a friendly slap on the back. "That's what brothers are for, right? I haven't forgotten how you were there for me when Alex was in the ICU. We're family. We stick together. That's just the way it is."

Emotion welled up in Tom's eyes and tightened his chest. He blinked away the tears and cleared his throat. "Yeah, well, anyway. Like I said, I appreciate it."

It seemed like Tom waited a lifetime and it was more than four hours before the porter and a nurse came to take him down to the operating rooms. Brandon shook his hand and then leaned over and gave him an awkward hug and promised to be there when he woke.

Despite the early hour, upon his arrival at the hospital, Tom had visited the ICU to check on Lily before heading to where he needed to be. He was told by the staff that she'd had a restful night. They were pleased with her progress. Everything looked good. Her vitals were strong and stable.

If only she'd wake up.

Tom kissed her soft cheek and left, hoping they'd both come out of their respective ordeals okay. Now, he was headed down to the operating theaters, situated in the bowels of the hospital. The temperature dropped a few degrees and he couldn't help but shiver. He was dressed only in a light hospital gown and was covered with a sheet.

"It's cold down here," he commented to the nurse who walked by his side. The porter merely smiled and continued to push the gurney.

"We keep it cold on purpose," the nurse explained with a friendly smile. "Our equipment runs better in the cool air and it also helps to keep the germs at bay. Traditionally, it's the reason why most operating theaters were built below the ground. It's cooler and we don't need any windows. It's the optimum place to be."

Tom nodded. Her explanation made sense and he was grateful her chatter had taken his mind off what was to come, if even for a little while.

"I can ask for a blanket when we get there, if you like?" the nurse offered.

"No, it's fine. I can manage."

The porter wheeled the gurney out of the elevator and down a short corridor. A moment later, double glass doors slid open and they entered the reception area. Tom looked around him, but saw little other than a couple of other staff with soft blue caps on their heads, similar to the one he wore. The nurse had put it on his head before they'd left the ward. After seeing them on the staff, he could only imagine what it looked like on him. He thought of his kids and stifled a grin, wishing they could see him. They'd laugh and tease him and it would feel good because it would feel normal. He couldn't remember the last time he'd felt normal.

Another nurse dressed in blue scrubs approached them and the nurse from the ward spoke to the newcomer.

"This is Tom Munro. He's here for a lumpectomy. His consent's been signed, he's had his pre-med and he's all ready to go."

"Great," the other nurse replied and then moved closer to Tom. "Hi, Tom. I'm Gemma. I'm one of the nurses and I'll be looking after you until you go through to the operating room. I just need to ask you a few questions and then we'll be right to go."

"Is Doctor Slee here?" he asked, looking around.

"Yes, she certainly is. She's scrubbed and ready to go. You'll see her before the anaesthetist puts you under."

Fresh nerves churned in Tom's gut, but he drew in a deep breath and did his best to relax. "Okay, good. I just want to get it over and done with."

Gemma smiled in understanding. "It will all be over before you know it and you'll be back up in the ward. Do you have family waiting?"

"Yes, my brother, Brandon."

"Do we have his contact number?"

"Yes. I gave it to the nurse on the ward."

"Great. We'll call him and let him know as soon as it's over. You'll spend an hour or so in recovery and then we'll take you back to the ward. How does that sound?"

"Fine."

"Good." She leaned forward and squeezed his arm in reassurance. "You'll be fine. Trust me. I'm a nurse."

He forced a smile and silently prayed that she was right.

Lily swam through the deliciously cool water and enjoyed the way it caressed her skin. She'd been swimming for hours, but she didn't feel tired. Even the pain in her belly had subsided. It was like the heaviness that had been weighing her down for so long had suddenly lifted and she felt lighter than a cloud. She rolled and dived and frolicked and laughed at the sheer fun of it. The only thing that was missing was Tom.

Tom. It felt like forever since she'd seen him, touched him, kissed him. She longed to share this paradise with him. They'd been together more than sixteen years. They'd shared everything. Somehow, having him there made everything better. It didn't feel right that he wasn't with her now, enjoying the glorious water.

A bright light beckoned in the distance, far above her. It sparkled off the water, shooting diamonds. The brightness hurt her eyes and she squinted. Yet still, it called to her. She turned her back and dived deep, reluctant to leave the sheer pleasure the water afforded her. Heat from the light behind her touched her skin, warming her and all of a sudden, it didn't seem so bad.

With a soft sigh of farewell tinged with regret, she turned and headed toward it.

CHAPTER 13

Seventeen years earlier

Tom stared at the computer screen in front of him and did his best to concentrate on completing his report. Earlier in the day, he'd attended the scene of a break and enter in the leafy, northern suburb of Lindfield and was now writing up his findings. Fingerprint technicians had attended the scene and were lucky enough to find a single print from what looked like an index finger, but a suspect had yet to be identified. It was just another day in the life of a New South Wales police officer.

Tom had been transferred to Chatswood Police Station a couple of months earlier and was pleased at the change of scene. Too many of his colleagues at the western Sydney station knew about Lily and the broken heart she'd left behind. It was a relief to come to work and not be the subject of gentle chiding or even worse, sympathetic looks, from his colleagues.

Besides, Chatswood was closer to the city and he'd found a cheap, one-bedroom apartment not far from where he worked. The building was a little run down and sometimes the neighbors were loud, but it was clean and comfortable. Best of all, it didn't hold any memories of the woman who'd said she'd loved him then left him, all in a matter of weeks.

It had been seven months and three days since she'd told him it was over and he still felt the pain of it like it had happened yesterday. The swiftness of her change in attitude toward him still put his mind into a spin. He'd questioned her about it as calmly as he could, doing his best to keep his hurt and confusion in check, but he'd come away angry and dissatisfied with her answers and her vague references to needing time apart.

"I'm young, Tom. We both are. We owe it to ourselves to see what's out there, what the world has to offer. I don't want to get tied down like my mom did, at a young age, and then live to regret it."

Her words stung as much now as they had then and he gritted his teeth at the memory. It was time he moved on and forgot about her. He was young, fit, in the prime of his life. He needed to remember this every time he found himself moping about what had gone wrong. He needed to let go of it. He needed to let go of *her*. They were over. Whatever they'd once had was gone. Done. Finished. He had to cut his losses and move on. It was as simple as that.

"Got any plans for the weekend, Tom?"

The question came from Rusty Webb, one of Tom's colleagues. About Tom's age, Rusty had a smile that made even Tom's lips want to twitch upwards in response. Fit and toned with a cheeky grin, Rusty was a man on a mission.

He'd quite openly told his colleagues that it was his goal to sleep with as many women as he could in as short a time as possible. He was proud of the fact that at the ripe old age of twenty-three, he had more than two dozen notches on his belt.

Tom might not have agreed with Rusty's moral stance, but he enjoyed the man's company just the same. It was Rusty who managed to distract Tom even for a little from his daily doldrums by regularly insisting they go out drinking together and although Tom hadn't told Rusty the reason for his reticence, he was more than grateful for the efforts made by his friend.

At the thought of Lily, Tom's heart once again lurched

with pain. He thought he'd met the woman who would one day become his wife. Too bad she hadn't felt the same. He could have sworn she was as much in love with him as he was with her. She'd said as much more than once. He couldn't believe she'd proclaimed her love for him one day and within a month, she'd called it quits. It just went to show, where matters of the heart were concerned, he knew shit.

Aware that Rusty waited expectantly for his answer, Tom shrugged. "The weekend? Nothing special. I might go across to Manly on Saturday and catch some waves. The weather's supposed to be fine. What are you up to?"

Rusty's smile widened to his trademark mischievous a grin and he gave Tom a wink. "I'm heading into the city tonight and hitting the nightclubs. You have no idea how those places attract the women. It's only a matter of time before I strike it lucky."

Tom grinned back at him and shook his head. "Rusty, you're incorrigible. Why don't you choose just one girl for a change and actually get to know her a bit? There's more to a girl than her body or the way she performs in bed."

"Nah, mate. You've got it all wrong. Why restrict yourself to just one when you can sample the whole lot? Besides, I'm only in it for a bit of fun. The girls know that." He stepped closer and punched Tom lightly on the arm. "Come on, Tom, you're only young once. Come out with me and have some fun."

Tom shook his head. "No, mate. You go ahead. I'm not feeling in the party mood."

"Come on, it's Friday night. You can't stay home on a Friday night. Nobody does that."

"Nah, sorry, mate. I'm going to get an early night, for a change."

"What do you mean, for a change? It's been damned quiet all week. That B & E we attended today was the most excitement we'd had since Monday. What's been keeping you up all night?"

Rusty's tone filled with innuendo and he gave Tom another wink. "Don't tell me you've been holding out on me, Munro. Come on, what's her name?"

Tom shook his head and smiled. "There's no one. I just meant...I haven't been sleeping so well."

Rusty's expression sobered. "Is everything all right? I know I joke about this place, but the truth is, the kind of stuff we see, the things we do... It gets to all of us now and then."

Tom was touched by Rusty's concern, but he was quick to alleviate his friend's fears. "No, mate. It's not the job. I'm all good there. It's just something I'm working through. Personal shit. Family stuff. You know how it is."

Rusty nodded in understanding and his expression cleared. "Hell, yeah. My parents fight and spit at each other every opportunity they get. They wonder why I don't want to come home very often. They should have divorced years ago and given us all a break."

Tom shot Rusty a sympathetic look, but remained silent. Let Rusty think it was Tom's parents keeping him sleepless. It was better than admitting he was nursing a broken heart. He'd had enough ribbing from his previous colleagues to open himself up to another round.

"Tom, Rusty. What are you up to?"

Tom swung around in his chair and nodded to his boss. Superintendent Kyle Campbell ran a hand through his short gray hair and headed toward them from the direction of his office.

"Not much, boss," Tom replied. "I'm just finishing up that report on the break and enter we attended in Lindfield."

"Do we have a match on the fingerprint?"

"Not yet. I'll let you know if we get a hit."

"Good." He cleared his throat and encompassed both Tom and Rusty in his gaze. "I've taken a call from the Chatswood Elementary School. They're doing a *Safety in the Community* session with the kids. They've asked if we would have an officer available to attend the school and perhaps give a little talk about policing in the community." He looked at Tom and then switched to Rusty. "Any volunteers?"

"When?" Rusty asked.

"Soon. As in, an hour's time. They'd arranged for someone from Gordon to come in, but the blokes there have been called out on a job and there's no one around who can do it."

"I'll go," Tom offered, grateful for the distraction. It would give him something more to think about, other than Lily.

His boss looked at him in relief. "You're sure?"

"Yeah, why not? I have two primary school-aged sisters back home. They love having me around."

"Well, good. Thanks, Tom. Appreciate your offer. I'll call the principal back and let her know you'll be coming. Grab some of those stickers we have in that box in the storeroom and hand them out to the kids. I haven't met a kid yet who didn't like stickers."

———

Lily clapped her hands in a repetitive, rhythmic pattern to gain the attention of the group of third graders and then asked them to sit on the floor. It was a trick she'd learned from the class teacher. Lily was in the middle of completing her month of practical instruction at the Chatswood Elementary School and was loving every minute of it. She was more than halfway through the second year of her teaching degree and despite her pregnancy, had managed to keep up with her studies.

The baby was due in a matter of weeks and she was hopeful the birth would coincide close to her spring break. It would give her at least a couple of weeks to adjust to life with a newborn before college recommenced. She wasn't kidding herself that she'd conquer the challenges a baby would bring within the first fortnight. Sleepless nights and nursing were no doubt what she'd be in for, but at least the break would give her some time to adjust to the joys—or the sorrows—of motherhood.

She was determined to continue with her studies after the baby's birth. Her mom and Tony were more than supportive and had already volunteered to watch over their first grandchild when Lily went back to school. She was grateful for their offer and would be even more grateful when the baby arrived.

She was also pleased they'd finally accepted she wasn't prepared to talk about the baby's father. It was a relief not to have to field the endless questions when she refused to give them answers. The baby's father wasn't important. He was just a man she'd met. They'd been together once, but they weren't now and there was nothing more to be said.

It wasn't fair, but it was all Lily was capable of telling them. She'd cried herself to sleep for a month after she'd told Tom it was over. At last, David had knocked on her door in exasperation and had given her a piece of his mind. Either she had to shut Tom out of her life and get over him, or tell him the truth and see where it led.

The stern talking to had worked. Lily had pulled herself together and forced Tom Munro out of her mind. She'd made the right decision. Now, she just had to learn to live with it. Over the ensuing months, she'd buried herself in her studies and occasionally even managed to forget the man who'd lit up every corner of her life. It was only when the baby started stirring inside her that the memories came rushing back.

She was teary and upset for more than a week until once again, David snapped her out of it. She didn't know what she'd have done without him. He even attended her prenatal classes.

She was a little sad that it wasn't Tom by her side while she learned how to breathe in and out and she was embarrassed when the instructor assumed she and David were a couple, but she'd be forever grateful for his strength and support—and that's what really mattered.

Now, as the baby kicked impatiently inside her, she settled the class for the next session. The teacher, Mrs Reynolds, cleared her throat and spoke.

"Now, children, remember how we've been learning about safety in our community? We have a special treat for you this afternoon. A visitor from the Chatswood Police Station has come along for a visit. Would you all please put your hands together and welcome Constable Tom Munro."

The door behind Lily opened and she turned as if in a daze. Her heart began to thud. *Had the teacher really said Tom Munro?* No, she couldn't have. Lily must have been mistaken.

A tall form filled the doorway. She blinked and then blinked again. *It was him.* There was no mistake. He strode into the classroom like he belonged there and looked around the room.

His broad shoulders filled his pale blue uniform shirt the way it always had. She couldn't believe it had been seven months since she'd seen him. From what she could see of his hair beneath his police cap, it was a little longer than he used to wear it, as if it were overdue for a haircut. Or maybe that's the way he wore it now? She no longer had the right to know.

As if he heard her thoughts, his gaze collided with hers. Her heart skipped a beat and then pounded away. Nerves flooded through her and her legs went shaky with fear. Her hands splayed across her belly in an effort to conceal its bulge, but at eight-and-a-half months pregnant, the action seemed futile. With her shoulders back and her head held high, she let him look his fill. She knew the very instant he recognized her.

He blinked and blinked again, just like she'd done. It would almost have been funny if the situation weren't so serious. And then his eyes widened and his features flooded with shock. His mouth opened, but no words came out. He shook his head and then blinked again and then she saw the anger set in.

His gaze narrowed and his jaw clenched. She could almost feel the fury that radiated from him. She stepped backwards in an effort to escape its heat.

"Constable Munro, thank you for taking the time out of your busy day to join us. We're very grateful that you could come." Mrs Reynolds turned back to the class. "Let's all say a good afternoon to Constable Munro."

The class of third graders dutifully wished Tom a good

afternoon in a singsong chorus of voices. Lily took the opportunity to move further away from him and took refuge on the other side of the room. She snatched a breath and did her best to get her heart rate back under control. It wasn't good for the baby to get so worked up.

To say that she was shocked was an understatement. Never in her wildest dreams had she thought he might see her like this. Their only mutual connection was a loose one between David and one of Tom's colleagues and David would never breathe a word to anyone. She'd foolishly thought she could get through the nine months and Tom would never be the wiser. Sydney was a city of nearly four million people. It was unlikely that they'd ever run into each other again.

But, here he was, a matter of yards away, looking just as stunned as she felt. From across the room, his gaze sought hers and from the hard look in his eyes, this was far from over. He wanted answers. She could see it in his face. She knew better than to imagine he might leave without getting them.

For now, however, she'd been granted a reprieve. Tom was expected to speak with the children for half an hour. Mrs Reynolds would handle the questions. Lily could slink back into the shadows and pray desperately for answers that might satisfy him.

Tom seethed. For an instant, he thought his mind was playing tricks on him. It couldn't possibly be Lily Strickland standing in the classroom, her hands crossed in front of an unmistakably pregnant belly. From the look of her, the baby could come any minute. Either that, or she was having twins.

The very thought of it sent another shaft of anger flowing through him. She certainly hadn't wasted any time. His side of the bed could have hardly grown cold before she found someone else to replace him. Hurt pierced through him and he nearly gasped from the impact. The faces of thirty expectant children stared up at him from their position on the floor and he suddenly remembered why he was there. Dragging his gaze away from Lily's, he cleared his throat and greeted the children with a smile. It was so forced, he thought his face might crack from the strain, but he managed it all the same.

A half hour later and it was all he could do not to sigh out loud with relief when the teacher eventually called for the last question. A cute little girl with blond pigtails gave him a toothy smile.

"What do you like best about being a police officer?" she asked.

Tom smiled back at her. This one was easy. He'd been born with law enforcement genes running through his veins. His father might not have been a police officer, but as a District Court judge, he was still very close to the law. Then there were his brothers.

"I love that I can help people," he replied.

"Doctors and nurses help people. Why didn't you become one of them?"

The same little girl spoke and this time, lifted a single fair brow in query. Tom's heart melted at the sight. She was going to be a handful someday. The thought left him yearning that things between him and Lily had worked out differently. He shot her a glance, but she'd turned away.

"That's a very good question, honey," he said. "I guess I wanted to keep people safe. It's like I've been telling you—there are a lot of bad things that can happen and it's important to have people like me you can call. We're there to scare the baddies away."

"And lock them up in jail!" a young boy seated in the front row shouted amidst cries of laughter.

"Exactly!" Tom laughed and then turned back toward the teacher who had introduced herself earlier as Mrs Reynolds.

"Okay, grade three, I want you to say thank you to Constable Munro. It's been lovely having the constable here to talk to us about safety in our community. Please put your hands together and thank him for coming."

While the children dutifully clapped, Tom gave the teacher the box of stickers. He'd almost forgotten about them. She thanked him with a smile and then turned back to the class. With firm efficiency, she directed the children back to their seats. Tom glanced at his watch. It was almost time for the bell. Lily hadn't moved from her spot up the back and he could hardly talk to her in front of a roomful of kids.

Biting back a growl of impatience, he threw her a hard stare and then turned away. With his cap in his hand, he strode to the door and left as quietly as he'd come.

———————

Lily blew out a surreptitious sigh of relief, unable to believe Tom had left without approaching her. Perhaps his initial shock was over? Perhaps he no longer cared enough to want to find out if the baby growing inside her was his? The thought pained her and she pressed her hand against her mouth to hold back a sob.

It was her own fault if he'd stopped caring. She was the one who'd lied to him. Okay, so she hadn't actually said the words, but when he'd asked if she was pregnant, her silence had been telling. She'd been too shocked by his question and had struggled for something to say. By then, it was too late and he'd drawn his own conclusion. Knowing it was for the best, she'd blown him off by telling him she wanted to play the field.

The lies had nearly killed her, but she'd said them for both their sakes. She refused to marry a drinker and Tom was one of them. He'd also feel honor bound to marry her and she'd be no man's obligation. It was the last decade of the twentieth century. Women now had more choices than that and thank goodness they did. Lily shuddered at the thought of what it must have been like for a woman who found herself pregnant and unmarried in the fifties.

As if on autopilot, she helped the children pack up the colored pencils and workbooks in anticipation for the end of the day. Not only the end of the day, the end of the week. Lily smiled in relief at the thought of having two days to put her feet up. As much as she loved teaching, she looked forward to the break.

She wasn't the only one looking forward to the weekend. Right on cue, the bell went and the children streamed from the class amidst shouts of excited good-byes. She finished tidying up the classroom and then went to the cupboard where she stored her handbag.

"Thank you for all of your help this week, Lily," Diane Reynolds said with a smile.

"No problem, it was a pleasure. They're a great bunch of kids. You have them all very well trained."

"Not without a lot of effort, let me assure you," Diane laughed. "You'll get the hang of it. You're a natural."

Lily blushed, pleased with the woman's praise. Diane had been teaching for twenty-five years. Her approval meant a great deal.

"Thank you. I-I've always wanted to be a teacher. I can't wait to finish college and get out into a school. I can't tell you how much I've enjoyed being with you, in your classroom. You've passed on practical knowledge that can't be learned from a book and...I just wanted to tell you how much I appreciate you going the extra mile. I've been with other teachers in other schools during my pracs and no one has taught me as much as you."

The woman smiled and accepted Lily's compliment graciously. "You're an interested pupil and a quick learner, Lily. Why wouldn't I be willing to help you out?" Diane finished cleaning the board and then turned back toward her.

"I was lucky when I was your age, just starting out, to have a teacher who became my mentor. She'd been teaching all her life and she had to be in her sixties. She taught me things I hadn't even thought of, little ways to connect with the children. It made a difference in my life and in my career. I'm always happy to pay it forward."

"Well, I for one am very appreciative."

Diane collected her handbag and together they walked to the door. "Have a good weekend, Lily. I'll see you on Monday."

"You, too, Diane, and thanks again for everything."

Together, they left the classroom and walked through the doorway that led outside. Lily looked up and gasped. Tom stood right outside the door.

"Oh, Constable Munro, I wasn't aware you were still here. Is there something I can do for you?" Diane asked in surprise.

"No, I'm fine. I was wondering if I could have a word with Lily?"

Diane turned toward her, a slight frown deepening the lines across her forehead. "With Lily? Of course. That is, if it's all right with you?"

She directed her last question toward Lily and it was all Lily could do not to turn tail and run. Here was her chance to escape. She could simply decline to speak with him and leave with Diane. There would be nothing he could do about it, short of running her down and she was sure he wouldn't do that.

"Um... I...I have to—"

"I won't take a minute, I promise." His grin was pure charm. Even his eyes twinkled. But Lily wasn't fooled. She could see the tension in every line of his body, the way his jaw was clenched. It was too bad Diane didn't know him as well as she did.

"I'll catch you next week, Lily. Have a good weekend." Diane nodded toward Tom and left.

Nerves thrummed like kettle drums in Lily's stomach, turning it upside down. Her hands clenched into fists and she drew in a deep breath, bracing herself for what was to come.

"You look well, Lily. Even more beautiful than I remembered."

It was the last thing she expected him to say and her breath left her body in a rush. Heat spread from her neck to her cheeks and she couldn't bring herself to look at him.

"I-I... Thank you." Her thoughts were in turmoil.

"I must admit, I was shocked to see you here. I thought you were still in college."

"I am. I...I'm doing a practical placement. I've been here a fortnight and I have a fortnight to go."

"When is your baby due? It doesn't look like it's going to wait that long."

Lily bit her lip, still unsure what to tell him. Her reasons for keeping it from him in the first place hadn't changed, despite the months that had passed.

"I...I..." She shook her head hopelessly and tears pricked her eyes. She didn't want to lie to him again, but she was terrified she didn't have a choice.

Mistaking her reticence, Tom's gaze narrowed and his lips went taut. "It's been seven months since you left me. You sure didn't waste any time."

She closed her eyes in an agony of indecision, hating the hurt that rang out in his voice—hating even more that she was responsible for putting it there. The knowledge that he thought so little of her—that she could go from his bed to another's with barely a breath in between—cut her heart to pieces. Torn, she stared at him for a long moment and finally decided upon the truth.

"The baby's due in a little over three weeks." The words tumbled out of her mouth and she was suddenly lightheaded with relief. The strain of keeping something so huge from the man she still loved had taken their toll. While the heavy feeling of dread she'd carried around inside her for the past eight months hadn't disappeared, it had certainly eased.

She watched a gamut of emotions chase themselves across Tom's face. Distrust, confusion—and finally comprehension—followed one after the other.

"You mean you're... You're more than eight months pregnant? Is that what you're saying?"

Lily nodded and clasped her hands protectively around her belly.

"But... That means you fell pregnant while we were still

together." He frowned. "Oh, Christ, the condom... The baby's mine?"

She nodded again, a little confused at his mumbling, but relieved that he'd comprehended the truth. She would have offered him a smile if his demeanour had given her the slightest hint that he was happy about the discovery he was about to be a father. But instead, Tom's expression darkened and his frown grew fiercer.

"You *lied* to me? How could you have done such a callous, cold-hearted thing? I asked you if you were pregnant and you told me no!"

She opened her mouth to respond, but he spun away from her, shaking his head in disbelief. A second later, he strode back to her, anger and hurt still clear on his face.

"You claimed to love me," he scoffed. "Lies and subterfuge. They aren't the actions of someone in love. During the last couple of weeks we were together you told me your feelings had cooled, that you were too young to be in a relationship—that you wanted out. Stupidly, I believed you and I gave you out, even when everything inside of me wanted to beg you to stay. I loved you enough to let you go...and in return, I discover you lied to me about something so huge... I-I can't believe you did it."

His breath came fast. "The truth is, Lily, if you loved me, you would have told me. Nobody keeps news like that from the person they love. We're talking about a *baby! Our* baby! It's totally ludicrous."

His anger seemed to grow with every turn of phrase until his face was red with shock and disbelief. The more he spoke, the more the reality of the situation appeared to sink in and finally, he shook his head in disgust. It nearly broke Lily's heart to watch his reaction.

"I'm sorry, Tom. I'm sorry I didn't tell you. The truth is—"

"*Truth?* How can you talk about truth? I've just discovered you're the instigator of the most monstrous lie of my life and you have the audacity to speak to me about truth?" With a vicious curse, he turned away from her again, as if he couldn't stand the sight of her a moment longer.

Desperation clawed at her insides and she searched around frantically for something to say—anything to wipe the look of shock and betrayal off his face. She looked around them, grateful to discover the schoolyard was mostly empty. Apart from a solitary child crossing the oval to meet a parent at the bottom gate and the groundsman who was emptying trash cans at the far end of the building, they were alone.

"I don't know what you want me to say, Tom." Her voice cracked and the tears she'd tried so hard to hold at bay slid silently down her cheeks.

He cursed again and when he lifted his gaze to hers, she gasped at the hurt and desolation that shadowed his eyes.

"There's nothing you can say, Lily. I... I'm sorry. I can't deal with this right now. I need to get away. I need time to think. I..."

With his lips compressed into a tight thin line, he stopped talking and closed his eyes. A moment later, he opened them and her heart skipped a beat. He stared at her with a look so cold, the chill of it sent shivers coursing through her body. Desperate and defeated, she wondered if she'd ever see him look upon her with love again.

Oh, God, what had she done? She'd lost the only man she'd ever loved. With a fist pressed against her mouth, she tried to keep the pain of it inside.

"I need to go," Tom muttered and turned on his heel.

Lily watched him disappear. With a shuddering breath, she leaned against the side of the building and let the deluge of hot tears fall.

CHAPTER 14

Chatswood, Sydney—present day

Cassie twisted a length of dirty blond hair around her finger and swallowed a sigh. It wasn't that long ago when she washed her hair every other day and now she couldn't remember the last time she'd attended to it. Her usual glossy locks hung dull and lank around her face, but she couldn't find the energy or enthusiasm to do anything about it.

Her mom was in hospital, struggling to overcome the damage caused by a bullet wound. Her dad was in surgery. They were operating on him right now to remove a cancerous lump. He hadn't given her the details, but she'd overheard him talking to her grandparents. It angered her that he didn't think she was old enough to deal with such news. She was seventeen. She wasn't a baby. She had a right to know that any moment in her godforsaken life, one or both of her parents could die.

It was a hell of a thing for anyone to face and she wasn't dealing with it well, although if she were honest, she'd concede the downward spiral had started months before. Every time she closed her eyes and even during some waking hours, she relived with increased ferocity that time she was snatched in broad daylight from the netball courts and taken to a secluded cabin in the woods.

Sometimes, it was a noise, a spoken word, or even a smell

that could trigger the flashbacks and she'd relive in crystal-clear detail the horror she felt as the man used a knife to cut open her shirt. The nightmares were escalating beyond her control and she didn't know what to do about them. And now, both of her parents were clinging to life in the hospital. Her life had gone to hell.

Reaching underneath her bed, her fingers closed around the neck of the rum bottle and she sighed aloud with relief. At least she had something stable in her life. The diminished capacity she got from swilling alcohol was more than worth the thumping headache she'd suffer.

It didn't matter, anyway. No one expected her to go to school while her parents were both so seriously ill. She'd tell her grandmother she didn't feel like going, which was the truth. Grandma didn't have to know it had nothing to do with her mom and dad and everything to do with the bottle of rum she'd all but consumed.

And now she had a little something extra to lift her from the doldrums. Richard Wales, one of the boys in the twelfth grade, had sidled up to her a week ago, before her mom had been shot, and offered her some pills. She'd been a little surprised at his bravery—everyone knew her dad was a cop—but it hadn't seemed to matter to Richard.

At twenty dollars a pop, they were on the expensive side, but he assured her the buzz she'd feel would be far superior to chilling out on alcohol and she wouldn't have to deal with the headache afterwards.

She'd been tempted—Richard was kind of cute and one of the more popular boys in school—but in the end, she'd smiled politely and thanked him and had declined his offer. Then, yesterday, after sleeping off another hangover, she'd remembered what he'd said. A call to a friend, who called a friend and Richard had turned up at her door. He'd told her grandma he was a friend of Cassie's and was there to see if she was all right. He also wanted to give her some study notes from school.

Grandma had fallen for the ruse and the charming smile Richard flashed her way. Cassie had taken him upstairs and within minutes, they'd conducted the mutually satisfying transaction in the privacy of her bedroom. Now, she sat up and tugged open the drawer of her nightstand.

The five little white tablets lay in a small plastic bag, tucked under her English novel. It was lucky she'd stashed her birthday money in her wallet, rather than putting it in the bank, or she'd have never been able to afford so many. Now, she reached out and grabbed the bag and opened it and pulled out one of the pills. She'd already had most of what was left in the rum bottle, but the alcohol seemed to be taking longer to kick in. A little bit of speed was probably just what she needed.

Opening her mouth, she set the pill on her tongue and swallowed it down with a mouthful of rum. With one final gulp, she screwed the lid back on the bottle and tossed it beneath her bed. With a sigh, she lay down on her pillow, closed her eyes and waited for the ecstasy to do its magic.

―――――――――

Royal North Shore Hospital

Tom heard a murmur of voices and then someone called out his name. The tone was gentle, but insistent. He was zoning out, still mostly asleep and did his best to ignore it, but the voice came again, disturbing a state of comfort he hadn't felt for days.

"Tom, can you hear me? It's Tessa. I'm one of the nurses. You're in recovery, Tom."

It was a woman's voice, but it wasn't Lily. He'd know her voice anywhere. All of a sudden, his memory resurfaced and he frowned. Lily had been shot. Lily was in hospital, Lily still hadn't woken up.

His chest tightened on a surge of fear and his heart picked up its pace. The nurse—Tessa, he thought she'd said—must have been hovering because her voice had a little more urgency when she called out to him again.

"Tom, open your eyes. The operation's over. Everything went well."

Someone shook him and then Tessa spoke once again.

"Open your eyes, Tom. Let me see that you're okay."

Tom gritted his teeth against the intrusion. He didn't want to open his eyes. If he opened his eyes, he'd have to acknowledge the truth—that Lily might never be all right. It had been four days and still she lay unconscious. Nobody could tell him how much longer it might be. The not knowing was driving him mad.

"Tom!"

"Okay, okay," he muttered and cracked his eyes open. "I heard you the first time."

A black woman with a short cap of thick curly hair stood over him, shaking her head. An exasperated smile tugged at her lips. Tom stared at the whiteness of her teeth, stark against the dark purple of her lips.

"You gave me a little fright," the nurse confessed, shaking her head. "Everything went well with the operation. Doctor Slee will speak to you later this evening. She has a full theater list today and we're only halfway through. Your family's probably wondering where you are. You've been down here a little longer than we expected."

"How come?"

The nurse shrugged. "You took awhile to come out of the anaesthetic. Sometimes it happens. Everyone's different. But now you're awake and talking, I can call the ward. They'll send a nurse down and a porter who will transport you back to your room."

Tom digested the information in silence. He'd never been under an anaesthetic before, so he had nothing to compare it to, but it didn't matter. He was awake now and that was good. The surgery was over and it all went well. It was a comforting thought. Now, he could turn his attention and energies toward Lily. She was going to make it. She was. He wouldn't have it any other way.

———————

Roseville, Sydney

Brady lay back in his bed and pulled the pillow over his head. Still, the noise of his parents arguing downstairs filtered through. He clenched his jaw and held the pillow tighter. He hated it when they fought. It reminded him of the time his dad had hit Brady's mom. It had only happened once. But it was enough.

His mom had come through the doorway of his bedroom holding her face, tears gathering in her eyes. She'd snatched him out of bed. She thought he'd been asleep, she thought he hadn't heard. The truth was, he'd heard everything.

Right now, they were arguing over the fact his dad had given him the gun and had left him with the box of ammunition. His mom was shouting at his dad that this whole mess was his dad's fault, even the police felt so. His lack of judgement giving Brady the gun had led to this senseless shooting and now their son was facing possible jail time and a lifetime of regret and misery. Brady would never have shot his teacher if it hadn't been for his dad.

His dad was having none of it, refusing to accept Brady's actions had anything to do with the gun. The boy was defending himself against classroom bullies. It was understandable, given the hell they'd put him through. Yes, his dad knew all about Ian Little and his cohorts. Brady had told him. His dad then turned the tables and accused his mom of being an unfit mother for not protecting their son.

"The boy wouldn't have had a reason to defend himself if you'd paid a little more attention to what he was going through. He told me he'd tried to talk to you about it, but you brushed away his concerns, like they didn't matter. You could have used your influence as deputy principal to move him to another class, spare the boy some of the heartache he's had to deal with over the years. You gave him no choice but to retaliate in a way that he thought would work."

Brady's mother protested and tried to argue back, but his

dad was having none of it. Brady pressed the pillow tighter against his face until it was a struggle to breathe. His lungs burned and lights flashed behind his eyes. Blood thumped in his ears, blocking out the sound of his parents.

And then he shoved the pillow away and gasped desperately for breath. *What the hell was he doing?* If he wasn't careful, he'd suffocate. Is that what he wanted? Did he want to die?

The thought took root in his mind. It was so awful that at first he pushed it far away, but in the dark, amidst the shouted arguments and accusations of his parents, it didn't seem like such a bad idea.

If he wasn't around, they'd have nothing to fight about. Life could go back to normal. His mom could return to school and the career she loved. His dad could get back to his new family. It would be a perfect solution for everyone—even him. His days of torment and torture at the hand of Ian Little and others of his kind would be over. He'd float away on a cloud. They wouldn't get him from there, no matter how hard they tried.

He sat up and pushed the bedclothes out of the way and then climbed out of bed. He padded across to his closet. The sunlight that shone brightly through his window seemed incongruous with his dark thoughts, but it didn't deter him. The huge fig trees lining the street below whispered gently in the breeze, the same breeze that now ruffled his hair. It was a nice day.

With careful deliberation, he opened the sliding door of his closet and riffled through one of his drawers until his hands closed around a belt. It was a nice leather belt. Soft, but strong. His mom had bought it for him last year to wear with his pants at her sister's wedding.

He tested it now by pulling it hard between his hands. The leather gave off a satisfying snap and he tugged it a couple of more times to be sure. It was good and strong, just like he remembered. It ought to do the trick.

He looked around his bedroom and debated about where he could do it. He needed something high enough off the floor that he wouldn't muck it up. There'd be no failing this time. He might have become a laughing stock after all that had happened at his school, but he had no intention of making the same mistake twice. He needed to do this right.

A moment later, he found it. The brace that hung from the roof, supporting his TV. It was made of steel and should hold his weight. He climbed up on his bed and swung off it, testing it. The bracket didn't move.

Standing on the bed, Brady threaded the belt through the buckle and pulled it tight, leaving enough room to take his head. With the belt now loose around his neck, he reached up to the TV bracket and pushed one end of the belt through the steel. It pulled tight around his neck and he stood high on tiptoe to ease the pressure. It wouldn't work until he'd secured the belt around the bracket.

With a grunt, he managed to knot the belt—only once, but it would have to do. It wasn't long enough to loop through again. He dragged in a breath through the tension around his throat and eased it out. He was almost done.

On tiptoes again, he thought through his plan. The bracket was almost not high enough. He'd have to throw himself out and pull his knees up if he wanted it to work the first time. He wondered if he'd be brave enough to do it.

He heard the sound of breaking glass and his mother's scream of fear. A second later, she was shouting at his father, ordering him out of the house. With another deep breath, he swung hard off the bed and the belt pulled instantly tight.

Hannah Sutton poured herself a neat scotch from the modest selection of bottles in her liquor cabinet and threw it back in a single gulp. It was the middle of the day. She shouldn't be drinking, but she needed something to fortify her. The last few minutes spent with her ex husband had left weak and trembling. Her hands still shook, despite the fact Colin had left more than an hour earlier. She should have called the police. She had a restraining order out on him, after all. He wasn't supposed to come within a hundred yards of her house.

She'd called him and asked him over because she needed to speak to him about Brady. The charges, the pending court hearing, the fact that her son's own father had given him the gun. Brady hadn't left the house since it happened and she could hardly leave him alone. So, she'd taken the risk and called his dad and now she wished she hadn't.

It had turned ugly almost immediately. She should have known that's the way it would go. She was foolish to think her husband would apologize or even be sorry for what he'd done. No, of course he wasn't repentant. He'd put all the blame on her. When he swiped at the crystal vase in a fit of anger, sending it hurtling to the floor, she'd suddenly had enough.

She'd shown him to the door, shaking with anger and fear. She was only thankful Brady hadn't witnessed it. He'd been in his room since breakfast.

The stress of the past days suddenly crept up on her and overwhelmed her. She poured herself another scotch and blinked back the tears. Her chest went tight and she blinked hard again, but there was no way she could hold them back. They slid down her cheeks in a silent path, a witness to her pain.

What if her husband was right? What if she was at fault? Brady had accused her of as much a couple of days before when he'd reminded her how she'd done nothing to help him escape the notice of the schoolyard bullies. She remembered him complaining to her of course, on more than one occasion, but she hadn't been lying when she told him she wasn't in charge of the classes.

She probably could have done more to ensure he wasn't in a class with Ian Little, but she'd wanted him to learn how to deal with the bully, rather than running away. There were bullies everywhere, even in the workplace. Like it or not, they'd come in and out of his life and there was no escaping them. It was important her son know how to deal with them, not run away and hide. No, moving Brady to another class would have only been a bandaid solution. Hiding didn't achieve anything.

And yet, her son cried like his heart had broken when he'd told her it was all her fault and now, with the husband's accusation ringing in her ears, she wondered if it was true. The thought sent an agony of pain spiralling through her. Lily Munro—a fellow teacher and a friend—had taken a bullet and Hannah was responsible for putting it there.

She cried out at the idea and slid down onto the sofa. The empty glass fell from her fingers and crashed onto the floor. Just like the vase, it hit the ceramic tiles and splintered into a thousand pieces. They glinted like diamonds in the sunlight.

With a gasp and a sob, she stepped carefully around the shards and stumbled up the stairs, unable to cope with the thought of cleaning up the mess just yet. She'd attend to the carnage in later.

With her footsteps muffled by the carpet, the only sound in the still afternoon was her crying. She needed to hold her son, her little baby boy. She needed to tell him how she was sorry and how she'd watch out for him, protect him from now on.

The tears were coming in earnest and she swiped a hand across her nose. She sucked in a ragged breath and did her best to control her pain. She didn't want to frighten him. Besides, he might even be asleep. She stopped outside his closed door and took another moment to compose herself.

Filling her lungs and letting it out slowly, she blew her nose on a tissue she had tucked inside her bra. Feeling marginally better, she turned the doorknob and stepped quietly into the room. His curtains were thrown wide. Blinking, she let her eyes adjust to the brightness. A moment later, she saw him.

———————

There was something in Lily's mouth that was causing her no end of trouble. Every time she tried to swallow, the thing got in the way. She turned her head one way and the other in an effort to dislodge it, but to no avail. She brought one hand up to her mouth and felt something hard and plastic. A tube of some kind. It went into her mouth and pressed uncomfortably against her tongue.

She moved her head and must have made a sound because all of a sudden, there were people leaning over her. Her mother-in-law, Marguerite, and a woman dressed in a nurse's uniform.

"Mm, mm." She tried to speak over the tube, but the effort was far too great. Her heart hammered against the strain.

"Oh, my goodness, she's waking up! Lily's waking up!"

Lily frowned at Marguerite's joy-filled words. Her mother-in-law sounded like it was nothing short of a miracle.

Why wouldn't she wake up? Just how long had she been asleep? Had they thought she was going to die? The questions came at her fast and furious until she squeezed her eyes shut to block them out. A moment later, a man spoke in a voice she didn't recognize.

"Lily, can you hear me? It's Doctor Reeves. Nod, if you can hear me."

She nodded and was rewarded with a cry of relief that came from Marguerite's direction. Lily opened her eyes again and looked around for her husband.

"Tom?" she managed in a voice so hoarse she tried to clear her throat.

"He's here...in the hospital," Marguerite replied a little hesitantly. "I'll call Brandon. He can pass the news onto Tom and let him know you're awake. Tom will be beyond thrilled and excited. Everyone will be. I can't tell you how wonderful it is to have you back with us."

Lily tried hard to concentrate on her mother-in-law's words, but they were confusing and made no sense. If Tom were here in the hospital, why would she call Brandon? Had something happened to Tom's phone? She thought about it a moment and then decided it must be that. Nothing else made sense.

She opened her mouth to make another attempt at conversation, but was scolded by the doctor.

"Save your energy, Lily and don't try to speak. You have a tube down your throat that will make it nearly impossible. The tube has been helping you breathe, but we don't need it any longer. Now that you're conscious, we can get rid of half this stuff that's been crowding up your bedside."

He offered her a reassuring smile that softened the hard planes of his face. He was probably a little younger than she was, but fatigue and countless long and stressful hours had aged him. Not that it mattered what he looked like. All that mattered was that he'd managed to save her life.

Marguerite patted Lily's hand and murmured something about going outside to make some phone calls. A few minutes later and doing her best not to gag, the breathing tube was removed and Lily got a chance to speak.

"Th-thank you, Doctor Reeves. I-I appreciate everything you've done."

He smiled and accepted her thanks, graciously. "Call me Matthew. We don't stand on formalities around here."

She smiled back at him and then lifted her arm still connected to the IV. "What about this? When can it come out? I hate needles."

Matthew grinned. "You'll have to wait a little longer for that one. Besides, the needle's removed right after it's been inserted. All you have in your arm is a thin plastic tube. If you continue to improve, we'll move you out of the ICU and onto a ward, but the IV will have to stay in as a precaution. It appears we're no longer in danger of losing you, but you still have a long road to recovery."

His expression turned serious. "Bullet wounds are often slow to heal and yours caused considerable trouble as it passed on its way through. Give your body the time it needs and before you know it, you'll be as good as new."

Lily held his gaze a moment longer and then slowly turned away. She'd been shot by a pupil in her class. A boy who was all of eleven. The shock of what had happened washed over her again. If there was one thing she was certain, she'd never feel new again. The thought was beyond depressing. She swallowed a sigh. She wanted Tom. She needed Tom. *Whatever could be keeping him?*

CHAPTER 15

Seventeen years earlier

From his position on his battered couch, Tom stared at the phone in his hand and cursed softly under his breath. The afternoon was as good as done and soon it would be nightfall. It had been a whole week since he'd seen Lily and he was just as confused as ever.

One minute, he wanted to push thrust aside her deception and just welcome her back with open arms. The next, he wanted to strangle her for keeping something so important from him and not loving him enough or not trusting him to make things right. No matter how many times the thoughts chased themselves around inside his head, he still didn't understand it.

Why hadn't she simply told him she was pregnant? Okay, a baby hadn't been in their plans—at least, not in the immediate future—but they loved each other. They'd get married because that's the way it had to be and they'd live happily ever after. What was wrong with that?

It appeared Lily had seen things differently. In fact, if he hadn't run into her at the school, he might never have known. Had she been planning to tell him at *any* stage that they'd made a baby? The fact that he didn't know the answer was deeply troubling.

Perhaps she didn't love him in the way that he loved her?

Perhaps she loved him, but loved him for *now*. Perhaps she didn't think her love would last a lifetime? There were so many questions left unanswered. The turmoil was turning his life upside down.

Ever since he'd discovered she was going to have his baby, he'd been at odds with the entire world. His lack of sleep had him tired and irritable and he was embarrassed to admit his colleagues had borne the brunt of it.

He snapped at the slightest thing. He couldn't concentrate enough to conduct even the most basic of interviews in a halfway competent fashion and he had half-finished reports piled up all over his desk. His professional life was beginning to mirror his personal life and Tom didn't like that one bit. He'd always relished the fact that he could control all facets of his life with relative ease. Each part compartmentalized, separated one from the other. The discovery he was about to be a father was doing his head in.

It wasn't the thought of being a dad that tortured him. It was the fact that the baby's mother had kept it from him. It would never occur to him to keep the existence of a baby from the woman that he loved. Okay, so he hadn't told her about the broken condom and he still felt a measure of guilt over that, but as far as he knew, it hadn't been an issue. They were together a couple of months. He assumed the malfunction hadn't resulted in anything but a little stress on his part.

Thinking back, he'd given cursory thought to whether or not she'd had a period during their time together, but the fact was, they hadn't slept together regularly enough for him to know for sure. He'd done a stint of night shifts for a week during both months and had barely seen her during that time.

He'd relied on the fact that she'd tell him if she was pregnant, particularly given he'd put the very question to her. Maybe it was stupid and looking back, it was definitely naïve, but that was the truth of it. He couldn't imagine keeping the existence of a baby from its father. Lily had done just that and it infuriated him.

With another curse, he scrolled through his contacts and found the number he was after. To his relief, it was answered after the second ring.

"Dad, it's Tom. How are you doing?"

"Tom. Good to hear from you, son. How's the city treating you?"

"Yeah, you know, busy. There's no shortage of criminals around here, although, I must admit, since moving to the north shore, things have quietened down a bit. Or maybe I should say the focus has changed. Not so many callouts to scenes of violence, but plenty of drug-related crime."

"Well, I'm proud of you son, for being willing to put your life on the line to keep the rest of us safe. Now, what's really going on?"

Tom bit back a smile at his father's bluntness. As the first-born son, he and his dad had always been close. Duncan, his father, knew him better than anyone.

"Why do you say that?" Tom countered, not quite ready to spill his guts.

"It's six o'clock on a Friday night. No single, young man calls his father at that time of the day unless something's wrong. If everything was all right you'd be down at the pub having a few beers with your mates."

This time, Tom let the smile take over his face and immediately felt better. He'd made the right decision to call his dad. Now he just had to find the courage to talk to him about what had happened. He cleared his throat of a sudden rush of nerves.

"You're right, Dad. I...I need your advice."

"Sure, son. What's the problem?"

His father's easy attitude relieved a little more of Tom's tension and he drew in a deep breath and eased it out. He hadn't told his family about Lily. They'd only been together a couple of months. They were still in the getting-to-know-each-other stage when she'd called it quits. At the time, he'd been grateful he hadn't mentioned her to his family. It meant he hadn't had to endure the embarrassment of telling them it was over.

Now, he wanted to tell his dad everything and he wanted his opinion, maybe, his advice. Tom was going to be a father any day and he wasn't even on speaking terms with the baby's mother. It was time to come clean.

"It's about this girl called Lily."

"Ah, somehow I guessed it was going to involve matters of the heart."

"Yeah, well, I don't know about that. We're no longer together, but...I ran into her a week ago and she's... She's pregnant. We split up more than seven months ago, but she tells me the baby's mine."

There was a pause before his father responded. "Do you believe her?"

"Yes, Dad. I do."

"Because you can always get a DNA test after the baby's born."

"No, I believe her. At least, I think I do. There was a hole in the condom and—" Tom's face flamed, but he forced himself to continue. "Anyway, the timing works out. The thing is, I thought I knew everything there was to know about her. She was the most honest and genuine person I'd ever met. I would have trusted her with my life. Now...I'm not sure that I'll ever trust her again."

"That's understandable, Tom. Keeping a pregnancy from the baby's father is way up there on the scale of deceit."

"Yeah, you can say that again. It's why I'm so damned mad at her. Why didn't she tell me? I loved her. I told her over and over again. I might not have mentioned the word marriage, but she sure as hell knew how I felt. A baby wasn't in our immediate plans—hell, I'm only twenty-two and she's in her second year of college—but it wouldn't have been the end of the world. We could have gotten married long before she started showing. Now, it's all too late."

"Have you asked her why she kept it from you?"

"Yes! No! Hell, I don't know. I don't know what I said. I was shocked to discover she was pregnant and hadn't told me. I-I got angry and shouted at her and then I kind of stormed off. The only thing I remember her telling me was that she was sorry, whatever the hell that's supposed to mean. That was a week ago, I haven't heard from her since."

"Do you still love her?"

"Of course I do! My life's been shit these last seven months. Just ask the people I work with. Even the boss had a word with me the other week about my short fuse. He's concerned it's delayed shock to something I've witnessed on the job." Tom's bark of laughter was humourless. "Ha! Work-related. I wish it was that easy. Work's the least of my worries."

Duncan Munro was silent for a moment and then spoke again. "You say you still love your Lily. I take it then that her deception isn't unforgivable?"

Tom opened his mouth instinctively to voice a protest and then closed it again. Could he forgive Lily for not telling him? Did her dishonesty matter that much? Or was his dad right? Did he love her enough to find a way to work beyond it?

"I...I guess so, Dad. If I'm honest, I'm more hurt than angry. I thought we had something really special. I thought she felt the same way. Finding out that she kept the baby from me is a huge shock. It feels like she didn't really care for me at all. What kind of person keeps something like that from the one they love?"

Tom's voice hitched on emotion and he struggled against the lump that had lodged in his throat. Even a week later, the knowledge of Lily's deceit still choked him up.

"It's all right, son."

Duncan's gentle tones soothed Tom over the phone. He dragged in a ragged breath and blew it out slowly.

"You have every right to feel angry and hurt," his dad continued. "You're the father of her baby. You have a right to know. I understand exactly how you feel and I'm behind you all the way, but I know you as well as I know myself, Tom. You wouldn't have fallen in love with just anybody and for you to *still* be in love with her and be prepared to forgive her tells me a lot about the kind of person she is."

Tom heard his father draw in another breath before continuing.

"She must be someone very special to bring out so much loyalty in you. You don't give your heart easily. You've always had standards that shoot up to the sky. She didn't do the right thing by keeping the news from you, but...perhaps she had her reasons? I think you owe it to her to let her explain."

"But, Dad—"

"Relationships don't follow a nice even path, son and the road to true love is often plagued with potholes. If you believe in your heart you can forgive her and still love her with everything that you are, you need to talk to her. She must have reasons why she kept the baby from you and if I had to guess, I'd bet those reasons are good."

Duncan paused. "Everyone has baggage, Tom and not everyone believes in love at first sight. It was like that between me and your mother. I fell head over heels the moment I saw her, but let me tell you, she took a little more convincing." He chuckled and Tom's lips tugged upwards in a smile. "Perhaps your Lily is the same?"

The question didn't require an answer and Tom didn't reply. Instead, he thought about what his dad had said and conceded it made sense. Lily had never struck him as the kind of girl who would be flippant with his feelings and she'd been more than upfront about the fact that her childhood had been less than ideal.

Perhaps there *was* something there that had caused her to keep the news to herself? *Did he love her enough to want to find out?*

Tom swallowed a sigh and quietly thanked his dad for his advice. After asking after his mom and with a promise to call again soon, he ended the call. He didn't know why Lily had deceived him, but he owed it to both of them and their unborn child to find out.

———————

Lily pressed a hand to her bulging belly and hoisted

herself up the last stair. When she moved into the apartment with David more than a year ago, the two flights of stairs to get to their front door hadn't bothered her, but now, due to give birth in a fortnight, the effort it took to climb them was taking its toll.

Digging into her handbag for her keys, she unlocked the door and struggled into the hall. Setting her bags down on the kitchen counter, she breathed a sigh of relief. Some last-minute purchases for the baby had taken her out to the mall and despite the crisp winter temperatures, she was sweating beneath her clothes.

It was Friday evening and, had circumstances been different, she would be out having fun with her friends, or even Tom. At the thought of him she sighed in resignation and braced herself against the stab of pain. She was too tired to do battle with her conscience. Besides, hadn't she convinced herself that there was no use walking down that path?

The thought of spending time home alone with her feet up on the couch watching movies was comforting and too inviting to ignore. She'd shower and change into her pajamas and order in takeaway Chinese. It sounded perfect.

She headed into her bedroom and started stripping off her clothes. David had gone away for the weekend, so she had the apartment to herself. As much as she loved sharing it with him, it was nice to be alone. For months, she'd kept up a brave face to him and to the rest of the world and it was a relief to give up the façade, if only for a little while.

Running into Tom so unexpectedly had been a shock of mammoth proportions and her heart had reacted before she could stop it. Just the sight of him standing strong and sexy and confident, surrounded by a roomful of children had melted her insides.

Though she still believed her decision to keep the baby news from him had been made for good and solid reasons, those reasons had quickly crumbled the moment she saw him at the school. She recalled every nuance of him, his smile, his touch, his kisses and they proved to be no match for the defensive wall she'd erected around herself by not telling him the truth.

Not that he'd exhibited any tender feelings at the school. In fact, his attitude toward her had been anything but friendly. Even now, the memory of his anger, the sound of his harsh words, sent an ache deep in her heart. She couldn't help but wonder if he'd ever speak to her again.

As if it was attuned to her thoughts, the baby inside her kicked hard against her ribs and she gasped from the impact.

"Hey, there, little one, you don't have to be like that. I might have made a mistake not telling him, but don't worry, your daddy will come around. One look at you and he'll soften like a marshmallow in the sun. Just you wait and see."

Lily cradled her belly in her arms and prayed a little desperately that what she said was true. She pulled off her sweater and T-shirt and unsnapped the top of her maternity jeans. Her belly protruded over the waistband. She still marveled at her body's ability to swell and expand to protect her growing baby. It was a miracle all in itself.

The sound of her phone ringing from where she'd left it in the kitchen elicited a frown. Not bothering to adjust her clothing, she walked into the other room and picked it up. She glanced at the Caller ID and her heart skipped a beat.

Tom Munro.

His name was typed across the screen, added to her contacts so many months ago. Her chest tightened with nerves that warred with elation. He was calling her. That had to be a good sign, right? As if in agreement, the baby kicked again and Lily smiled on a half sob before she forced a deep breath into her lungs. She didn't want to sound overwrought and emotional when she answered the phone.

With a hand that shook, she pressed the button to take the call and did her best to sound normal.

"Tom, how are you?"

"Lily, hi. I'm fine. Actually, I'm not fine. We need to talk."

His tone was so grave she wasn't at all sure she was going to be happy to hear what he had to say.

"Right," she said cautiously.

He blew out a breath over the phone and when he spoke again, his tone had softened. "I'm sorry, Lily. I should never have yelled at you like that. I should have at least given you a chance to explain. I didn't mean to upset you. Will you meet with me and tell me what happened?"

Lily closed her eyes against a sudden surge of emotion. Tom wanted to meet and talk. He wanted an explanation. Would he understand when she gave him her reasons and...what would happen if they were just not good enough?

"Please, Lily. I...I've had time to think and I don't believe you kept the existence of the baby from me out of maliciousness. There's a reason you didn't tell me and I'd really like to know what it was."

His quiet, desperate plea loosened the tight hold she had on her emotions. Tears gathered in her eyes and silently slid down her cheeks. She bit her lip in an effort to still its trembling, and nodded.

"Okay, I'll meet you. When?"

"Is now too soon? Do you have any plans tonight?"

Lily looked down at her half-clothed self and grimaced. "No, I was looking forward to staying in. I was just about to step into the shower..."

Her words drifted off as she remembered another time many months ago when she'd taken a shower at Tom's apartment. He'd joined her halfway through and they'd had a wonderful time loving each other under the hot spray, laughter and soap in abundance. From the silence on the other end of the phone, Lily couldn't help but wonder if he were remembering the occasion, too.

She blushed and fished around for something to say, more than grateful when Tom cleared his throat and spoke.

"It's okay, I'm living over on the north shore now. This time of night, it will take me the best part of an hour to get there. You're still living in Newtown, aren't you?"

"Yes," she replied and wondered when and why he'd moved from the western suburbs. Perhaps he'd been transferred to another station? That would explain why he'd attended a safety talk at an elementary school in Chatswood.

"Good. I'll see you in an hour, then."

Another surge of nerves went through her, but she forced them aside. "Okay. See you soon." She ended the call and exhaled on a rush the breath she hadn't even realized she'd been holding. She turned as quickly as her awkward belly would allow and hurried to the shower. Despite the fact she'd ended things with him, she wanted to look her best when he arrived.

The sound of the doorbell ringing, in what seemed like an impossibly short time later, sent her pulse skittering. *It couldn't have been an hour yet?* She glanced at her watch and realized the time had slipped away. Spritzing herself with her favorite perfume, she patted her still-damp hair and gave herself a final once-over in the bathroom mirror.

No matter which way she turned, her belly was enormous. The sunshine-bright yellow stretch-knit T-shirt dress outlined its rounded shape, in sharp contrast to the flat stomach she used to possess, but there was nothing she could do about it. Besides, Tom had already seen her. There would be no more surprises tonight.

The nerves she'd managed to hold at bay suddenly surged again inside her and turned her legs to jelly. Even the baby was kicking up a storm, no doubt sensing her turmoil. As much as she was dreading the upcoming confrontation, she had no choice but to get it over with. Straightening her shoulders, she left the bathroom and walked through the hall to the entryway. Slipping off the chain and unlocking the door, she drew in a deep breath and pulled it open.

His hair was as damp as hers. He must have also taken a shower. His long-sleeved, navy blue T-shirt sported a Police Academy logo, printed in a contrasting white. The fabric stretched taut across his chest and clung lovingly to the muscles clearly delineated beneath it. Heat scorched her cheeks and she swallowed, remembering the feel of his broad chest pressed tightly against hers.

Her gaze drifted lower and took in his jeans and the brown leather loafers he wore on his feet. It seemed like forever before she finally found the courage to meet his eyes. When she did, her heart skipped a beat.

His eyes burned with an intensity that snatched her breath away. Fear and uncertainty, mixed with a hint of anger, appeared at war with the white-hot desire that darkened his eyes to the deepest blue. Her heart pounded, both with excitement and a lashing of renewed nerves. He looked so gorgeous, so sexy, so alive. *So Tom.*

She'd missed him like crazy and she suddenly realized the countless weeks and months when she'd done her best to convince herself she'd made the right decision now counted as nothing. She loved him as hard and as fierce as she'd done since the early days of their relationship. Seven months or more of distance and endless pep talks hadn't changed that. She wanted him, she needed him and she was suddenly terrified all the reasons why she'd turned away from him in the first place were about to explode back in her face.

"Hi, Lily. It's good to see you again."

His murmured greeting was enough to break through her panicked thoughts and she blinked and nodded by way of acknowledgement, for a moment beyond speech.

"Th-thank you. It's… It's good to see you, too." The words seemed so mundane compared to the chaos that raged inside her. She ducked her head so that he wouldn't see the effect his presence had on her. They had important matters to discuss. She was a fool to let her physical reaction to him cloud the real reason for his visit.

With the harsh reminder now front and center in her mind, she cleared her throat and stepped back, allowing him to enter. Turning as quickly as her cumbersome body would allow, she walked into the kitchen.

"Coffee? Tea?" she murmured and moved to switch on the kettle, grateful for the distraction.

"Thank you. Coffee would be great."

She opened the cupboard near the stove and pulled down two mugs. She spooned coffee and a teaspoon of sugar into one and then reached for a teabag.

"You remembered," Tom said quietly, a tender smile on his lips.

"Remembered what?"

"The coffee. You remembered how I take it."

Lily frowned at his words and then realization struck. She hadn't given the makings of his coffee any thought. It was like she'd made him coffee only that morning, not seven months earlier. It just went to show how everything about Tom Munro lingered in her subconscious.

A short time later, the water boiled and she filled their cups. After adding a dash of milk, she stirred both mugs and then handed the coffee to him. Their fingers collided and she shivered from the contact. It had been way too long since she'd touched him.

For two glorious months, they'd touched and kissed and fondled and there hadn't been an inch of his tanned skin that she hadn't known. But that had been a lifetime ago and she no longer knew if she had the right to even think about touching him, let alone acting upon it.

That awareness was beyond depressing and with determination, she thrust it aside. Tom had called her. He wanted to talk. She'd focus on the present and hope that the outcome of their conversation would work out for the best for everyone, whatever that might be. But right here, right now, with Tom strong and sure and sexy, smiling at her in her kitchen, she was more confused than ever about what she hoped that outcome would be.

"Shall we sit down?" Tom asked. "You might find it a little more comfortable."

Lily collected her mug and walked to the couch in silence. It was a three-seater sofa in a brown faux leather fabric that she and David had bought at a yard sale not long after they'd moved in together. They'd got it for a bargain and the owners had even had it delivered when they discovered Lily and David didn't own a car. What Lily loved most was that it was comfortable. After a long day on her feet, there was nothing that could compare to its softness.

Now, it almost looked too small for the two of them to fit on. With Tom's broad shoulders taking up more than his share, and her protruding belly, she wondered if it would be better if she sat on a kitchen chair. The thought had barely formed when Tom moved over and patted the space beside him.

"There's plenty of room. I won't bite."

His grin should have relieved the nervous energy that was somersaulting way deep inside her, but it didn't. The humor on his lips didn't reach his eyes and Lily clenched her fists together at her side to keep them from trembling. It was obvious he was still upset. She hoped, once she'd given him her explanation, he'd understand.

Gingerly, she perched on the edge of the couch and drew in a deep breath. Tom moved closer, until their thighs were all but touching. Lily jumped.

"It's okay, Lily. I meant it when I said I don't bite. There was a time not that long ago when you couldn't get close enough to me on this very couch. Surely, I haven't changed so much?"

Lily shook her head. "No, of course not. You haven't changed. You look as gorgeous as you always did." When she realized what she'd said, she blushed to the roots of her hair. *Where had that come from?* They were meant to be having a serious, possibly life-altering conversation about their future. She shouldn't be getting hot and bothered about his appearance.

Tom merely smiled a tiny, pleased smile and Lily was grateful when he didn't pursue her comment any further.

"I'm sorry," she said quickly. "I shouldn't have said that. You're still upset and I didn't mean to make light of any of this."

"I know. And you're right. I am still upset, but I also miss you. I miss *us*. And I don't think I've ever seen you looking so beautiful. So, now we're even. Let's get on with the hard stuff."

Lily swallowed the ball of nerves and blinked back sudden tears. Her love for him was as strong as ever and she didn't know how she was going to find the courage to walk away from him a second time if he wouldn't see things her way.

"Talk to me, Lily."

It was the gentleness in his tone that brought her unstuck. She caught her breath on a sob, but the tears came anyway. The stricken look on Tom's face made them fall even harder.

"Lily, please... Please don't cry." He scooted closer and pulled her gently into his arms. He caressed her back and she leaned into the warm strength of him and prayed that things would turn out all right. After a moment or two, she drew in an unsteady breath and pulled away from him.

"I'm sorry. I didn't mean to fall apart on you like that. It's... It's the pregnancy hormones. They play havoc with my emotions."

He reached for her again, but she put her hands up to stop him and moved even further away.

"I'm fine, Tom. I promise. Now, let's get this over with." After another deep breath and in halting sentences, she began.

"You're a good, kind, honorable man, Tom Munro and that's one of the reasons why I didn't tell you. We might have only been together a couple of months, but even then, I knew the kind of man you were, the kind of man you are."

Tom shook his head in confusion. "I don't get it. I mean, I'm far from the paragon of virtue you've just described, but I was certainly brought up right. I don't get how that became the reason why you kept the baby from me."

Lily frowned and looked away. "I'm sorry, I'm not explaining myself very well. What I mean is, it's your very upbringing, your code of honor that's the problem. I was pregnant, but we barely knew each other. Okay, we were in love and having a great time, but that doesn't equate to being ready for marriage. If I'd told you I was pregnant, you would have wanted to get married."

"Of course I would have! It's the right thing to do. What's wrong with that?"

Lily held his gaze. "And then there was the drinking."

Tom frowned. "What the hell are you talking about? After that night when you told me about your father, I never drank in your presence again."

"But, you did drink. I saw you. One night outside your apartment. I saw you through the window. I saw you surrounded by empty bottles, moments before you sent them flying all over the room. They shattered against the floor. There was broken glass everywhere and you didn't seem to care. It scared me, Tom. It reminded me of my father. I couldn't take the risk of bringing our baby into that world, a world I vowed never to go near again."

"Lily, that's not fair. I was upset, I was hurting. We hadn't long been over. I did what a lot of men do—I got roaring drunk. I'm not proud of it, but I didn't even know you were there. How could you think I'd ever be violent around you or our child?"

Lily shook her head, hopelessness surging through her at his anger and bewilderment. *How could she make him see?* Before she could find the words, Tom leaped to his feet and began to pace the floor in front of her. He ran a hand through his hair and then uttered a curse.

"For Christ's sake, Lily, I still don't understand. Why did you walk away? You saw me drunk, but I'm not your father! I'm not a violent, abusive man. I loved you and you loved me. Okay, I get that a baby wasn't exactly in our plans, but it wasn't a deal breaker. At least, not for me. And it's not like you didn't want to keep it. You're a couple of weeks away from giving birth." He shook his head, his frustration evident, but his voice softened. "Please, Lily. Help me out here. I'm struggling. I really am. Help me to understand."

She closed her eyes briefly and prayed for the words that would help him see.

"You're right. A baby wasn't in our plans. When I found out I was pregnant, I panicked. You know a little about my childhood. It was far from ideal and in my defense, I think it goes a long way to explaining my reaction to your lapse in judgement."

She paused to gather her courage. "But, there was more to it than that. What I didn't tell you was my mother was pregnant with me before she married my father and he never let her forget it. My father was a nasty, vindictive man. He resented her for trapping him into marriage. He threw it in her face nearly every single day."

She risked a glance in his direction and was relieved to see the anger in his face had eased and was replaced with sympathy and understanding. "I didn't want that for us, Tom."

"You have to be kidding? I would never—"

"Like I said, you're a good and honorable man, Tom Munro. Once you learned about the baby, you'd want to get married. Not a moment ago, you said as much. You say now you wouldn't resent being forced into marriage before you were ready, but you don't know that for sure. What's more important is that *I* don't know that for sure."

Tom shook his head in disbelief and cursed again. "How can you even think something like that, let alone say it? I love you, Lily. I fell in love with you the moment I saw you across the room in Charlie's noisy, crowded apartment. I didn't even know your name. I was ready to propose after our first date, but I restrained myself, knowing I'd probably scare you off."

He shook his head again. "You're nineteen years old with the world at your feet, on your way to a professional career. I figured marriage was the last thing on your mind, so I kept it to myself. I was happy to have you on any terms and when you were a little older, or had come around to the idea of being with me forever, I was going to propose. Baby or no baby, I'll love you until I die. I can't explain it. Most people wouldn't believe it. But *I* do. I *know*. It's *real*. And it's never ever going to go away."

He drew in a ragged breath and she did her best to keep the happiness that was bubbling up inside her from escaping. *Could he be telling the truth? Could their love survive forever?* She wanted desperately to believe it could.

Tom stared at her and then returned to the couch and took both of her hands in his. "That's how *I* feel, Lily. I no longer have a clue if you feel anywhere near the same. Once upon a time, I thought you loved me. Now…" He blew out his breath on a heavy sigh. Lily couldn't bear the sight of his desolate expression a moment longer.

"Tom, oh, Tom." She reached out for him awkwardly and was relieved when he pulled her into his arms.

"I love you, Tom. I've always loved you."

"But, you said—"

"I know what I said and I was stupid to think a baby would change things. I should have trusted you and your love for me and told you the truth right from the start." Fresh tears filled her eyes.

"*Shh*, Lily. Please, honey. Please, don't cry. I hate it when you cry. Think about the baby, *our* baby."

Lily gasped on a sob. "I deprived you of so many things. You missed the first scan; going to classes. I cried the first time I felt it kick and I wanted so much to share it with you. Will you ever be able to forgive me?"

"Please, Lily, let's not talk about forgiveness. I understand the reasons for your misgivings. You grew up in a household filled with fear and hatred. Who would want to risk being in such a position again? Besides, you're not the only one with a guilty conscience."

She looked up at him and frowned, not knowing what he meant. He stood and moved away from her, his gaze directed toward the window that overlooked the street. He was silent for a long moment and then finally, his shoulders slumped on a sigh. He came back to her and took his seat beside her. The solemn look in his eyes sent a shiver running through her.

"What is it, Tom? What happened?"

"Do you remember the first time we made love?"

She blushed and looked away. "Of course."

"I asked you if you had a condom and you didn't."

"But you did. I remember. It's why I couldn't believe it when I realized I was pregnant. We'd been careful. We'd used protection every single time. I still don't understand how it happened."

"I do."

She stared at him and shook her head. "What do you mean?"

"It was the condom. It was old. I'd had it in my wallet for months. Somehow, it broke."

Surprise surged through her. "It broke? You mean, while we were...?"

"Yes. You fell asleep right afterwards. When I pulled the condom off, I discovered there was a hole in it."

"You didn't think to tell me? To warn me that there was a risk I could fall pregnant? And what about diseases? You didn't think I'd want to know?"

Tom shook his head. "It wasn't like that and I knew I was clean. We have regular medicals through the police service." He shrugged and looked uncomfortable. "I'm sorry. I should have told you. I was going to, but you were asleep. We'd just shared something beautiful. I didn't want to spoil it. Besides, the odds of you getting pregnant had to be a thousand to one. When the weeks went by and you said nothing, I assumed we'd gotten lucky."

Lily felt his words like a knife to the heart. He hadn't wanted a baby, after all. "Gotten *lucky*? Is that what you thought?"

Tom frowned at the quiet sobriety of her tone. "That's not what I meant, Lily. It was a figure of speech. Neither of us were planning on becoming parents. Now that we are, I couldn't be happier. I'm not going to let you use against me the fact that I felt relief when I thought I hadn't gotten my nineteen-year-old girlfriend pregnant."

Lily stared at him and knew with a certainty that she believed him. What he said was true. She'd been devastated to discover she was having a baby. It didn't mean she didn't want it or that she wouldn't love it and protect it with her life. It was a shock, but one she'd adjusted to and now she couldn't wait to meet the little person growing inside her. She was glad Tom felt the same way.

He leaned forward and took her face between both of his hands, his skin warm and rough against her cheeks. His gaze was intent on hers, as if pleading with her to understand.

"I want you and I want our baby. I'll love both of you until the day that I die. I'm not your father, Lily. I'll never be that man. In fact, I'll swear to you here and now, on the head of our unborn child that I'll never get drunk again. The thought of what you and your mom endured angers me beyond words. How could he blame your mom for getting pregnant when he knew darn well he was equally at fault? His utter selfishness and conceit—it's beyond my ability to comprehend."

His eyes burned into hers. "Do you believe me, Lily? I will love you and honor you heart and soul, body and mind until the day that I die. Please, believe me."

The intensity of his expression thawed the icy fear that had encased her heart for as long as she could remember. Without consciously being aware of it, she'd kept part of herself buried beneath a layer of fun and laughter. The most popular girl in high school, the life of the party. It was all an elaborate façade.

Not until Tom Munro had forced his way into her heart was she compelled to confront the demons of her past. And now that she had, she felt like a caged bird that had been suddenly set free.

Her smile turned into a grin and then laughter bubbled up from way down deep inside. Tears coursed down her cheeks. Tom stared at her, confused, unsure if she was laughing or crying.

She tightened her arms around him and then pulled back and took his head between her hands. Pressing her lips against his, she kissed him with all the love in her heart. Within moments, her passion ignited his and he pulled her as close against him as her belly would allow.

The past, the future; the here and now... Everything faded away. There was nothing and no one but the two of them and that's how it would always be.

"I'm still not going to marry you."

Tom's jaw dropped from sheer astonishment. He'd barely caught his breath from their extended, albeit careful session of lovemaking and Lily was dropping another bombshell. He pushed aside the bed sheets that were twisted around his legs and turned to stare at her.

"What do you mean, you're not going to marry me? Of course we're getting married. The baby's due in like a fortnight. There's no way he or she is going to be born to single parents."

To his chagrin, Lily only looked more determined. Her jaw set in a stubborn line. "We can still raise our baby together in love without doing the whole marriage thing. Plenty of people do it. It's not like our child will be the only kindergartner with parents who aren't married."

Tom forced a deep breath through his clenched teeth in an effort not to say something he might regret. When he felt a little more in control, he responded.

"Marriage is not a *thing*. It's a lifelong commitment, a proclamation to the world and to God that we'll love each other, support each other, trust each other, in sickness and in health, until the day that we die. Please tell me you believe in that?"

Lily shrugged, but the shadows in her eyes belied her casual attitude. "I haven't seen a lot of happily-ever-afters among the married people I know. As well as my parents, there were plenty of kids at my school who'd lived through a divorce. A *defacto* relationship just seems so much more civilized. It's almost as if it would make us work harder to stay together, to keep our love strong, if we knew one or the other of us could leave in an instant."

Tom's horror grew by the minute. He thought they'd totally addressed the issue of marriage out on the couch. He'd been certain they were in agreement with the way things would be. Their love was strong enough to withstand the test of time.

Isn't that what *both* of them believed? She'd just given herself to him, in the sweetest, most magical way and now she was questioning once again whether what they had together would last!

He shook his head in disbelief and prayed it was nothing more than the hormones that had her reasoning going off in crazy directions. The very possibility that she was actually contemplating living together, raising their baby outside the sanctity of marriage went against everything he held dear and true.

Forcing his body to relax, he closed his eyes and breathed deeply, concentrating on the softness of the pillow beneath his head. He counted to ten in silence and then opened his eyes and turned to her, pitching his voice low. "What are you afraid of, Lily?"

She blinked and then averted her face. A moment later, she reached down and pulled the sheet up over her head. "Who says I'm scared?"

Her muffled voice elicited a grin and his fears eased. Of course the thought of marriage scared her. She hadn't exactly had the ideal role models in her parents and even though she'd told him her mother and stepfather had made it work, he understood her reticence.

The scars of her childhood ran deep and wouldn't easily be forgotten. It was up to him to replace those memories with better ones. Gently, he pried the sheet out of her fingers and moved it away from her face. Taking her chin in his hand, he turned her around to face him.

"After being a witness to your parents' marriage, it's only right that you're scared. Hell, if I'd witnessed that much heartache and resentment, I'd feel the same way. The only reason I don't is because I got lucky. I grew up in a home filled with love and trust and respect. I'm not saying there were never any arguments, but they were handled in a mature way and there was always room for an apology and forgiveness, if it came to that.

"Twenty-plus years down the track and my parents still have a strong and loving marriage. It's the kind of marriage I want for us. One that I've always dreamed of. It's not just for fairy tales. Happily-ever-afters are possible. I know they are and I'm lucky they've shown me how. Think of your mom and Tony. That's how it can be for us."

He reached for her hand and held it tightly between both of his own, hoping to convince her with his words and his touch that what he said was true. Pressing kisses against her fingertips, he continued.

"I'm not saying I'm going to be the perfect husband or that I won't make mistakes, but I believe with everything that I am that we can make it. We can be one of those couples who love each other 'til death do us part. But I can't do it alone. I need you to believe in us, too. Do you? Do you believe in us, Lily?"

He stared at her, trying to make her see how much her answer meant to him. When she offered him the tiniest, most hesitant nod, his breath left his mouth in a rush. Wild jubilation flooded through him and he squeezed her so hard she was gasping for breath. Remembering the baby, he eased his hold and then kissed her softly, lovingly on the lips.

He began to caress her belly, marveling at the roundness and firmness of her body. The very feel of it reminded him of the precious cargo that lay within. He was going to be a father, and there safe and snug inside of Lily was his child, a child he would love just as much as it's mother.

Tom was overcome with emotion, a feeling of joy so profound it hurt. *Was it possible to love one, now two people so much that it hurt beyond any physical pain he'd ever endured?* While continuing to stroke her belly, he said, "I want you to meet my parents, Duncan and Marguerite. They've been married twenty-four years and still look at each other with love. I'm going to show you just how wonderful marriage can be and by the time I'm finished, you're going to be begging me to walk you down the aisle."

Tom grinned at her and was relieved when she smiled back.

"Really? Begging? I'm not too sure about that."

Tom hugged her again, but gently this time and pressed another soft kiss against her lips. "Okay, I don't give a damn about the begging. Just as long as you're willing to say 'I do.' That's the only thing that matters."

Chapter 16

Roseville, Sydney—present day

Hannah Sutton stared at the blue and red and white strobe lights that bounced off the walls of her modern townhouse. Police and ambulance vehicles littered the front lawn. Another van, this one parked closest to the walkway that led up to her front door had the word "morgue" stenciled across it in reflective gold lettering. A small crowd had gathered in the far corner, right beneath the ancient gum tree, its bark curling from the unseasonable spring heat.

A murmur sounded from the onlookers and Hannah turned in time to see the morgue workers pushing a gurney that held her son. Not that she could see him. He'd been zipped into a bright blue, plastic body bag, the smallest hump on the long steel structure that was the stretcher.

An arrow of pain shot through her and forced its way out through her mouth. She cried out at the sight of Brady, so small and so dead. She'd never forget the way he'd looked when she'd found him, with his eyes bulging in his head. His tongue hung from his mouth, dry and swollen. His skin was blue and cooling.

She didn't know how long he'd been hanging there, but it was obvious it had been long enough. She'd screamed and raced to pull him down, feeling frantically for a pulse.

Even as she did it, she'd known it was an exercise in futility. She was too late to save him. Brady, her little boy was dead and there was no bringing him back.

In a daze, she'd called the police and had then found the number for Brady's dad. She couldn't even remember what she'd screamed at him, but her anger had found its head. It was all his fault. Instead of providing guidance and being a good role model for their son, he'd given him the gun and then allowed him to play out his fantasies with a violent video game where the heroes shot others indiscriminately for pleasure and sport.

What kind of man and father would misguide his son in such a way? And to think it had all been done in secret behind her back. The guilt of not knowing what her son had been involved in would be with her for the rest of her life. She'd taken out her despair and anger on her husband and had cursed and slung every possible venomous word that came to her. She'd ended the conversation by telling him that Brady's blood would forever be on his hands.

A low howl of pain now started deep inside her and worked its way through her bones. With her head in her hands, she fell to her knees and screamed out her agony and desolation. Despite her ranting and raving at her ex, it was *her* fault Brady was dead. He'd said as much when she'd last tried to discuss it with him. If she'd intervened at school, if she'd listened and given credence to his pleas... How would she ever forgive herself? How would she live with the guilt?

She couldn't.

It was as simple as that.

Royal North Shore Hospital

Not long after the nurse had called for someone to escort Tom back to his ward, an elderly male porter with a grizzled face and kind eyes arrived in recovery, accompanied by a nurse. After the nurse collected his paperwork from Tessa, the man eased off the brakes on the gurney and began pushing it out the door. Relieved, to be heading back to the ward, Tom stared at the white paneled ceiling above his head and prayed for good news about Lily.

Now that his medical emergency had been dealt with, he was eager to return to her side. With a *ding* and a *swish*, the doors to the elevator swung open and he did his best to reign in his impatience. The porter whistled a quiet tune and seemed in no hurry to arrive at his destination. Tom guessed it was probably hard work pushing him and the gurney and tried to distract himself with conversation.

"So, have you worked here long…Mohammed?" he asked, spying the man's name on his hospital identification.

"Twenty-five years this summer," the man replied with a toothy grin, his teeth as white as his hair.

"Wow, you must have seen a lot of people come and go. Have you always worked around the theaters?"

"Nope. I had a stint in the X-ray department back in the nineties. Even worked in rehab for a short while, but I like the theaters the best. I take people down from their wards, all stressed out and concerned about their pendin' surgery and then I get to take them back again when they've woken up and it's all over."

He gave Tom a wink. "Take you, for example. I pushed you down here a few hours ago and you never said a word. I bet you didn't even notice me. I was just some dumb old man pushin' your gurney. Now, when the drama's over and you're headin' back to your loved ones, you're all talkative and friendly."

"I didn't mean to—"

"Hey, don't get me wrong. I ain't complainin'. I'm just makin' an observation. It's not just you. It's everyone. I've learned not to take it personally."

Tom's smile was a little strained, still embarrassed that what the porter had said was true. He hadn't paid any heed to the man who transported him to the operating room. His head had been full of the upcoming surgery and the risks involved. Now that it was over and had apparently gone well, his thoughts were on anything but.

"You're right, Mohammed, and I'm sorry. I was a little distracted earlier, but I want to thank you for what you do. A lot of people forget about all the staff behind the scenes. When we think of hospitals, we think of the doctors and nurses, but without people like you and the kitchen staff and even the cleaners, the place wouldn't run. You need more recognition, Mohammed." This time, Tom's grin was genuine.

"Ain't you right about that, Mr Munro," Mohammed grinned back at him.

A moment later, the elevator dinged again and the doors slid open. Mohammed wheeled Tom outside and into the corridor that led to his ward. Another nurse met them at the entryway.

"Welcome back, Mr Munro. You're looking good."

"Thanks. I'm relieved it's all over."

"You'll need to take it easy for the next little while. I'll get Mohammed to take you to your room. I think your brother's there waiting for you."

Tom nodded. At the mention of Brandon, his thoughts flew to Lily and he couldn't help but wonder if there had been any news. He'd been away from the ward a good chunk of time. Anything could have happened. Good or bad.

His mind shied away from the possibility that she'd gone downhill in his absence. He had to remain positive. After all, his operation had gone well. There was no reason Lily couldn't be so lucky.

Mohammed swung the gurney into the private room and Tom spied Brandon in one corner, lounging against the wall. The television was on but tuned so low it was nothing but a murmur. Upon registering Tom's arrival, Brandon pushed himself off the wall and came toward him.

"Tom! It's so good to see you. I take it the operation went well?"

Tom slid across from the gurney to his bed and nodded.

"Yeah, at least, that's what everyone's been saying."

In silence, Mohammed pushed the gurney out of the way and headed toward the door. The nurse who had accompanied him pulled out a thermometer.

"Hey, Mohammed?" Tom called and waited for the man to turn around. "I just wanted to say thanks. For everything. None of this," Tom waved around the hospital room, "would be possible without you."

"Thank you, Mr Munro. I appreciate your sayin' so."

Tom acknowledged his thanks with a nod. "You have a good afternoon, Mohammed."

"You, too, Mr Munro. You, too."

The minute Mohammed cleared the door, Brandon moved closer to Tom's bed. "I'm so glad to see you and to hear that everything went well and I can't wait to tell you the news."

"I'm just going to take your temperature and blood pressure, Mr Munro. I won't be a minute."

Tom stared up at Brandon and took note of the grin that widened his brother's lips. Chafing at the delay caused by the nurse, he counted the seconds while she recorded his vital signs. Brandon seemed to be humming with excitement and a tiny spark of hope ignited deep down in Tom's gut. He did his best to tamp down on it in case the news had nothing to do with Lily, but as soon as the nurse departed, the words fell out of his mouth in a rush.

"News? About Lily? Did she... Did she wake up?"

Brandon's grin turned into a *whoop* of glee and he punched the air. "Hell, yeah, she woke up! And not only woke up, but is asking for you. She's going to be all right, big brother. She's going to be all right."

Brandon's voice turned husky with emotion and he leaned down and gave Tom a fierce hug. Tom winced from the pain in his breast, even as a tumult of emotions battered him from all sides. He blinked away a sudden rush of tears.

Lily was awake. Lily was okay. Lily was asking for him.

"I need to see her," he croaked. "Bran, I need to see her."

"Yeah, mate. I understand. I'll go and speak to the nurse

and tell them what's happening. Maybe they can work something out."

It seemed like forever until Brandon returned with the same pretty young nurse in tow who had accompanied him from the operating room. Her shiny brown hair had been pulled back in a bun that nestled at the top of her spine. Her badge identified her as Sarah. Tom sat up a little higher in the bed and waited to hear what she had to say.

"Wow, is it true, Tom? Is your wife in the ICU?"

Tom nodded. "Yes, she was shot by one of her students earlier in the week. She's been unconscious since they brought her in. My brother..." He indicated Brandon who stood a few feet away. "Just told me she's awake. I-I really need to see her."

Sarah nodded, her blue eyes flooding with compassion and understanding. "It's wonderful that she's regained consciousness. Terrible that she's in the ICU, but great that it sounds like she's on the mend. I understand why you want to see her, but you've just undergone some fairly major surgery. You've barely been back on the ward five minutes. I think you might need to take a moment and catch your breath. It's probably not such a good idea to be rushing down to the ICU. Let's give it awhile, all right?"

Disappointment surged through Tom at the nurse's response and his hands clenched into fists.

"No, Sarah, please. You don't understand. I don't just *want* to see my wife. I *need* to see her. I've been sitting by her bedside night and day, not knowing if she's going to pull through. Now that I know she's awake, I can't lie here another minute without talking to her. I need to see her, touch her, kiss her. I need to find out for myself that she's okay."

The nurse made sympathetic noises, but continued to shake her head. "I'm sorry, Tom. I can't have you up and about like that just yet. Bathroom visits only, you understand, but I tell you what. I'll speak to the doctor and see what we can do. If you feel up to it, I'd like to see you eat. You've been fasting all day."

At the mention of food, Tom was suddenly ravenous. He

hadn't eaten since the meal he'd shared with his parents the night before. Now knowing that Lily was going to be all right, his appetite returned in full force.

"I'll eat whatever you give me," he said and then begged her one more time. "Please, Sarah. It's really important I see my wife. I would appreciate anything you can do to make the doctor agree. I mean it."

Sarah smiled gently and turned to leave the room. "I'll do my best. I promise." With that, she disappeared from view.

Tom slumped back against his pillows and sighed.

"Hey, don't feel too bad. Don't worry, you'll get to see her."

"Yeah, thanks. And thanks for being here, Bran. I really appreciate it."

"No problem, bro. You'd do the same for me."

"Who's with Lily?"

"Mom. She's been with her for most of the day. She was the one who called me with the news."

Tom nodded and thought about how lucky he was to be surrounded by a family who loved him and offered their support whenever they could. There were plenty of people a whole lot less fortunate than he.

"Hey, Bran. Have you spoken to the kids?"

"No, I wanted to tell you first."

"Can you call them for me? Tell them both their mom and I are okay? I didn't tell them last night about my surgery, but let them know something about it now."

"What do you want me to say?"

"Just tell them I had to have a small operation while I was waiting for their mom to wake up. They'll know there's more to it, but I'm sure the excitement of having their mom awake and talking will keep their curiosity in check. I'll tell them more about it later, after we're all back at home safe and sound."

"No problem, Tom. I'll do it right away."

"Thanks." Tom closed his eyes, all of a sudden overcome with weariness. He guessed it had something to do with the residual effects of the anaesthetic, not to mention his lack of sleep since the shooting. He couldn't remember the last time he'd slept the night through. Maybe now that the stress of the past days was over and both he and Lily were on the mend, he could relax and finally catch up on the rest he desperately needed.

With a sigh of relief, he succumbed to the succor of sleep.

Cassie heard the distant ringing of the telephone down the hall and buried her face in her pillow. Her granddad was around somewhere and Joe had stayed home from school. Surely one of them would answer it?

Her head felt thick and foggy after the alcohol and the pills. She didn't know why people took the stuff. She'd felt a little better for a short while, but that had worn off hours ago. Now all she felt like was *yuck*.

Opening her eyes, she rolled onto her back and peered through the sheer, white lace curtains that covered the floor-to-ceiling window that stood beside her bed. With a frown, she noticed the sun had crept way low in the sky. The day was nearly over. She hadn't even noticed.

She reached for her phone where it sat on her nightstand and held the button down to switch it back on. Her friends would no doubt have been trying to reach her. She'd switched it off right after swallowing the second pill. She didn't want to have to make conversation with anyone while she was trying to get wasted, not even her friends.

The phone buzzed with message after message, vibrating against her hand. She scrolled through them and bit her lip. Most of them were from her best friend. She'd known Madeleine since kindergarten and they were still as close as two friends could be. After reading through Maddy's increasingly concerned texts, Cassie was flooded with guilt.

Maddy knew about Cassie's abduction at the hand of

her mother's stepbrother and Cassie had shared a little of the horror of it with her, but not the full story. Never the full story. To tell anyone the truth of what really happened that day would tear open her wounded soul and throw her into a dark oblivion from which she'd never return. Better to live life dulling the pain than risking losing what little life she had.

She'd spoken to her parents right after it had happened and had told the therapist most of it, but the sickening feel of his hands on her breasts, the terrifying way he'd pinched her nipples... No, no one would ever know about that. And that's the way it would stay.

Brandon stared down at the phone in his hands and frowned, wondering why no one at Tom's house had answered his call. According to his mom, both of the kids and his father were home. One of them should have been able to come to the phone.

He glanced across at his brother and was relieved to see that he was asleep. Brandon knew how much Tom wanted to see Lily, but the truth was, he needed the rest. Opening a new message screen on his phone, Brandon sent his mother a text.

Tom back from surgery. All went well. Called Tom's home number. No answer. Where's Dad?

A moment later, his phone buzzed and he read the incoming text from his mom.

Great news about Tom. Lily asleep right now. Sleeping, not unconscious. Told her about Tom's operation. She kept asking for him. Thought it was better to tell her why he wasn't there. She was shocked, but okay. Not sure why Dad or the kids aren't answering the phone. Perhaps they went out? Will call Dad on his cell.

Brandon read the message and nodded. Of course, the day was almost over. He'd spent all of it inside the hospital, waiting with Tom and then waiting for Tom. Brandon's belly rumbled and he was reminded that he'd had nothing to eat all day but a packet of crisps and a couple of candy bars from the vending machine in the hall.

It was almost dinner time. It made sense Dad had taken Cassie and Joe out to eat. It explained why no one was answering the phone. His cell buzzed in his hand with another incoming text and he glanced down at the screen.

Just spoke to Dad. He's at Tom's, along with the kids. He was asleep. Didn't hear the phone ring. Maybe the kids had their music too loud or headphones on? Dad thrilled all okay here at the hospital. What's Tom up to?

Brandon read the text, relieved that nothing untoward had happened at home. The Munro family sure as hell didn't need any more drama. He shot off a quick reply.

Tom's asleep. I told him about Lily. He wanted to come right down and see her of course, but the doctor won't allow it, yet. Best for Tom to get some rest, anyway. Glad to hear all good with Dad and the kids.

A moment later, his mom sent back a smiley face emoji and Brandon grinned.

Joe Munro sat hunched over on the cold brick steps that led down into the paved outdoor area situated in his backyard and tried not to think about how quickly his life had spiraled out of control. Night was closing in and he wrapped the dusk about him like a comforting cloak. In the dark, he was anonymous, insignificant, nothing of importance. The dark could hide him, help him disappear.

His dad and his mom were both in hospital. His granddad hadn't wanted to tell him why Dad had left with Uncle Brandon in the early hours of the morning, but Joe had pleaded with him and cajoled him, unwilling to be put off. Eventually, he'd worn Granddad down and he'd admitted Dad needed an operation.

Granddad hadn't given Joe any details, but if it wasn't serious, it wouldn't have been kept from him in the first place. It wasn't like he was a baby. He was fourteen. Almost fully grown. At least, that's what his dad always said whenever they stood side by side.

Joe was proud he looked like his dad. He had way darker coloring than his sister. Cassie had taken after their mom—all blond hair, fair skin and petite. Joe's hair was a dark blond, like his father and his skin color had also come from the Munros. His granddad was a full blooded aboriginal. The height had also come from the Munro side. Joe was still a teenager, but he towered over most of the boys in his class. He liked being tall. It made him feel strong, invincible. Braver than he dreamed he could be.

It was one of the reasons why he was mad at himself for hiding outside. He should have been inside, demanding an explanation from his sister. Joe had opened the door earlier that morning to some skanky, scary kind of guy who said he was Cassie's friend. Joe recognized him as being one of the senior boys at their high school who was known to run with a wild crowd. What he was doing with his sister, Joe really didn't want to know.

His thoughts shifted to his mom and dad and a band of emotion squeezed him around the chest, so tight he couldn't breathe. Was his mom ever going to wake up? Would he get to speak to her again? As for his dad—what awful thing was wrong with him?

Joe blinked back a sudden rush of tears and wrapped his arms around his legs. He hugged them to his chest. Dropping his head, he rested it on his knees and dragged in a shaky breath.

There was no use crying about stuff like this. Crying was for babies and little kids. He had to man up and face whatever came his way. The first thing on his list was finding out just what the hell was wrong with his dad.

CHAPTER 17

Seventeen years earlier

"**I**s it always so green around here? And look at those majestic trees. They must be over one hundred years old."

Tom glanced across at Lily where she sat in the passenger seat of his pickup. She had taken a little convincing, but she'd finally agreed to come with him to Grafton to meet his parents. The baby was due in seven days, but he was determined to show her the way marriage could be. Even after more than two decades of togetherness, his parents still had the same level of commitment and devotion towards one another that they'd had at the beginning of their married life.

His parents were expecting them and he was relieved when his dad had assured him he'd broken the news of Tom's impending fatherhood to Tom's mom. Even though he was sure his mom was too well bred and well mannered to ask awkward questions, he didn't want any uncomfortable scenes when he introduced her to Lily.

"It looks like they've had some recent rain. It's freshened everything up, but yes, it's often green around here. Those trees lining the river are jacaranda trees. Grafton's famous for them. They even have a Jacaranda Festival and crown a Jacaranda Queen. It's held later in the year. Mom can't wait for the day my younger sisters are old enough to take part. The trees come out in big clusters of pale purple flowers. It's really kind of special."

"You love this place."

Tom blushed and kept his gaze fixed on the road. "Yeah, I guess I do. It's home, you know?"

"No, I don't. When my mom left my dad, we moved around so much, I didn't ever have a home. I never had the chance to lay down roots or get attached to any one place enough to call home. At least, not until Mom married Tony."

Her soft words caught him in the chest. "I'm sorry. It must have been hard for you."

"It was, but I was so young when we left, I never really knew what I was missing. Watching you, listening to you talk about your hometown, I realize how much I lost."

He offered her a gentle smile and reached over to squeeze her hand.

"Don't get me wrong," she hurriedly continued. "I don't blame Mom one bit. I'm grateful she was courageous enough to leave that abusive relationship and she certainly did it with my best interests in mind. Who knows what my dad might have done if we hadn't run away? I can't even bear to imagine how things might have turned out. Certainly not for the better; I'm sure of that."

"I'm sorry you had such a tough childhood. I wish I could make the memories disappear," Tom said quietly and meant it.

His heart ached at what she'd endured...and what she'd missed out on. His own childhood had been so full of fun and laughter and love. His parents had loved and respected one another and it had showed in many little ways. If he were honest, he'd admit he'd taken the security of his childhood a little for granted. It wasn't until he entered the police force that he truly realized not everyone grew up in an idyllic home environment.

Lily turned to him and tears sparkled in her eyes. "Thank you, that means a lot to me. My only hope is that our baby never knows a moment of fear, of uncertainty, of insecurity. It's what scares me about the whole marriage and happily-ever-after thing. What if it doesn't last? How can we be certain it will? Neither of us has a crystal ball. We can't see into the future."

"You're right, we can't. All we can do is trust in each other and trust that the love and respect we have for each other will last the distance."

"But—"

"Hey," Tom interrupted and squeezed her hand. "Let's not talk about it now. You're about to meet my parents." He offered a cajoling grin. "We don't have to solve the problems of the world right now."

To his relief, she smiled back and gave his hand a reassuring squeeze. One-handed, he negotiated the turn into his parents' driveway on the edge of town and brought his truck to a stop. Leaning across the console, he pressed a soft kiss against her lips.

"What was that for?" she murmured.

"Just because."

"Because?"

"Because I love you and you're the most beautiful, pregnant woman in the world and you're mine. Nearly."

She smiled and kissed him back. Within moments, the kiss turned heated and Tom reached out to draw her close.

"Ouch!"

He drew back. Lily rubbed her stomach. Tom frowned in concern. "Are you all right?"

"Yes, our baby was just making his presence felt, that's all. Perhaps he doesn't approve of his parents making out in the car?"

"He?" Tom asked, his heart beating fast.

Lily shrugged. "Or she. It was just a figure of speech. I didn't find out the sex."

Tom smiled and excitement shot through his veins. "I'm so glad. It gives us something to look forward to."

They stared at each other for long moments and the blood ran back to Tom's groin. With a groan, he wrenched his gaze away, knowing that they couldn't possibly take things any further in the car.

"We'd better go inside," he said with reluctance.

"Yes, we'd better. A woman I assume is your mom has been watching from the front window ever since we arrived. She'll be wondering what's keeping us."

Heat crept up Tom's neck and spread across his cheeks and he busied himself by climbing out of his truck. He didn't know why the knowledge of his mom spying on him while he made out with his girlfriend in the car embarrassed him, but it did. All of a sudden, he felt like a seventeen-year-old, stealing kisses from his childhood sweetheart. It was stupid, but true.

Walking around to the passenger side, he helped Lily from the car and then collected their bags from the back. They'd barely reached the front steps when the front door swung open and his mom rushed out across the porch.

"Tom! How wonderful to see you. I can't believe how much you've grown." She pulled him into a vigorous hug.

"Mom," he laughed and hugged her back. "I'm nearly twenty-three. I stopped growing a long time ago."

"Nonsense, you get bigger and broader every time I see you. You haven't been home since Christmas and that was eight months ago. And you must be Lily," she added in the same breath, turning toward her and opening her arms.

They embraced a little awkwardly, then Marguerite Munro stepped back graciously and offered Lily a welcoming smile.

"You must be tired from your travels. Come in and put your feet up. I'll put the kettle on."

Tom swallowed a sigh of relief, only just realizing he'd been more than a little nervous about the meeting between Lily and his mom. He should have known his mom would welcome his heavily pregnant girlfriend—a girlfriend she'd only just been told about—with her usual affability.

His dad sat in his usual place by the fire and Tom bit his lip against a sudden surge of emotion when Duncan Munro stood and greeted him with a wide smile before pulling him in close for a hug.

"Son, it's good to see you."

Tom cleared his throat of its huskiness. "You, too, Dad. You look good."

"Well, you know me, the day I'm too old to climb out of bed and go for my usual three-mile walk along the river is the day I'll tell them they might as well put me in the ground."

Tom laughed and his dad joined in. They'd always been close and as Tom had grown into adulthood, they were almost like mates rather than father and son. It was a relationship Tom cherished and was more than grateful for. He had plenty of friends and colleagues who could barely bring themselves to be civil to their father, let alone seek out and enjoy their company.

Turning, Tom reached out for Lily and drew her against his side. His arm lay protectively, possessively around her shoulders.

"Dad, this is Lily."

Like his mother had earlier, Tom's father greeted Lily with a genuine smile and shook her proffered hand.

"It's lovely to meet you, Mr Munro," Lily said quietly.

"And you too, Lily, but please, call me Duncan."

Lily tilted her head in acknowledgement. Tom squeezed her hand.

"You live in a beautiful city, Duncan. I've never been to Grafton before but it certainly has an appeal. The river's so wide and lovely. I bet you never get tired of watching it."

"Yes, it is and you're right. I love to sit out on the back porch and watch the ebb and flow of the Clarence. It's tidal, you see. It runs all the way to the Pacific Ocean."

"It looks great for water skiing. Do you have a boat?"

Duncan shook his head. "Not one with enough power to pull skiers, unfortunately. I have a little runabout that I like to take fishing whenever I can. I spend quite a lot of time on the court circuit, so I don't have the freedom to fish as often as I wish."

"Dad's a District Court judge," Tom explained and Lily nodded.

"Tom, Lily? Would you like a cup of coffee? Or perhaps tea?" Marguerite asked.

"Tea would be lovely, Mrs Munro," Lily replied.

Marguerite waved Lily off. "Please, call me Marguerite. We don't stand on formalities. Tom, what would you like?"

"I'll have tea too, thanks, Mom. White with one. Lily takes hers the same."

Marguerite bustled off in the direction of the kitchen and Tom looked over at Lily. Dark lines of fatigue had etched themselves into her face and he remembered how long the car trip had been. They'd left Sydney mid-afternoon. It was now going on for ten. While Tom had done all the driving, the trip had still taken its toll. It couldn't have been comfortable for her to sit for such a long time with a full-grown baby on board.

"Why don't you take a seat and put your feet up?" he suggested quietly, rubbing the back of her hand with the pad of his thumb. "I'll go and see how Mom's doing with the tea."

With a grateful smile, Lily let him lead her over to the armchair that matched the leather sofa in the living room. It was far enough from the fire that Lily wouldn't overheat, but close enough for her to feel cosy.

"She'll be all right, son." Duncan winked at Lily. "I'll take good care of her."

Tom chuckled and shook his head and then turned and headed toward the kitchen. The house was much as it had been during the years he was growing up. The pictures that lined the hall still evidenced the life stages of him and his siblings, from framed baby pictures and school photos to shots of the whole family. The latest picture to make it to the wall was one of him in his full police uniform. It had been taken by a professional photographer at his graduation ceremony from the Academy. He couldn't believe that was nearly three years ago.

"There you are," his mom smiled softly. "Come in and talk to me while I finish making the tea."

Fresh nerves swirled around in Tom's gut and he forced his

feet forward. His mom might have welcomed Lily with open arms, but she wouldn't stop until she had all the details of how he came to arrive back at home with a very pregnant girlfriend in tow and not have clued her in on a single thing.

Knowing there was nothing he could do but get the inquisition over with, he tugged out a wooden stool that stood beneath the breakfast bar and sat.

"So, tell me about Lily. She seems sweet and she's incredibly beautiful. How old is she?"

Tom tried to bite back a grin. Trust his mom to get straight to the point. "She's nineteen, mom. Nearly twenty."

"*Mm*, nineteen. Yes, I thought she looked young. When's the baby due?"

"In seven days." He looked at his watch. "Actually, I think it's probably closer to six now."

Marguerite shook her head. "Six days? How could you have kept this quiet for so long? It's my first grandchild! You know I'd be excited, no matter what the circumstances! I should turn you across my knee or—or ground you for keeping something so important from me."

"Mom..."

"I know. I'm sorry, there are far more important things to talk about, including the how and why and when. Your father told me a little about what happened. You didn't know about the baby either, until two weeks ago, is that right?"

Tom drew in a deep breath and let it out slowly. "Yep."

"So, you two had broken up, or something? Is that what happened?"

"Yes, we were only together a couple of months. We met toward the end of last year. When we... When we ended things, I had no idea Lily was pregnant. I ran into her by accident at a school where she was working and realized she was about to have a baby. At first, I assumed it was someone else's. It was only after we'd talked that she told me it was mine."

"I hate to sound indelicate, but are you sure you're the father? I mean, these days—"

"No, Mom. The baby's mine."

"Well, if you're sure. I mean, you could always do a DNA—"

"Mom, please. Dad suggested the same thing. Lily said I was the father and I believe her. It's as simple as that. The baby's mine. Besides, the dates line up to the time when we were still together. Unless she was cheating on me way back then, which I don't believe for an instant, there's no other possibility."

"Okay, then, just as long as you're sure. I'm only trying to look out for you, Tom. That's all."

"I know, Mom, and I appreciate it. But let's just move on. Where are the others, by the way? I thought Clay and Riley might still be awake?"

"Your brothers are at a birthday party out of town. They're staying the night. The girls are asleep in bed. At least, I hope they're asleep. It's a school night for them. I didn't tell them you were coming.

"When you texted to say you hadn't left Sydney until three, I expected you to arrive late. If they'd had an inkling you were on your way, I'd have never gotten them to bed. It will be a nice surprise for them in the morning."

Tom grinned at the thought of his mischievous younger sisters. Josie was twelve and in her final year of primary school. At nine, Chanel was an authority on everything from space travel to psychedelic fingernail polish. He never got tired of listening to her dissertations on one subject or the other. She was old beyond her years. He pitied the man she'd finally end up with.

"Now, stop changing the subject and tell me about Lily. How did the two of you meet?"

Lily watched Tom disappear from view on his way into the kitchen, leaving her alone with his father. She swallowed her panic. It wasn't like Duncan Munro had been anything but welcoming, but the fact was, he was a District Court judge. Even without knowing what he did for a living, she'd have guessed immediately it was something important. He had an air of authority about him that demanded respect and attention.

Tom had told her his dad was a full blooded aboriginal, but it still came as a surprise to discover how dark skinned he was. Although Tom looked like he had a perpetual tan, his dark blond hair offset the golden color of his skin and it wasn't until he'd told her about his aboriginal heritage that she even guessed he was biracial.

Still, she could see the resemblance to his father in the mutual proud bearing, the impressive height, the wide smile and the kindness that glinted in his father's dark brown eyes.

"So, Lily, tell me about yourself. What do you do in Sydney?"

She took a deep breath and eased the air out between her lips and took a moment to brace herself for the inevitable run of questions. "I'm at college. I'm in the second year of my teaching degree."

"I see. Teaching. A very noble profession. What are you going to do when the baby arrives? It looks like it could arrive any minute."

While Duncan's tone was gentle, Lily couldn't help but feel embarrassed. Tom had inherited his traditional values from someone. She'd bet her life's savings on the fact that he'd gotten them from his dad. Averting her gaze, she did her best to stem the blush that spread from her neck and then moved across her cheeks.

"The baby's due in a week. I've finished my mid-year exams and all of my assignments have been completed to date. It's not long until spring break. It's only three weeks, but it's something. I'm hoping if the baby arrives on time, I'll have at least the holidays to get a bit of a handle on things. I've rearranged my study schedule so that I can attend the majority of my lectures online."

Duncan smiled. "It sounds like you're going to be a very busy young lady for the next little while, but good on you for continuing with your studies. It's important to have something behind you, especially these days. Do you have any family living close?"

"Yes, my mom and my stepfather live in Sydney, although they're doing a little touring around Australia right now. I received an email from them last night. They're in the middle of the Nullarbor Desert, so cell phone coverage is sporadic at best, but mom's promised she'll be home for the birth and at least for the first few months afterwards."

"Good. That's good. I remember when Tom was born. Marguerite and I had moved from Sydney to Grafton. Neither of us had any family nearby. I was working sixteen hours a day in a law office and Marguerite was left largely alone with a new baby. I'm the first to admit it was tough and we were quite a bit older than you and Tom."

"But you got through it and went on to have another six kids, right?" Lily smiled.

Duncan grinned back at her. "Yes, we did. And in fairly quick succession, too, I might add. At one stage, we had five children under five, and all boys at that!"

Lily laughed and shook her head in disbelief. "Wow, I can't even imagine what that must have been like. You both deserve a medal."

"It was Marguerite who did the brunt of the work. As I said, I spent a lot of hours at work. I'd help out on the weekends to give her a break. I'd take the boys fishing down the river or play ball in a nearby park. It gave their mom a chance to rest and recuperate so she could face the oncoming week."

The fondness in his voice was reflected on his face and Lily couldn't help but feel a pang deep down inside her. Here was a man, a good man, who loved his family with everything that he was; who still loved his family. He was so different from the man she'd once called Dad.

She'd only been six when she'd left the only home she'd known and her memories of the years she'd spent under that dark and dangerous roof were hazy, but she hadn't forgotten how it had felt. The fear that overrode even the smallest of actions, right down to creeping down the darkened hallway in the early hours of the morning to use the bathroom, remained with her all these years later.

Here, in the Munro family living room, with its comfortable couches and cosy fire, she couldn't imagine a cross word being spoken. Duncan Munro might be large in presence, but he was far from intimidating. Even now, knowing nothing about her but that she was carrying his son's baby, he'd treated her with kindness, courtesy and respect and his wife had done the same.

Lily had only exchanged a few sentences with Tom's mom, but she could tell the woman loved him unconditionally. It was the way parents were supposed to be, but sadly sometimes weren't. Lily could see why Tom was so well-adjusted and why he believed in true love right up until the very end. She hoped some of his confidence would rub off on her and help her accept that what they had together was strong enough to survive.

The baby kicked hard and she jumped a little in the chair. The kick was followed by a tightening of her belly.

"What is it? Are you all right?"

The immediate concern in Duncan's voice was touching and she couldn't help but open her heart. He was her baby's grandfather. The only true grandfather her baby would have. While Tony would always be there, at least in some way, it wasn't like a blood tie.

As she thought of all the things Tony had done for her and her mom, she felt a little guilty, but it didn't change the truth. She'd always love her stepfather for giving them a new life, but he'd never be her dad. That was just the way it was.

Besides, Tony had no interest in babies. He'd always said as much. She was sure the arrival of her own wouldn't change his mind and that was perfectly okay, because she had Tom's family in her life. With six siblings, he had more than enough numbers on his side. She couldn't wait to meet the rest of them.

Another tightening gripped her stomach, this one stronger than the first. The pain was like nothing Lily had ever felt before, quick and sharp. She tried to take a deep breath to calm herself. Increasingly alarmed, she rode another wave of pain. A moment later, she felt a rush of warm water between her legs.

"Oh, oh... Oh, no! I'm so sorry!"

Duncan was on his feet immediately and rushing to her side. At the same time, he yelled for Tom and Marguerite.

"What is it, Lily? Are you okay?"

She shook her head, unable to form the words. Another contraction took hold of her body and she gasped in surprise at the intensity of the pain. From the corner of her eye, she spied Tom, followed closely by his mom.

He knelt on the floor beside her and took her hands in his. "What's happening, Lily? Oh, Christ. Is it the baby? Please, talk to me, honey. Is the baby coming?"

She nodded, her head moving up and down on autopilot. "Yes, I-I think my water just broke."

The color leached from Tom's face and he glanced down at the floor. If it were possible, he turned even paler. "Oh, shit. Oh, mom. Lily's all wet. Her water has broken. The baby's coming."

Marguerite gently moved him aside and put her hand on Lily's stomach. Taking in the damp stain pooling on the floor, she smiled calmly and nodded. "I think you're right, Tom. Your baby's on its way."

Tom stood quickly and began to pace. "It can't come now. It's too early. We have another six days and we're not married yet. I don't want my baby being born out of wedlock." He spun on his heel and began to pace in the other direction, pulling at his hair. "Shit. I had it all planned. We had a week. Way long enough to propose and make it all legal."

"Really?" Duncan drawled in a dry voice. "You need to apply for a marriage license at least one month before the day."

Tom came to a sudden halt and turned to face his father. "A *month*? You're kidding me? You can't just walk into a Registry office and sign your life away?"

"No, son. You can't just walk into a Registry office. It doesn't work that way."

Tom looked aghast. "Can't you do something? You're a judge, after all."

Lily watched the exchange in confusion and did her best to breathe through the pain. The contractions were coming faster and harder and were lasting longer. She didn't know how much longer she could put up with it.

Her moan was loud and full of pain. "Tom, please. Hold my hand. It hurts so much."

"We need to call an ambulance," Marguerite announced. Both men fell silent and stared at her.

"An ambulance," Tom repeated, his face blank.

"Yes, Tom. An ambulance. Lily's labor is progressing rapidly for a first birth. We need to get her to the hospital. Now, stop this nonsense about marriage and Registry offices and babies born out of wedlock and go and call an ambulance."

Her words seemed to finally penetrate his brain. He patted his pockets frantically, in search of his phone. "Where the hell did I put my phone? Dad, do you know where I left it?"

"No, Tom. Why would I know where you'd left it?"

"I had it just a—"

"Tom!" Marguerite said sternly, her tone brooking no argument. "We have a phone on the side table in the hallway. Pick it up and call an ambulance."

He stared at his mom for a few moments and then did an about turn and strode out of the room. Yet another contraction gripped Lily and she gritted her teeth and panted. She tried to concentrate on what she'd learned in the classes she'd attended over the past few weeks, but everything the instructor told her had dissolved into thin air. Her mind was like a sieve and refused to focus on anything other than the pain.

Another fierce contraction took hold of her and she cried out. Tom materialized again and reached for her hand and Lily squeezed it for dear life. It didn't take the pain away, but it helped her think about something else. She sighed in relief when the wave of pain was over.

"You're doing fine, Lily. Breathe deeply, catch your breath, relax until the next one," Marguerite encouraged her. "The ambulance is on its way. You're going to be fine, honey. I promise."

Marguerite's soothing words and calm manner helped ease some of Lily's fears. She did as Tom's mom suggested and by the time the next contraction seized her, she was ready for it. The pain was the strongest yet and the contraction seemed like it lasted forever. She panted and squeezed Tom's hand and did her best to breathe through it.

A stinging sensation burned between her legs and despite her best efforts, she screamed. Marguerite knelt down between her legs and lifted her dress. Lily would have died with embarrassment if she hadn't been in so much pain.

"Okay, here's what we're going to do," Tom's mom stated in a calm, but firm voice. "Tom, move Lily carefully and lie her down on the couch. Duncan, go to the linen press and get me four or five clean towels."

Tom stared at his mother, his face dark with confusion. "Mom, the ambulance will be here soon. Surely we can wait until then?"

"I don't think so, Tom. The baby's head has crowned. In another push, maybe two, your baby's going to be here. I don't think it's going to wait for the ambulance."

Lily heard Marguerite's quiet words and fear gripped her heart. She was going to have her baby in the Munro family living room! As if tuned in to her thoughts, Tom picked her up in his arms and murmured reassurances in her ear. Gently, he deposited her on the couch. In the distance, she heard a siren and was overwhelmed with relief.

Oh, thank goodness! The ambulance wasn't far away. Perhaps she could just wait... A few seconds later, another wave of agony gripped her belly and Lily cried out against it. The urge to push came upon her and there was nothing she could do but go with it.

"Push, Lily. Push." Marguerite's encouragement gave her confidence.

"Oh, hell. I can see the head!" Tom shouted, his eyes wide with a combination of fear and excitement.

All at once, the burning sensation eased and Lily gasped on a breath.

"That's it, Lily! The head is out! You're nearly there, honey. One more push and it will all be over."

With her chin pressed to her chest and her knees bent high, Lily clung to Tom's hand and braced herself for the next contraction. It came hard and fast and she pushed with all her might.

"Quick, Tom! Get down here and help me. Your baby's about to be born!"

Tom threw a panicked look at Lily and then toward his mom. Lily groaned and breathed and groaned again. Tom rushed to take the spot beside his mother. With something akin to wonder and terror warring on his face, he leaned forward and reached for their child.

"You've done it, Lily! You brilliant girl! What do we have, Dad. Is it a boy or a girl?"

Tom looked down at the squalling red mass of humanity in his hands and tears filled his eyes. He stared at Lily and shook his head, as if at a loss for words.

"It's a girl," he croaked, his voice husky with emotion. "We have a daughter!"

The pain that had held Lily's body in its grip miraculously receded and her breath slowed. She collapsed against the pillows, exhausted and relieved. She watched while Marguerite expertly swaddled the tiny bundle in a towel and then handed her back to Tom. With reverence and awe flooding his face, Tom turned and brought their daughter to Lily and laid the baby on her chest.

The next while passed in a blur and in what seemed like no time at all there were strangers in uniform beside her, urging her to remain calm while they cut the umbilical cord and she delivered the placenta. A little while later, the paramedics urged her to shuffle across to the stretcher. She kissed the petal-soft skin of her daughter's cheek and then handed her back to Tom. He took the baby from her and grinned so hard she thought his lips might split in two. She offered him a tentative smile in return.

"Is she… Is she all right?" she whispered.

"She's beautiful, just like her mother and perfect in every way." He bent down and brushed the damp hair off her forehead and kissed her softly on the lips.

"I love you, Lily Strickland. I'll love you for the rest of my life."

"I love you, too, Tom Munro."

Tom's eyes grew darker with emotion and he took her hand and raised it to his lips. "Will you marry me, Lily?"

Lily stared at him and her heart swelled with a love so deep and powerful she was surprised she could contain it. The people in the room faded away until there was no one and nothing, but Tom. She might have had a shitty childhood, but he'd shown her families weren't always like that. He'd had the best of role models and together, they'd learn to deal with whatever life tossed their way.

"Yes, Tom. I'll marry you."

His eyes widened in shock. A split second later, he *whooped* his exhilaration so loud it rang out through the house. "You'll marry me? You mean it?"

"Yes, Tom. I mean it." And she did.

CHAPTER 18

Royal North Shore Hospital—present day

Tom opened his eyes and blinked them, feeling a little groggy from the residual effects of the anaesthetic. His chest was sore and his mouth was dry. A headache persisted across his forehead. But Lily was awake. She was going to be all right. And that was all that mattered.

He stirred in the bed and lifted his arm, noticing the IV tube than ran into the vein on the top of his hand. Brandon sat in a chair in the corner of the room, looking more than a little disheveled as he watched his brother open his eyes.

"Tom, you're awake," he said and stood and came over to the bed. "Good to have you back with us, mate. You slept more than four hours. How do you feel? Can I get you anything?"

"Water, please," Tom rasped and licked his dry lips.

"Sure, there's a water jug right here."

Tom watched while Brandon picked up a blue plastic jug and poured water into a glass. Handing it across the bed, Tom took the glass and swallowed a mouthful, sighing in relief.

"Ah, that tastes fantastic. I feel like I haven't had a drink for a week."

"Well, you hadn't eaten all day and you were asleep when your dinner arrived. No wonder you're thirsty. The nurses have been in and out through the night checking on you and replacing the bag of fluid running through your IV, but they decided not to wake you."

"How's Lily? When can I see her?" Is she still in the ICU?" Tom glanced out at the window that took up most of the far wall. The night sky was littered with tiny stars, barely illuminated against the lights of the city.

"She's doing great. She's supposed to be moving to a ward tomorrow, if she remains stable overnight."

"Great. What time is it? Can we go now?"

Brandon smiled. "It's seven-thirty in the evening. The nurses might not be so keen to let you out at this time of the night."

"Bran, please. I need to see her. The ICU staff will understand. I've been a fixture at her bedside since it happened."

"I understand, mate. I'll go and talk to one of the nurses. I'll see what I can do."

Tom nodded in gratitude, but inwardly, he chafed at the delay. If he weren't feeling so under the weather himself, he'd just up and get out of there now.

"Oh, the doctor stopped by earlier to check on you. She was pleased with how the operation went, but she needs to wait for the results of the pathology to ensure they got all of the cancer. She also said it's important for you to mobilize as soon as possible. I'm happy to help you out of bed. We might not be able to walk to see Lily, but we could take a short turn around the ward."

Tom looked at his brother and realized Brandon had spent the day by his side. His chest tightened with emotion. It made him feel good to know how much his brother cared.

"Yeah, thanks, but I might leave it a little while. I-I still have a bit of a headache and my chest feels like it's been run over by a truck. I want to save my strength so I can see Lily."

"Sure, I get that and we can always take a wheelchair." Brandon yawned and stretched his arms way out over his head and then shot Tom a grin. "Let me tell you, that hospital seat sure leaves a lot to be desired in the way of comfort."

"I want to thank you for staying with me, Bran. I-I don't know what to say. I really appreciate it." Tom cleared his throat. "It... It means a great deal."

Brandon merely nodded, as if he was also struggling for words. Eventually, he said, "No worries, bro. You'd have done the same for me."

"What about Lily? Was anyone able to stay with her?"

"Lily's mom—Fiona, I think she said—took over from Mom this afternoon. Mom went to your place after she arrived, to help Dad out with Cassie and Joe. He's been with them all day. Not that they're babies, but...you know. As far as I know, Fiona's still with Lily."

"Yes, of course and I'm glad Lily hasn't been left alone. She's probably wondering where the hell I am. Has anyone told her about...?"

"Yeah, Mom did. She wasn't going to, but Lily kept asking for you and wondering why you weren't there. She was getting more and more distressed about your absence. Eventually, Mom decided it would be better to tell her the truth."

Tom was flooded with guilt. He should have told Lily about the lump months ago. It shouldn't have been left up to his mom. He remembered how hurt and betrayed he'd felt when Lily had hidden the truth about being pregnant with Cassie. Now that the tables were turned, he prayed Lily would be understanding of the situation and his reasons for keeping it hidden from her for so long.

"How did she take it?" he asked.

"Okay, I think. I only spoke to Mom briefly when she called in to see you and to tell me she was heading back home.

Tom sighed. "I'm so grateful to everyone for chipping in and helping out. It's been such a relief knowing the kids have been taken care of and someone's kept Lily company. You can't know how much it means to me."

"Of course. We're family. It's what we do."

"Still—"

"Would you stop thanking me? It's not necessary. You're my brother. Of course I'm going to do all I can to help you when you need me, okay? End of story."

"Okay," Tom smiled. "I get it." Tom's thoughts shifted to his children. "Do the kids know their mom's awake?"

"I assume Mom's told them by now. I tried to call earlier when you asked me to, but I couldn't get through to them. Mom called Dad on his cell phone and he admitted he'd fallen asleep and hadn't heard the phone. I'm not sure what the kids were up to. Mom thought they were probably listening to music with their headphones on."

Tom frowned. "What time was this?"

"I don't know. Four, maybe five o'clock?"

"You'd have thought one of them would have heard the phone."

"Hey, don't stress about it. I'm sure it was nothing."

"Yeah, I hope so." Tom blew out his breath on a heavy sigh.

Brandon's forehead creased on a frown. "What's the matter? You look like you've got the weight of the world on your shoulders."

"I'm... I'm a little worried about Cassie. Even before the shooting, things weren't quite right."

"What do you mean?"

"I don't know. Nothing in particular. I've just noticed a change in her attitude. She used to love school, she's always been a straight A student. She's always had lots of friends, been involved in sport. The last year or so, it almost seems like another girl has taken over inside her body. She looks the same, but she's not my Cassie."

Brandon pursed his lips in thought. "Do you think it might have something to do with that shit with Gibbons?"

Tom closed his eyes and tried to suppress a shudder. The memory of the sheer terror he'd felt when his daughter had been kidnapped by a pedophile still haunted him. Brandon had worked on the investigation. He knew firsthand the horror they'd all been through.

Tom rubbed a tired hand across his eyes. "I don't know,

Bran. Maybe. It was four years ago. The first couple of years were pretty rough, even with the intensive therapy, but she seemed to have come out the other side of it. A year ago I'd have even said she was the same old Cassie from before. Now, I don't know. I don't know what's going on with her anymore."

"Well, you've got a lot on your plate. You're busy at work and Lily's been busy, too. She's working all day and now she's gone back to school at night—neither of you have special powers to deduce what's going on in your daughter's head. I don't have teenagers yet, thank Christ, but I'm sure sometimes it's far from easy to know what's going on with them."

Tom laughed without humor. "You have that right. Hell, you want to brace yourself for the day your kids hit their teens."

Brandon chuckled. "I'll know where to come to for advice. The three of them are growing like weeds. The teenage years will be upon me before I know it."

Tom forced a smile, but his thoughts were still on Cassie. "Do you mind going over to the house tomorrow and just checking to see if Cassie and Joe are both okay?" he asked.

"Sure. No problem, but I'm assuming they'll come and visit here, anyway. With Lily awake and you out of surgery, I'm guessing Mom and Dad will have a hard time keeping them away."

"Yeah, you're right. They might even drop by tonight. I'm probably apprehensive for no reason."

"Hey, you're their dad. You're allowed to care and be concerned, particularly if Cassie's been giving you cause to be worried. I tell you what, I'll take them back home after they've been to visit and spend a bit of time with them. I'll see if I can work out what's going on with her. How does that sound?"

Tom sighed in relief and reached up to squeeze Brandon's arm. "That sounds great, bro. Thank you. I really appreciate it."

Brandon shook his head, even as a smile tugged up his lips. "Don't tell me we're back to that thank-you shit?"

––––––––––––––––––

Lily took a moment to check out her new surroundings. Her stomach still hurt like hell and every part of her body ached, but she was awake and lucid and had been transferred out of the ICU, so she couldn't complain.

The ward she'd been taken to was so much nicer than the ICU. Not that she could fault the ICU staff—their care of her had been beyond reproach—but there were no windows in the ICU, no connection to the outside world. It was a blur of pale walls and white sheets and machines that beeped all night. It was cool and calm and efficient and everyone spoke in hushed tones. There was no life, no sunshine no...anything. She couldn't wait to leave.

The private room she'd been taken to had a window that looked out onto a park. The trees stood tall and fresh and green with their new leaves and even from a distance, the grass looked soft and inviting. The gentle hum of traffic filtered in and a scattering of people wandered through the grounds, heading to wherever.

Obviously, the world outside the hospital continued. For many people, it was just another day. Lily rejoiced in the normalcy of it. Normal was good. She'd had enough excitement and drama over the past week to last a lifetime. Being shot by one of her students wasn't even the half of it.

She still couldn't believe Tom had not only been diagnosed with breast cancer, but he'd also been operated on and the tumor removed. That alone would have been enough to send her mind into a spin. On top of the fact she was still recovering from a bullet wound, she was surprised she could function at all.

She prided herself on being someone who could remain calm in a crisis, but it was different when the crisis was so close to home and happening to someone she loved. In a way, she was grateful she'd been unconscious when Tom's health drama had unfolded. She'd been spared the agony of fear and uncertainty that surely their kids and his family must have suffered.

At the thought of Cassie and Joe, Lily smiled in anticipation. Tom's mom phoned her earlier and had assured her the kids would drop by as soon as they could. It seemed like a lifetime since Lily had hugged them. It felt even longer since she'd held Tom.

Tom. A rush of love and gratitude flooded through her with the knowledge that he'd come through his surgery okay. When Marguerite had finally told her the reason for his absence, she'd been almost paralyzed with shock and fear.

Breast cancer? How could he have breast cancer and she not even have a clue? It didn't seem possible and yet it was. The odds of him getting it had to be miniscule. Most people thought of breast cancer in terms of the sufferers being women, but that wasn't always the case. She was beyond relieved it had been discovered in time and dealt with. She shuddered at the knowledge it could have been terminal and pushed the negative thought away.

He was fine. Marguerite had assured her he'd come through the surgery well. That his doctor was pleased with the operation. That he was going to be all right.

She didn't know what she'd do if she lost him. He was her rock, the very foundation that she balanced her life and existence on. To lose him, would be to lose her footing and she had no doubt that without him, her life would come crumbling down. They might have started off a little rocky, but the years had proven their love could stand the test of time, just like Tom had promised.

She smiled a little at the memory of their wedding. It had been the most wonderful day of her life. Tom had wanted to get married the minute she returned home from the hospital with baby Cassie by her side. Of course, she loved that he was so eager, but Cassie was already there. His concerns about their daughter being born out of wedlock had been moot.

She made him wait for more than a year before she finally walked down the aisle. She wanted the day to be perfect and refused to be rushed. She had no intention of marrying again—this was it, for life. Besides, she'd gained nearly twenty pounds of baby weight and there was no way she was getting married until she'd lost every one of them.

Tom agreed with huge reluctance to let her have her way, despite his passionate arguments that he didn't care what she looked like. Baby weight or not, she'd always be beautiful to him. She loved his sentiments, but held her ground. By the time she slipped into her custom-made white satin-and-pearl embroidered wedding gown, she was back to her usual shape and was pleased she'd remained firm.

The door to Lily's room opened and she looked up in time to see her mom returning from a trip down the hall in search of decent coffee. Lily smiled when she noticed a Styrofoam cup in either hand.

"You brought one for me?"

"Yes, honey. I can't imagine how you must feel after going nearly a week without a hit of caffeine. I'm just so grateful you pulled through and are here for me to deliver one to you."

Fiona Gibbons' voice was husky with emotion and her hand was a little unsteady when she offered Lily the cup. A sudden surge of tears burned behind Lily's eyes. She knew all about gratitude.

"Thanks for being here, Mom. For staying through the night. For the coffee. For…everything. I really appreciate it."

Fiona came closer and perched on the edge of the bed. "You're my daughter, my only child. There's nothing I wouldn't do for you." She reached out and laid a soft hand against Lily's cheek. A moment later, she shuddered.

"You won't believe how terrified I was when I received the call from Tom. I couldn't believe you'd been shot, didn't want to believe it, but Tom said there was no mistaking what happened. He had no reason to lie. I could tell from the panic and fear in his voice that it was true."

She drew in a ragged breath and clasped the coffee cup

with both hands. "I told Tony right away and made him turn around. We were halfway along the Birdsville Track, but it didn't matter. All I could think of was getting to you and seeing you before you... Well, it doesn't matter any longer. You're awake and the doctors say you're going to be fine. It's only a matter of time."

The tears that Lily had tried to hold back now ran slowly down her cheeks. She swiped at them with her free hand, but they kept coming.

"Don't cry, baby," her mom whispered. "It's all over now. You...Tom. You're both going to be fine."

Setting her coffee cup down on a nearby table, Fiona took Lily's cup and set is aside, too. Then she leaned over and carefully drew her daughter close. Lily sighed and rested her head against her mom's soft breasts, like she used to when she was a kid. Her mom had always been able to make everything right, no matter how wrong everything seemed.

"I'm so glad it's all worked out for you, Lily. Not only this, but with Tom and the kids. You're surrounded by people who love you. All of Tom's family have been here, taking turns keeping you company, providing each other with support. I'm so happy for you, baby. I'm so happy you have such a good life. It's... It's all I ever wanted for you."

"Oh, Mom," Lily gasped and the tears fell even harder. "I can't imagine what you went through before...with Dad. I was so young when we left, but I've never forgotten the feeling...the fear, the anxiety, knowing he could blow up in an instant. And I was only a child hiding in the shadows. It must have been so much more terrifying for you, walking on eggshells all the time."

Her mom stroked her back and hushed her and Lily felt even worse. *She* should have been the one offering comfort, not her mom. Fiona Gibbons had seen the worst the world had to offer and still gave something back. Lily hoped her mom knew how much she loved her and then she made sure of it.

"I love you so much, Mom. You've always been there for

me, keeping me safe, keeping me happy, loving me. Even when I was nineteen and single and pregnant with Cassie, you were there for me. Not once did you judge me or turn me away. In fact, if I'd listened to your very wise counsel, I would have told Tom about her long before I did.

"You tried to tell me not every man was like my dad, but at the time, I was too scared to listen. I'm sorry that I didn't. I should have known not to doubt what you said."

"Hey, baby, it doesn't matter anymore. Everything turned out all right. I love Tom like the son I never had and he adores the ground you walk on. He's a good man and you both deserve the happiness you have with one another. It brings me comfort and peace of mind knowing you're so well taken care of."

Once again, the door to her room opened and this time it was Tom who stood there. Lily cried out at the sight of him. He looked pale and a little unsteady on his feet, but her heart filled with love and relief.

With slower steps than usual, he closed the distance between them. Her mom stepped discreetly away.

"Lily, honey. Christ, you're awake! You don't know how scared I've been." Tom took her carefully in his arms, mindful of the tubes that were still attached to her body. Lily clung to him and the tears that had nearly stopped came flooding out again.

"Tom, oh, Tom! You're here. You're okay. I...I can't believe all that's happened."

He held her gingerly against his chest, mindful of their injuries. She breathed in his scent, but it was tainted with the smell of the hospital. Instead of pajamas, he was in a hospital gown and she smiled when she realized one of the ties had come loose. She slipped her hand lower and cupped his naked buttocks.

His butt cheeks flexed. He pulled slightly away and looked down on her, a smile tugging at his lips. "Lily Munro, you *must* be feeling better."

She winked at him and grinned. "I feel on top of the world."

He smiled at her again and then drew her in close for

another hug. "You had me so scared. Watching you lying there so still, on the gurney at school and in the ICU, with tubes coming out every which way. I've never felt so helpless. All I could do was sit there and hold your hand and pray that I'd get to talk to you again. Even last night, when I came down to see you, you were asleep. I wanted to wake you, but I didn't."

"You came by last night? Oh, Tom! You should have woken me."

"It was okay. I knew you were sleeping at least and not unconscious. It made a world of difference."

"And what about you?" Lily murmured. "Your mom told me you've had surgery to remove a tumor. I can't believe it, Tom. How did you discover it? How... How long have you known?"

Tom looked away and Lily saw him take a deep breath. Something stirred in her chest.

"What is it, Tom? What haven't you told me?"

"I've known about the lump for a year, but I only found out it was malignant a couple of days ago. I-I'm sorry. I should have told you."

Lily frowned and shook her head, confusion flooding her pores. "A year? What are you talking about? Why didn't you tell me?"

Tom's shoulders slumped and she noticed the fatigue around his eyes. She felt a stab of guilt. He'd just come through major surgery. He probably shouldn't even be out of bed. But she needed to know how it had happened and why he'd carried the secret around with him for so long.

"Talk to me, Tom. Tell me what happened."

"I don't know where to start."

"How about from the beginning? How did you find the lump?"

"I'm not sure. It was a long time ago. I think I just felt something when I was in the shower. It wasn't painful and not very big, so I just kind of ignored it."

Lily shook her head. "How could you do such a thing? You've seen the TV ads, read the stories. Hell, your mom is a breast cancer survivor. You of all people know that early detection is vital."

"I know, honey and I was stupid to ignore it for so long. I discovered it not long before Dad suffered the ruptured brain aneurysm and there were much more serious things going on in our lives. For a while, we didn't know if Dad would pull through. A tiny lump that was giving me no trouble was the last thing on my mind."

"But that was last Christmas, almost a year ago. Why didn't you see a doctor when you returned to Sydney?"

He shrugged and his cheeks turned red. "I don't know. I guess I was busy and...you know. Days turn into weeks into months..."

Lily shook her head. She wasn't buying it. Sixteen years of marriage had taught her a lot about her husband.

"You were scared it was going to be cancer, like your mom's, weren't you? That's the real reason you ignored it."

To his credit, he didn't refute it. With another sigh, he grimaced and met her gaze. "Yes."

"Oh, Tom. Why didn't you tell me? I'm your wife! It's my job to help you in your hour of need. We could have gone to the doctor together, I could have supported you through it. Did you even tell *anyone?* Your brothers, your mom?"

"I told Dad, but he was still in a coma. I don't know if he heard. He's never said anything to me about it, so I guess he didn't. Anyway, it doesn't matter now. It's all over, thank Christ."

"What did the doctor say?"

"I haven't seen her, yet. She came in late yesterday afternoon while I was asleep. Brandon spoke to her. She was happy with how the surgery went and is confident she got all the cancer. She's waiting on the results from pathology to know for sure."

"I'm glad Brandon was with you. I'll have to thank him."

"Yes, he was with me all day yesterday. He even drove me to the hospital. He's right outside if you want to see him. He came in again early this morning and brought me back down here from my ward."

"Please, send him in."

Tom left the room and Lily's mom stepped forward and pressed a kiss against her cheek.

"I might leave you to it, honey. It seems like everything's going to be okay. You get some rest now, you hear me? I'll see you a little later."

Lily smiled. "Thanks, Mom. You go home and get some rest too, okay? And thank you again, for everything."

"There's no need for thanks, Lily. I'm just glad you've pulled through. Tony will be thrilled to hear it. He'll want to take you out to Watsons for dinner to celebrate, just as soon as you're able."

Lily smiled again and nodded. "Tell him I'll keep him to it."

The door opened and closed behind her mom and a moment later, it opened again. Tom walked in, closely followed by Brandon. Knowing that he'd spent all day with her husband just because he cared, brought tears to Lily's eyes.

"Brandon," she murmured.

"Lily. It's good to see you awake. You look almost as good as new."

"Thanks, Brandon," she said with a smile. "I don't feel that way, but I'm grateful just the same. It's good to be awake."

"You can say that again. You had us all worried there for a while. And then this one books himself in for surgery—hell, there's never a dull moment in the Munro family."

He laughed and Tom and Lily joined in. It felt good to make light of their serious circumstances. It felt normal.

"I want to thank you for everything you've done for Tom," she said sincerely, holding Brandon's gaze. He turned his head and scuffed his boot and suddenly found something fascinating on the floor. His embarrassment only served to endear him to her further.

"It was nothing. Any of us would have done it. It was just that I had a few rostered days off and Alex had her mom to help take care of the kids. Declan and Riley have been calling around the clock and Clayton will drop in after work. Chanel flew in from Brisbane last night and Josie's on her way down from Grafton. They knew you were in the ICU and the hospital staff were restricting visitors, but they're about to arrive *en masse*—so brace yourself."

Tom chuckled and Lily grinned. This was what their family was all about. People who loved and cared deeply for one another and who were willing to put themselves out. She loved every member of the Munro family and wouldn't trade her life for anything.

"Where's Chanel staying?" Tom asked, interrupting her reverie.

"I think Mom said she's staying at your house. She wanted to help out with Cassie and Joe. It's been awhile since Mom and Dad had anything to do with teenagers. She didn't want the kids wearing them out. She keeps reminding me that Mom and Dad aren't getting any younger and Dad did have that scare last year…"

Tom nodded. "Yeah, you're right. It's good of her to come."

"Anyway, now that I've done my bit, I might leave you to it. The kids were in bed asleep when I got home last night and I haven't spent decent time with Alex in what seems like forever." Brandon stepped closer and pecked Lily on the cheek. "She sends her love, by the way. It's good to see you awake, Lil. Take care."

He turned to Tom and shook his hand. "Will you be all right getting back to your ward? If you want, I can stay until you're ready to leave."

"No, go. I'll be fine. The nurses know where I am. I'm sure they'll come looking for me when it's time to head back. Right now, I'm going to enjoy spending time with my beautiful wife."

Chanel Munro pushed back a loose strand of blond hair and climbed the stairs up to her niece's bedroom. She'd arrived late last night and both children had been asleep. But it was now going on for eight-thirty in the morning and

Cassie still hadn't made an appearance. When she'd questioned Joe about it over breakfast, he'd shrugged and muttered that he didn't know what was up.

Her mom had spoken to Lily earlier and her sister-in-law was understandably eager to see her kids. The rate Cassie was going, it would be lunch time before they arrived. Reaching the top of the stairs, she walked down the carpeted hall and came to a halt outside the door with a colorful, handpainted, carved wooden sign announcing it was Cassie's room. She knocked quietly on the door.

"Cassie? It's Aunty Chanel. May I come in?"

She was greeted with silence. It was way past time when Cassie should be up. On a normal day, the teenager would already be at school. Wanting to make sure she was all right, Chanel slowly turned the knob and opened the door.

The room was dark, despite the early morning sunshine that did its best to push through the closed blinds. It also smelled musty. The window was shut tight and dirty laundry was piled all over the floor. The scene was so different from the last time Chanel had been in her niece's room that she was taken aback.

She understood that Cassie was going through a difficult time, with her mom being shot and her dad undergoing surgery for cancer, but this drastic change was unexpected. As her eyes adjusted to the dimness, she made out Cassie's form in the bed.

"Cassie? Are you okay?" Chanel moved forward and reached out toward her niece. She gently turned her by the shoulder to face her and was overcome by alcohol fumes. Cassie's eyes were closed.

She shook her niece harder. "Cassie? Wake up! What the hell is going on?"

Her niece remained silent and limp and Chanel's panic ratcheted up another notch. Racing across the room, she pulled up the blind and turned on the light. Prying Cassie's eyelids open, she was stunned to see her niece's dilated and unfocused pupils. She slapped the girl against the cheek and called out louder.

"Cassie! Can you hear me? Wake up!"

Still the girl remained unresponsive and Chanel's medical training kicked into gear. She'd seen enough people affected by drugs to know what it looked like. Mixed with the alcohol, it could be a deadly cocktail.

Turning Cassie onto her back, she quickly checked for a pulse. The slightest fluttering under her fingers sent a surge of relief flooding through her, but the danger was far from over. She held her hand above Cassie's mouth and was grateful to feel warm breath. Cassie was alive, but unconscious. Chanel was worried her niece's condition had been caused by something far worse than alcohol.

Tugging her phone out of the pocket of her jeans, she called for an ambulance, stumbling a little when she tried to remember Tom's address. After what seemed like a lifetime, she got the information right and then checked Cassie's pulse again. It was faint and erratic, but it was still there.

She set Cassie's hand down gently on the sheet and started searching the room. The necks of at least two empty rum bottles poked out from under the bed. Plates and bowls and coffee mugs littered the floor and desk, most of them covered in remnants of dried food. It was no surprise the place smelled so bad.

On a sudden hunch, Chanel returned to the bed and pulled open the drawers of Cassie's nightstand. She searched through a collection of junk: notebooks, pens, an iPod and earbuds; candy wrappers, half a stick of gum, an old copy of *Wuthering Heights*.

"I know they're here somewhere, Cassie," she mumbled. "It would be a hell of a lot easier if you woke up and told me where."

Knowing no answer would be forthcoming, Chanel gritted her teeth and kept looking. She picked up the novel and flipped through the pages. Almost instantly, a small plastic bag fell out of it and tumbled onto the floor. Chanel bent down and picked it up.

Three small, white tablets lay in the bag. Ecstasy. She was sure of it. She blew her breath out on a heavy sigh.

Shit.

Though she'd suspected as much, to have the proof in her hand was a tough blow. This was her niece. Her brother's daughter. The very brother who was recovering from surgery. How could Chanel burden him with the knowledge his little girl was taking drugs? He'd be devastated, and Lily, too. What if it set back her recovery? She'd been shot, for goodness sake.

But their daughter was lying unconscious from an overdose of alcohol, drugs, or both. They were her parents. They had a right to know. Besides, assuming Cassie was going to pull through, she'd need a lot of support if they were going to break the cycle of dependence.

Chanel had no way of knowing how long her niece had been getting high, but the fact that she still had three pills stashed in a book in her nightstand was telling. Most kids experimented with one tablet at a time. Having a stockpile told her this probably hadn't been the first time.

Getting hooked on illegal drugs was easier than most people thought. It often started with a less ominous "party drug" like speed, but very quickly it could escalate to a whole lot more. Chanel had seen her fair share of ice—or crystal meth—addicts to know the total dependence it demanded in a very short space of time and the effects of an ice addiction were heartbreaking for everyone. She couldn't help but send up a silent prayer of thanks that Cassie's curiosity hadn't extended that far.

The faint sound of sirens drifted up from the street and she breathed a sigh of relief. Realizing she hadn't notified the rest of the household, she checked for Cassie's pulse again and then hurried from the room.

Chapter 19

Royal North Shore Hospital—present day

Tom packed the last of his things into the small suitcase Brandon had dropped by earlier and zipped it up. Glancing around, he did a quick check of his room to make sure he hadn't left anything behind. After visiting with Lily, he'd gone back to his ward and had met up with his doctor as she did her rounds. She was pleased with his progress and had given him the all clear. Within an hour, his discharge papers had been completed and he was now waiting for a member of his family to drive him home. A brief knock on the door snagged his attention. He smiled when he spied Chanel.

"Hey, little sister, it's great to see you and thanks for flying down. I can't imagine how busy you must be working in the biggest hospital in Brisbane. It was good of you to make the effort."

She barely lifted her shoulder in the slightest shrug of acknowledgement. Her mouth was tight, like she was doing her best to hold something in. Tom frowned and looked at her a little more closely.

He hadn't seen her since last Christmas. Her normally impeccable appearance had undergone a vast transformation in the intervening months. Her eyes were red and tinged with fear, her hair and her clothes were disheveled. He opened his mouth to make a joke of the rough night she must have had when he noticed she was on the verge of tears.

Halting beside her, he gave her a light hug, mindful of his stitches. With the pad of his thumb, he wiped away the moisture that had gathered in her eyes and was now spilling down her cheeks.

"Hey, sweetie, there's no need for tears. The surgery went well. The doctor's happy. You of all people know that has to be a good thing. In fact, they're letting me out of here today. Isn't that why you're here?"

"T-Tom. I-I…"

Tom's frown deepened. A shard of concern went through him. "Chanel? Is everything okay?"

Chanel shook her head and drew her breath in on a gasp. "No, Tom. No, it isn't. I-I… Cassie…"

Fear held Tom immobile. His mouth went dry. "What's the matter, Chanel? What's happened to Cassie?"

"She-she… Oh, Tom. She's been brought in by ambulance. She's in the ER."

"For Christ's sake, what happened to her? Is she hurt?"

Chanel remained mute and he shook her with increasing urgency. "Chanel! Talk to me! What the hell's happened?"

"She overdosed… On speed and alcohol. I-I found her unconscious in her bedroom not long ago."

Tom reeled back in shock. *"What? Overdosed? You have to be fucking kidding? You can't be talking about Cassie?"*

His sister drew in another deep breath and the action appeared to calm her. When she spoke again, it was in a quiet, controlled tone.

"Tom, you have to listen to me. I'm as shocked as you, but I'm telling you the truth. Right now, your daughter is downstairs fighting for her life. Fortunately, I found her before it was too late, but there's still no guarantee. They're pumping her stomach and hoping the toxins haven't reached her liver. The staff downstairs need to make contact with her next of kin. I told them about your situation. Given that Lily's barely a day out of her coma, we agreed it would be best to speak to you. I-I wanted to tell you myself."

Tom shook his head, beyond words. His mind spun furiously. He tried to focus on what Chanel had said, but his brain refused to work.

Cassie, a drug user? It was impossible. And yet, from the look on Chanel's face, it was true.

"I need to see her," he said, spinning around and looking for his things.

"Of course, but there's no point in rushing down there. She's still being treated by the doctors. You'll only be sitting in the waiting room."

"I can't just sit here doing nothing!" he yelled and immediately felt guilty for his outburst. "I'm sorry, Chanel. That wasn't fair. I should be thanking you for finding her, not shouting at you. It's just that—"

"It's okay, Tom. You're not the first frightened relative to yell at me. I can handle it."

Tom smiled grimly. "Still, I'm sorry just the same."

"Why don't you go and see Lily? The news about Cassie might be better coming from you."

Tom ploughed a hand through his hair. "Yes, of course. She's Cassie's mother. She has a right to know."

Chanel nodded, but didn't reply. Instead, she put her arms around him and hugged him gently.

"I'm going back down to the ER. I'll call you as soon as I have any news."

———

Lily stared at Tom in shock, unable to believe what he'd told her. Their daughter, their beautiful, talented daughter had overdosed on alcohol and drugs. Even now, she was in the ER, with doctors working over her to save her life. If the news hadn't come from Tom, she'd never have believed it.

Hell, she *still* didn't want to believe it. How could something like this happen to her own daughter and she not be clued in that there was something terribly wrong? She didn't even know how long it had been going on.

Lily prided herself on having a close relationship with both of her kids, but she hadn't seen this coming. Oh, she'd noticed Cassie had become a little less like her usual sunny self, but she had no idea it had come to this.

Alcohol...and *drugs?* The knowledge still stunned her. Working in a school environment Lily had known that kids were exposed to such things, but she was certain that she and Tom had raised both their children to have enough self-confidence that they could avoid the temptation. How could they have failed their daughter when she needed them the most?

The awful truth made her shudder. Whatever was bothering Cassie was serious enough to make her turn to the type of solace that could have dire consequences. The only thing she could be grateful for was that Chanel had discovered Cassie before it was too late. At least, she hoped she had. They were still waiting for news.

As if on cue, Tom's phone vibrated on the nightstand by her bed. Lily caught his gaze and she was sure the fear and dread that shadowed his eyes was reflected in hers. Tom broke the contact by answering his phone.

"Chanel, how is she?"

He was silent and Lily could only assume he was listening to his sister update him on Cassie's condition. She gritted her teeth and clenched her fists and tried to breathe through her impatience.

The waiting and not knowing was killing her. Staring at Tom, she tried to gauge from his expression whether the news was good or bad, but it was impossible to tell. After what seemed like an eternity, he ended the call.

"What did she say? How's Cassie?"

"She's fine. She's going to be fine." As if the words were only just beginning to register, Tom's shoulders slumped and he leaned forward in his chair, with both elbows resting on Lily's bed, his head in his hands. She knew how he felt. She couldn't keep the relief from her voice.

"Oh, thank goodness!"

Tom raised his head and managed a weak smile. "Yes. They're keeping her in overnight for observation, but Chanel says it's more of a precaution than anything. Thankfully, she'd only taken a couple of tablets. Because her system wasn't used to coping with the pills and the alcohol, it depressed her nervous system and she fell unconscious. We're very lucky Chanel found her when she did."

Lily shook her head, almost beyond words. Tears of relief and gratitude that her daughter had been spared pricked her eyes. She set her jaw, determined to stay strong, but the tears built until there was no holding them back. They leaked down her cheeks and dripped onto her nightgown. Soft, silent tears that were long overdue.

"Hey, babe, don't cry. She's going to be all right." Tom awkwardly patted her arm.

"She was using *drugs*, Tom and drinking! How could we not know? She's our daughter, living under our roof. What kind of parents are we to be so out of touch with our kids?"

Tom shook his head, his jaw set at a determined angle. "Don't do this, Lily. We're good parents. You know we are. We've both been busy and Cassie's been extremely clever about hiding this from us. I'm not saying we couldn't do better, but we're far from neglectful of our kids. We love her and have always tried to do what's best for her, even after that terrible incident with your stepbrother."

Lily flinched at the reminder and Tom gave out a heavy sigh.

"I'm sorry. I didn't mean anything by that. You know I don't blame you."

Lily stared at him for a moment and then turned away. "I need to see her, Tom. I need to know she's okay. I need to ask her forgiveness. No matter how we try and justify it, we've let her down. She needed us and we weren't there for her. This thing hasn't happened overnight, or even over the past week. I'll bet she's been battling demons for longer than both of us think."

Tom dragged in a breath and looked up at her. His eyes

were bleak. "It pains me to admit it, but I think you're right. Our baby girl's been suffering and neither of us knew about it. We're so lucky Chanel found her in time. Christ, I don't know what I would have done if it had been too late."

His voice caught on a sob and Lily squeezed her eyes shut in an effort to contain a fresh wave of tears. "Where's Joe?" she said.

"Chanel said he's at home, with Mom and Dad. I can only imagine how desperate and confused our son's feeling."

A feeling of sadness and hopelessness overwhelmed her and it was all she could do not to cry. It seemed life had dealt one blow after another in quick succession and her mind was spinning. She didn't know which fire to put out, where to expend her energies. If only she had the energy to deal with all of it...

The sound of the door to her room opening snagged her attention and she lifted her gaze. Tom' partner, Andy Warwick, filled the doorway. She offered him a weak smile.

"Andy, how are you?"

Andy nodded a greeting and then caught sight of Tom. "I'm glad I caught you. I went up to your room, but they told me you'd left."

"I've been discharged, but I came down here to see Lily. We... We have some trouble with Cassie."

"Is there anything I can do?"

Tom glanced at Lily. She nodded. Andy had known Cassie for almost as long as he'd known Tom. Not only was he a trusted work colleague, he was a close family friend.

"Cassie OD'd on pills last night. She was brought in by ambulance this morning. She's downstairs, in the ER."

Andy's face filled with shock and he shook his head. "Christ, what a mess! That poor kid! How is she?"

"Thankfully, she's going to be all right. My sister discovered her unconscious this morning and immediately called the ambulance. They've managed to reverse the effects of the drugs."

"Why? How?"

"We haven't spoken to her, yet," Lily said sadly. "But we think it has something to do with what happened years ago, with my stepbrother."

Andy's expression turned grim. "I'm so sorry, for both of you."

Tom nodded. "Yeah, but at least she's going to be okay."

Andy looked away and Lily saw him draw in a deep breath, as if he was bracing himself against something. A frisson of fear filled her belly with dread, but she forced herself to ask.

"It's lovely of you to visit, Andy, but is there another reason for your presence?"

Once again, Andy drew in a deep breath and his gaze stayed fixed on the floor. Tom frowned.

"What is it, mate?"

Andy shook his head slowly back and forth. When he looked up at them, pain and sad resignation cast dark shadows across his face. "I wanted to tell you in person."

Lily's fear went into overdrive and her fingers turned white on the sheet. Tom's frown deepened into something more.

"Tell us what?" he asked in a voice that was almost steady.

"It's about Brady Sutton. He-he's dead."

In a voice laced with sadness, Andy relayed the details of Brady's death. Lily turned to Tom, frozen with shock. She opened her mouth to speak, but the words wouldn't come. *Brady had killed himself. Brady was dead. Oh, God. Hannah, poor Hannah.*

"I-I have to call Hannah. She must be devastated. *I can scarcely take it in, how must she be feeling? She'll need as many friends around her as possible. I have to call her. I have to help.*"

Tom reached out to stop her from climbing out of the bed. "Lily, for Christ's sake, you're recovering from a bullet wound that tore you up inside. You're a day out of the ICU. You're not up to helping anyone, especially with something like this. You should be conserving your energy for getting well."

"I don't care about any of that," she shouted, almost blinded by her tears. "She's my friend. I have to be there and lend her my support. She'd do the same for me."

"Of course she would, but honey, please listen to me. You're lying in a hospital bed. If you were well enough to leave and take back up with your life you'd have been discharged."

Lily stared at him, her brain in a whirl of confusion and residual shock. First Cassie, now Hannah. She had to go to them and help them in any way she could. She understood Tom's reluctance to involve herself with Hannah. Her friend would be feeling worse than Lily could ever imagine. She remembered the absolute terror and soul-destroying fear that had ravaged her when Cassie had been kidnapped, but she'd clung to the hope her child would be found. Hannah had no such hope. Nowhere to turn. Nothing to pray for. Lily's agony for her friend intensified.

"At the very least, I have to call her, Tom. Please, try and understand. We know what it's like to face the possibility of losing a child—and we got ours back. Twice. I can't let her go through this alone. I have to at least let her know I'm thinking of her and praying. She's my friend, Tom. She's my *friend*."

Tom's jaw clenched and his hands tightened into fists, but eventually he relaxed and nodded. "Okay. I understand. I do. She's lucky to have you for a friend."

"She was there for me and I'll be there for her. It's as simple as that. Her son didn't intend to shoot me. I'm not absolving him of what he did, but it doesn't mean I'm not prepared to help her in her hour of need."

He nodded, though his expression remained grim. In silence, she turned down the volume on the television and reached for her phone. Scrolling down her contact list, she found Hannah's number. With a shaky breath and an even more unsteady hand, she made the call.

It rang out for so long, Lily tensed in anticipation of Hannah's voicemail message cutting in. She was already composing a few words in her head when Hannah answered.

All of a sudden, Lily didn't have the slightest idea what to say. She was spared making the initial contact when Hannah spoke.

"Lily? Is it you?" Her voice was so full of surprise and wonder, Lily was suddenly all choked up. This woman had just lost her son in the most horrific way and yet she could summon joy to discover her friend had woken from her coma.

"Yes, Hannah," she gasped. "It's me." Despite her best efforts to maintain her composure, tears poured down Lily's cheeks. She swallowed almost frantically. This wasn't about her. She wasn't the one who'd found her son dead.

"Oh, Lily, I'm so pleased you're okay. I-I hadn't heard the news that you'd regained consciousness. Are you all right? You're calling me, so I assume you're recovering. I—"

"Hannah, I... I just heard the news. I—"

A cry so full of agony and heartbreak cut through Lily's words. She wanted to block her ears against the desolation, but forced herself to hold the phone up close against her ear. Her fingers turned white from the pressure.

"My baby, my baby. My poor little boy. What have I done? Oh, God, what have I done?"

"Hannah, it wasn't your fault. You have to believe that."

"Of course it was my fault! All of it was my fault. Even the shooting was my fault. He told me it was because of the bullying. It had been going on forever. He'd told me about it and I ignored it, thinking it would go away. I *ignored* it, Lily, my own son!"

"You couldn't have known it would turn out this way, that he'd—"

"He *told* me so! He told me it was the reason he took the gun. I didn't do anything to protect him, so he was going to protect himself. I failed him, Lily, my own son. I failed him and now he's dead."

Her sobs grew louder and more out of control and Lily's pain intensified. The wounds in her chest and stomach were on fire and her mouth was as dry as wood. She licked her lips and tried to think, to come up with words of comfort, but she came up empty. She swallowed a moan of pain.

Tom stood and came nearer, a dark frown marking his face. She could tell he was upset because he was worried about how her conversation with Hannah was affecting her. It was obvious she was doing it tough.

But not as tough as her friend. Never as tough as that.

"I still can't believe it, Lily. I still can't believe it's true. I keep expecting to see him tearing down the stairs or hear him in the bathroom. I've been praying so hard since this happened—the shooting and…everything…and it's all been for nothing. He's dead, my little boy is dead."

The heartbreaking sobs renewed themselves and Lily cried just as hard. She jammed her fist against her mouth in an effort to keep the sobs in. Tom looked like a thundercloud, but there was nothing she could do. She would listen to her friend and be there for as long as it took.

"I remember when that awful thing happened to Cassie and you were beside yourself with fear. We prayed together for God to bring her home safe and sound. And He did. He *did*. Why, Lily? Why was your child spared, when mine was not? Why? Why? *Why?*"

The tears continued to pour down Lily's cheeks and she squeezed her eyes tight against the pain. Hannah didn't know about Cassie's latest brush with death, but it didn't matter. In fact, it was better this way. Nothing could change what had happened to Brady and no matter how much she wished it were different, she had no answers for her friend.

"I'm sorry, Hannah. I'm so, so sorry…"

Seated beside her niece's hospital bed, Chanel took Cassie's hand in hers and squeezed it. The warmth and healthy color of the girl's skin was reassuring and Chanel swallowed a sigh of relief. The doctors had given her niece a good report. They were confident they'd reversed the effects of the drugs. The alcohol in her system was also diminishing with every passing hour.

Chanel checked the monitor beside Cassie's bed and was relieved to see her vital signs were back within the normal range. A moment later, the girl stirred and her eyelids fluttered open. She frowned up at Chanel, as if trying to place her.

"Aunty...Chanel? Is that you? Where am I? What are you doing here?"

Chanel shook her head and bit her lip on a surge of emotion. They'd come so close to losing her and her niece had no idea. Drawing in a fortifying breath, Chanel plastered an encouraging smile on her face.

"Cassie, honey, you're in the hospital. I-I found you at home in your bed. You were unconscious, but you're fine now."

A frown marred the perfect, smooth skin of Cassie's forehead. "Unconscious? Are you sure? I didn't have that much to drink."

"Yes, honey. I'm sure. It wasn't the quantity of alcohol you consumed. Mixing the alcohol with the drugs caused the problem. I'm just glad I found you before it was too late."

"Too late? As in...I could have *died*?"

"Yes, you could have. But let's not think about that. We got you to the hospital in time and they've done what needed to be done to save you. I was lucky that I could tell them exactly what you'd taken. I found the bottles and pills in your room."

Cassie drew in a deep breath and let it out on a sigh. Tears of remorse filled her big blue eyes. "Oh, God! What are my mom and dad going to say? I'm sorry, Aunty Chanel. I'm so sorry. I-I didn't mean to start on that stuff. It's just that, there's been so much crap going on in my life lately, I thought I'd escape it for a while."

Chanel pulled her chair up closer to the bed. "Is it because of what happened to your mom and dad? Is that what you're talking about?"

Cassie lifted one shoulder in a shrug. "That's part of it."

"Well, I'm not sure if Grandma told you, but your mom and dad are fine. Your mom's awake and talking. They've moved her out of the ICU. Your dad had his operation and all went well with him, too. He's being released from hospital now. They're going to be fine. They'll be home soon and you won't have anything to worry about."

Cassie nodded. "That's good news, Aunty Chanel. That's really good news." She looked away, but not before Chanel caught the shimmer of fresh tears in her eyes.

"That's not all that's going on, is it?" Chanel hoped her gentle tone would coax something more from her niece.

Cassie shook her head in a jerky motion and swiped at her tears. Chanel reached for her hand and held it tightly.

"Talk to me, honey. What else has got you down? Tell me what's bothering you. Who knows, maybe I can help?"

Cassie looked up and her eyes flashed with pain. "No one can help. I should know. I've had plenty of people try. Mom and Dad spent a fortune on psychologists and counselors and self-help books full of positive acclamations. I lost count of all the people I talked to and all those who tried to help. They can't help. No one can. I'm going to live with what that man did to me for the rest of my life."

Chanel recalled the horrific events of a few years ago and suddenly understood. A feeling of uselessness flooded through her veins. What Cassie said was true. She'd probably never forget the trauma she'd been subjected to. Chanel couldn't imagine the terror the girl must have felt.

"I'm...I'm sorry, Cassie. I wish like hell there was some other way I could help you."

"Like I said, no one can help me."

The desolation in Cassie's voice tore strips right off Chanel's heart. Fury at the man who had caused it burned through her. It was just as well James Gibbons was still locked up in jail. The way Chanel felt in that moment, she could tear him limb from limb.

She prided herself on being a non-violent person, but the way she felt about child predators negated all that. They were the lowest form of life and she'd gladly vote to see them executed. No good could come from a society that believed in keeping them alive. It was a shame the politicians and civil rights activists didn't see it that way, but that's the way it was.

As if able to read her thoughts, Cassie rolled over in the bed and turned to face the wall. Chanel felt her rejection like an arrow through the heart. Her niece had been waiting for an answer, some hope that she could cling to, reassurance that she was wrong—that she would get over the shocking events of her childhood, that one day, things *would* be better.

But Chanel didn't have the words and couldn't give the reassurances. She clenched her jaw in frustration and her heart ached. She wished her sister, Josie, were here. Josie was a child psychologist. She had a PhD. She'd know what to say to help Cassie, to bring a smile back to her face.

But Josie wasn't here yet, and Cassie was crying out for help. Chanel had to do something, say something that would bring her niece even a modicum of hope.

"I understand the ghosts of your past and how they might still be tormenting you, but honey, drinking and using drugs aren't going to make them go away. Okay, the therapy didn't work out so well, but it doesn't mean we give up. It just means we have to work harder at finding a solution that will help you heal."

Cassie ignored her for long moments and Chanel began to despair. She couldn't force the girl to talk or to concede that it was worth trying something else. Then Cassie moved and Chanel eased out her breath. A moment later, her niece's shoulders shook on a heartrending sob.

"I'm sorry, Aunty Chanel. I'm so sorry. I don't know what I was thinking. No, that's not right. I knew exactly what I was thinking. I wanted a way to escape the pain, blur the memories that just won't go away. It started out with just the alcohol, but when Mom got shot and then Dad got sick...

"A boy from school offered me some pills. He said I'd float on a cloud so high, nothing would feel bad ever again. I wanted so much to believe him. I tried it and he was right. What he didn't tell me was that the feeling wouldn't last long enough and things would go back right to what they were."

"Honey, I don't need to tell you how dangerous it is taking speed. You don't have a clue who's made it and what they've put in it. I hear horror stories from the police about ecstasy tablets that are filled with paint thinners, acetate, rat poisoning and a heap of other toxic chemicals. Combine that with alcohol and there's a real possibility you'll wind up dead. It could have happened this morning if I hadn't stopped by."

Chanel stared hard at her niece and tried to make her understand. "Is that what you want, Cassie? To swallow a handful of pills and never wake up? Because it can happen. It does happen. More often than you think."

The girl was sobbing loudly now and Chanel's heart clenched with pain. The tough love lecture might have been warranted, but it hurt her to do it just the same.

"S-sometimes I do, Aunty Chanel. Sometimes that's exactly what I want."

Chanel cried out in shock and dragged Cassie into her arms. Her niece's sobs grew desperate and hot tears ran down Chanel's cheeks. Her beautiful niece had lost all hope and was hurting way down deep inside. Despite all the years of therapy, she still had moments that were of darkest black.

The knowledge was polarizing and so very sad. Somehow, somewhere every one of them had failed the young girl in her arms. They loved her, they wanted to help her, they'd found people she could talk to, but it hadn't solved the problem.

They had to try harder, find better therapists, never give up until they knew for sure it was done—that Cassie, their beautiful niece, daughter and granddaughter was in a truly happy place. Chanel wasn't a trained psychologist and she couldn't know for sure if it were even possible, but she was going to try her utmost to bring peace back into Cassie's life.

"Please, honey, don't cry. It's going to be all right. You'll see. You're surrounded by people who love you and we are all going to fight to the death for your happiness. Aunty Josie will be here soon and she'll do everything she can to help you through this. We all will."

Cassie lifted her tear-stained face, her eyes red and puffy. "Do you really mean it?"

"You'd better believe it."

Lily was still a patient in the hospital when Brady Sutton was laid to rest. The media had been on a feeding frenzy from the moment the news broke. They'd called her phone incessantly and had even tried to steal into her room. She was more than grateful for the vigilant hospital staff and their keen-eyed security.

The piranhas of the media all wanted the same thing: a sound bite for their news bulletin. She didn't know what they expected of her, but she'd be damned if she'd give them anything. The knowledge of Brady's death, and the fact he'd been bullied by his mates right under her nose, left a hole deep down inside her and it didn't matter that he'd been the one who had nearly taken her life.

He was a child, a boy of eleven. What did he know of the world? She still hadn't gotten all the details as to why it had happened, but the Brady she'd known for years hadn't been an evil child.

And Hannah. Poor, Hannah. How was she to cope with the loss of her only child? While Lily could still recall how she'd felt when her stepbrother had kidnapped Cassie, she hadn't had to deal with the realization her baby was never coming back. It was too much to ask of any mother and she prayed desperately that God would be there to comfort Hannah in these darkest of hours.

Tom and Cassie and Joe had attended the funeral and all three had been quiet and grim when they visited her later in the hospital. Lily was especially pleased to see her daughter up and about. She hadn't wanted Cassie to go to the funeral, but the girl had insisted, saying she wanted to show Ms Sutton her support. It was what Lily would have done had she been able and Lily had been proud that her daughter had found the courage to attend. There hadn't been an opportunity for Lily to have the heart to heart discussion with Cassie that was long overdue, but as soon as she was home again, she'd make sure it happened.

A nurse pushed open the door to Lily's room and ducked her head inside. "Lily, you have a visitor. She says her name's Hannah Sutton. I just wanted to check to see if it was okay before I send her in."

Lily's heart skipped a beat and then took off at a run. It had been three days since the funeral. Along with Tom and the kids attending the service, she'd arranged to have a bouquet of flowers delivered to Hannah's house, but she hadn't spoken to her since the morning she'd found out about the tragedy.

Now, she didn't know if she was ready to face her friend, here in the hospital bed, with nowhere to hide. She didn't know what to say to a woman who'd lost everything. Aware the nurse was waiting for her answer, Lily bit her lip and nodded.

"Please, send her in."

A short while later, Hannah walked slowly into the room. Bent over like an old woman, her hair was scraped back into a messy ponytail and her face was devoid of makeup. She seemed to have aged two decades since Lily had last seen her. Her dark-colored jacket and matching skirt hung off her frame and only added to the somber mood.

"Lily, thank you for seeing me."

The husky voice, rough with emotion barely sounded like the voice of her friend. Lily held a hand up to her mouth and tried not to show her shock.

"Hannah, I didn't expect you to come and visit. It's the last thing you should be concerned about. After all that's happened..."

Hannah made a sound in the back of her throat that could have been a gasp or a sob. "I wasn't sure if you'd see me. After what my son did to you, I'm probably the last person you want to see."

Lily gasped in shock, unable to believe for an instant

Hannah would think she'd feel that way. She said as much, her voice rising to keep up with her disbelief.

"How could you think such a thing? We've been friends for years! What happened wasn't your fault. It had nothing to do with you."

"But it did. That's where you're wrong. It had everything to do with me. If I'd listened to my son when he told me—no, *begged* me to do something about Ian Little and the other boys who were giving him grief, he'd have never gotten to the point where he thought the only solution was for him to sort it out with a gun. So, you see. It *was* all my fault."

Hannah's breath came fast and tears poured down her cheeks. Lily cried out against her friend's pain and for everything both of them had lost. At least Lily still had her life intact and that of her family's. Hannah's life would never be the same again.

Struggling to sit up in the hospital bed, Lily reached out for her friend. With a cry, Hannah closed the distance between them and together they clung to one another and sobbed. It was a long time later when Hannah pulled away and searched in her handbag for a tissue. After she'd wiped at her tears and blown her nose, she looked at Lily again.

"I've put in my resignation. I-I can't go back there again."

"Oh, Hannah!" Lily protested. "That job means the world to you and you're so good at it. Are you sure?"

"Yes, I'm sure. I'm very sure. I can't imagine ever wanting to step foot inside a class room again. I failed my son in his hour of need. It's not something I'll ever forget. I don't want there to be a next time when I let somebody down. I can't take the risk."

"Give it time. Take an extended leave of absence. I'm sure the administration will understand. You might feel differently a little further down the track. Promise me you won't make any hasty decisions."

Hannah merely shook her head. "I'm not going to feel any differently about returning to the schoolyard. I've made my decision. I'm not going back."

Lily's heart ached for her friend, but there was nothing else she could do.

"I've put the house on the market and moved in with my sister. She lives in the western suburbs with her husband and three kids. It's not ideal and hopefully it won't be forever. I've spoken to Colin. I told him I've filed for divorce. I need to bring this whole chapter of my life to an end. I can't bear to think about it another minute. As soon as the house sells, I'll move on."

"Where?" Lily asked, her voice gentle.

Hannah grimaced. "I don't know yet, but that doesn't worry me. I need to get out of Sydney, away from the memories. Every time I close my eyes, I see my baby hanging there..." Her voice broke on another heartbreaking sob.

"He's crying out for me to help him, Lily. When I reach him and try to pull him down, it's too late. It's too late..."

Fresh tears flooded Lily's eyes and she reached for Hannah once again, silently cursing her injuries that kept her confined to the bed. Her friend cried like her heart had broken in two and would never be whole again. Lily cried quietly with her. She'd never felt so helpless.

CHAPTER 20

Chatswood—present day

Lily sank into her favorite leather armchair that stood in its usual position in her comfortable living room and let out a sigh of relief. After four long weeks in a hospital bed, it was heaven to be finally home. The kids had returned to school and Tom's parents had returned home amidst a flurry of love and gratitude. Tom hovered nearby, an expression of concern on his face as he made sure she had everything she needed.

"Here's an extra cushion for your back," he said, pushing one gently in behind her. "And here's the TV remote and the one for Foxtel. I'm not sure if there's anything decent to watch, but you might find something. Now, can I get you a cup of coffee, or would you prefer a cool drink? It's damned hot out there today."

Lily smiled and reached out for him. She caught his forearm and tightened her fingers. Hard muscles bunched and flexed in response.

"Tom, I'm fine. Please, stop fussing about me like I'm a child. If I weren't well enough to come home, the doctors wouldn't have discharged me. I'm happy here, beyond content, back in my own house. I'll never underestimate the absolute gloriousness of being home again." She smiled to soften her words and was pleased when he smiled back.

Bending low, he kissed her gently on her lips. In what seemed like seconds, heat ignited between them and Lily pressed herself as close as she could get. She let out a sound of frustration when her position in the chair limited her in her quest. It had been so long since she'd felt his arms around her and even longer since they'd made love. Tom groaned and tried to pull away. Lily only tightened her hold.

"Babe, I'm not sure that the doctor had this in mind when he discharged you. He gave me explicit instructions to make sure you take it easy."

"*Mm*, you're right. Let's take this upstairs. That will make it much easier." She reached up and tugged his soft earlobe into her mouth. Years of togetherness meant that she knew exactly how to drive him wild. The guttural sound he made deep in the back of his throat was heavy with desire.

Releasing his ear, she nibbled her way down the side of his neck. Tom's next groan was laced with impatience.

"Let's go upstairs so we can finish this in comfort," she murmured, persisting with her sensual torment.

With one swift movement, Tom bent and scooped her up in his arms. His mouth met hers in a scorching kiss that sent her heart racing and made her ravenous for more. With her arms draped around his neck, she tortured him with kisses all over his face. Eventually, she fused her mouth to his and didn't come up for air until he kicked open their bedroom door.

The familiar sight and smell of the room nearly overwhelmed her. After so long in a hospital, surrounded by disinfectant and sickness, it was beyond wonderful to be back in their room, the place where they'd made so many memories.

Tom laid her gently on the bed and she dragged him down on top of her. Toeing off her shoes, she tugged up her knee-length, fitted dress to better slide her legs around him. With her foot, she rubbed up and down his leg, loving the feel of him through the denim of his jeans. Familiar, strong, secure—her husband, her rock.

Tom stroked up her ribcage and then cupped both of her

breasts. Staring down at her, he bent his head forward and laved them through her dress. The feel of his hot breath stole right through the linen and sent heat all the way to her core. She moved against him, needing so much more.

Taking her silent cue, he rolled her gently onto her side. Tugging the zipper down on her dress, he slowly pushed it off her shoulders. Within moments, her bra had joined the dress which now lay in a pile on the floor. Clad only in her panties, Tom's gaze rested on the fresh pink scars on her abdomen and his expression grew fierce.

"I can't believe how close I came to losing you," he whispered, his voice hoarse. "I don't know what I would have done without you. Please don't scare me like that again. I don't think I could survive another one."

Lily reached up and smoothed the frown lines off his face. "I'm here, my darling, alive and well and I'm not going anywhere. I'm going to be around for a long, long time to come. So come and love me and let's not talk about what happened ever again."

With that, she pulled him down until their lips met once again and she kissed him with all the love and pent up passion inside her. They might have had a rocky start in the early part of their relationship, but sixteen years later, their love burned stronger than ever. He was her husband, her life partner, her very best friend. He was her everything.

It was a long time later, breathless and exhausted, they collapsed back against the pillows. Tom had loved every inch of her with his mouth and his tongue and his body and she'd gladly returned each loving gesture. Now, utterly replete, she reached for his hand, threaded her fingers through his and sighed in contentment. "Happy anniversary," she murmured and leaned over and kissed him softly on the mouth.

Tom half-sat up and stared down at her, a frown marring his forehead. "Really? It's our anniversary? I'm so sorry, honey. I forgot all about it."

"That's okay. You've had a lot on your mind. I've had plenty of time lying around in a hospital bed to remember."

"The last time I thought about our anniversary was the day of the shooting. I remember talking to Andy and thinking about the gift I might buy. Then we got the phone call and everything went sideways."

Lily reached up and pulled him back down and he pulled her in close against his side. "I don't need gifts to remind me of your love, Tom. Every moment we're together reinforces how much you mean to me. Having you here with me, going through life with you by my side—it's all I'll ever want or need."

Tom's eyes darkened with emotion and he kissed Lily hard on the lips. "You can't imagine how lonely it's been without you. Lying in this big old bed alone. It was awful." His arms tightened around her almost painfully and she knew exactly how he felt. He pressed his lips against her hair and whispered, "I missed you so much."

Snuggling against him, she breathed in his familiar scent and thanked God they'd both been spared. Along with Cassie and their beautiful son, she had much to be grateful for. At the thought of their daughter, she sighed quietly.

"What is it, babe?" Tom asked, sounding like he was on the verge of sleep.

"I was just thinking about Cassie. Now that I'm home, we need to talk to her."

"She spent quite a lot of time talking with Josie while she was here. I think she benefited from that," he mumbled.

"I'm sure she did. Josie's an excellent child psychologist and, being family, Cassie might have found it easier to talk to her, but we're her parents, Tom. We need to talk to her."

He sighed heavily. "Yes. We do. Just, not right now. I'd like to have these few moments with my beautiful wife by my side and just kind of drift off for a while and pretend everything's right with the world."

She smiled, knowing exactly what he meant. Pushing her concerns about Cassie aside for just a little while longer, she curled up against the curve of her husband's back.

Tom heard the sound of the front door opening and closing and looked up from where he stood at the kitchen counter. Catching sight of Cassie's backpack as she disappeared up the stairs, he wiped his hands on a tea towel and went into the living room to find Lily. She was seated in her favorite recliner, reading a magazine.

"The kids are home from school. Do you think we should go and talk to them?"

"I guess now's as good a time as any." Setting aside her magazine, she dragged herself out of the chair, her expression somber. He put his arm around her and gave her a brief, hard hug.

"It will be fine. You'll see. Cassie will expect us to talk to her about what happened, including the drugs and alcohol. In fact, it will probably be a relief for her too, to have this over with."

"Yes, I'm sure you're right. And it's important for Joe to listen to what we have to say. I've been worried about how he's been holding up through all of this. We don't want a repeat of this in another few years."

"That's for sure. Let's do it."

They started up the stairs, Lily in the lead. Tom let her make the climb at her own pace, mindful that she was still recovering from her injuries. The door to Cassie's room was closed. Tom knocked on it and then opened it.

"Hey, Cass, can we come in?" he said.

She looked up at her parents from her place on the bed. A flash of fear, followed by resignation, clouded her eyes.

Tom cleared his throat. "We'd like to talk to you, honey. Do you mind if we ask Joe to come in? We think he might need to hear this, too."

Cassie shrugged and Tom nodded toward Lily, who quietly left the room. A moment later, Joe joined them looking cautious and a little bit scared. Lily closed the door and took up a spot next to Tom. He reached for her hand and gave it a reassuring squeeze. She shot him a grateful look.

"Cass, I think you know why we're here," he started and was relieved when she gave him a hesitant nod.

"I spoke to Aunty Chanel and Aunty Josie. We know about the alcohol and we know about the speed. I'm not going to lie and tell you we weren't shocked out of our minds when we were told you'd overdosed. It terrified us both. If Aunty Chanel hadn't stopped by to check on you when she did, who knows what might have happened."

"I'm sorry, Dad. Aunty Chanel already explained all the scary stuff. It was stupid. I shouldn't have touched the stuff—not the alcohol and definitely not the drugs. There... There was a drug raid at school yesterday. A bunch of kids were arrested. The boy who supplied me with the ecstasy was one of them."

Tom nodded with satisfaction. "Good. It's the least that should happen to him."

Releasing Tom's hand, Lily stepped forward and perched on her daughter's bed. "Aunty Josie told us you mentioned you were still having nightmares."

Cassie's nod was little more than a jerky movement of her head. She turned her face away to stare at the wall.

"I wish you'd told us you were struggling, honey," Lily whispered. "Your dad and I are cut up inside knowing how much you were hurting and we didn't know."

Cassie's shoulders shook with silent sobs. Tom clenched his fists, feeling beyond helpless to deal with his daughter's pain. Anger at the man who had caused it coursed through him and he savagely pushed it away. James Gibbons was rotting in jail, where he belonged. There was nothing more Tom could do. Right now, he had to focus on his little girl and help her as best he could.

He sat down beside his wife and reached for Cassie. She turned and threw herself in his arms.

"Daddy! Please help me! I don't know what to do. I can't stop thinking about what happened, even after all this time."

"*Shh*, honey." He held her head against his chest and stroked her long blond hair. She cried quietly against his shirt. He looked over Cassie's head and caught Lily's eye.

Tears ran silently down her cheeks. Joe stood quiet and

passive in the corner and Tom wished his son would show more emotion. It wasn't right that he be so stoic. Tom swallowed a sigh and made a mental note to make another therapist appointment for Joe, too.

He cleared his voice again. "We're going to get through this." His gaze encompassed the two of them. "I promise. Your mom and I will do everything we can to make this right. It doesn't matter how long it takes or how much it costs, we're not going to quit until you tell us you're better." He pulled slightly away from Cassie, forcing her to look at him. "Okay?"

She held his gaze, her expression grave. "Okay."

Lily squeezed Cassie's arm and beckoned Joe closer. He pushed away from the wall and came toward them. Lily opened her arms to him and he threw himself against her. Tom caught the flash of tears in his son's eyes and was quietly relieved.

"We're here for you, both of you," she said, her eyes as fierce as her expression. "Anytime, anywhere. I'm going to cut back on my classes, so I can spend more nights at home. It won't matter if I take a little longer to get my Masters. Its importance in my life pales to insignificance when I compare it to ensuring the welfare of my family.

" Like Dad said, we're not giving up until we've beaten this. We refuse to let that evil man win. We're Munros and we fight to the death. He's not going to dictate to any of us the way we live our lives. If you need to talk, about anything at all, we're here."

Tom nodded. "You might not believe this, but your mom and I were young once, too. We might not have gone through what Cassie has, but we had issues to deal with, just the same. It's easier to talk about a problem than ignore it. I'm sure you've heard Grandma say it more than once: A problem shared is—"

"A problem halved," Cassie finished with the tiniest ghost of a smile.

"You betcha," Tom said and gave her a wink.

His arms went around the three of them and he held

them close. They were his family, his everything. He'd do all he could to keep them safe.

As if sensing the wealth of fierce emotions that filled him up inside, Lily looked up and caught his eye. He leaned over their children until he could align his lips with hers and kissed her.

"I love you," he whispered. "I love us. I love everything we've created."

She smiled softly, her eyes filled with love. "You are my world, Tom Munro. My forever. We're going to get through this. Together, there's nothing we can't do."

NOTE TO READERS

I do hope you have enjoyed reading Tom and Lily's story. Please feel free to leave a review for The Shooting. Every review is very much appreciated and I thank you for taking the time to leave one.

The Maker—Book Ten in the Munro Family Series is the next book in the Munro Family Series and is Chanel and Bryce's story.

Here's a sneak peek:

Chanel Munro has landed her dream job as a junior resident doctor at the prestigious Sydney Harbour Hospital. Only two years out from medical school, she can't believe she's been chosen by the highly respected Doctor Leo Baker to be part of his team. She's stunned she's made it through the gruelling selection process. It's well known that he chooses only the best.

But an esteemed position on Doctor Baker's team doesn't come without sacrifice. It soon becomes clear the doctor expects her to provide him with certain favors in return for her position on his team and he's not talking about volunteering for the coffee run. His feelings couldn't be clearer: put out or leave.

Scared, angry and confused, Chanel is at a loss what to do. She refuses to give in to blackmail, but if she takes her complaint to the medical board and they don't believe her,

her career will be in ruins. The years of study and sacrifice will be for nothing. Vowing to steer clear of him until she can come up with a viable plan, she keeps a low profile and puts all of her energies into the job that she loves.

It's then that she realizes patients are dying in unseemly numbers under Doctor Baker's care and she can't help but wonder why. Despite his personal failings, he's a doctor with decades of experience. It's ludicrous to suggest he's at fault. As the death toll continues to climb, Chanel bravely confronts the doctor. Dissatisfied with his explanation, she takes her concerns to the police.

Detective Sergeant Bryce Sutcliffe of the City of Sydney Police Station takes Chanel's statement. Despite the fact he's drawn to her earthy beauty, he's sceptical of her claims and can't help but wonder if there isn't more behind her complaint.

When the elderly mother of a New South Wales senator dies under Doctor Baker's care, the resulting media circus and pressure from above forces Bryce to pay attention. Could the girl with the compelling eyes have been telling the truth? Could the Sydney Harbour Hospital's most highly respected doctor be a murderer?

The Maker will be released on 27 September, 2015 and is AVAILABLE NOW for pre-order from your favorite retailer.

If you would like to subscribe to my newsletter to receive news on upcoming Munro Family stories, release dates, book launches and other snippets, please go to my website at christaylor@antmail.com.au and follow the link. I love to receive feedback from my readers. Please feel free to contact me at christaylor@antmail.com.au. Let me know who your favorite Munro family member is.

About the Author

Chris Taylor grew up on a farm in north-west New South Wales, Australia. She always had a thirst for stories and recalls writing her first book at the ripe old age of eight. Always a lover of romance and happily-ever-afters, a career in criminal law sparked her interest in intrigue and suspense. For Chris to be able to combine romance with suspense in her books is a dream come true.

Chris is married to Linden and is the mother of five children. If not behind her computer, you can find her doing the school run, taxiing children to swimming lessons, football, ballet and cricket. In her spare time, Chris loves to read her favorite authors who include Richard North Patterson, Sandra Brown, Kathleen E Woodiwiss and Jude Devereaux.

You can find out more about Chris and sign up for her newsletter at her website:

http://www.christaylorauthor.com.au

Follow Chris on Twitter at:
http://www.twitter.com/christaylorbook

Join Chris on Facebook at:
http://www.facebook.com/christaylorwriter

www.ingramcontent.com/pod-product-compliance
Lightning Source LLC
Chambersburg PA
CBHW061530210726
48287CB00006B/1905